23492

This fascinating and often moving novel is set in Anglo-Saxon Britain just after the withdrawal of the Roman Legions. Gerontius, a young English nobleman, discovers Igerna, the girl whom he loves, tragically bereaved and herself the only survivor of a savage massacre. Though he rescues her and takes her to safety, the shattered Igerna takes the veil. Desolate, Gerontius helps to raise an army against the marauding Saxon bands to avenge the murder of Igerna's parents. The effect of the battle on the lives of the lovers is the substance of this story. Deeping's great understanding of human nature and his vivid style of writing bring the characters to glowing life.

THE SWORD
AND THE CROSS

by
WARWICK DEEPING

CASSELL & COMPANY LTD
LONDON

CASSELL & CO. LTD.
37/38 St. Andrew's Hill
Queen Victoria Street
London, E.C.4

and at

31/34 George IV Bridge, Edinburgh
210 Queen Street, Melbourne
26/30 Clarence Street, Sydney
24 Wyndham Street, Auckland, New Zealand
1068 Broadview Avenue, Toronto 6
P.O. Box 275, Cape Town
P.O. Box 11190, Johannesburg
58 Pembroke Street, Port of Spain, Trinidad
13/14 Ajmeri Gate Extension, New Delhi 1
15 Graham Road, Ballard Estate, Bombay 1
17 Chittaranjan Avenue, Calcutta 13
Macdonald House, Orchard Road, Singapore 9
P.O. Box 959, Accra, Gold Coast
Avenida 9 de Julho 1138, Sao Paulo
Galeria Güemes, Escritorio 454/59 Florida 165, Buenos Aires
Marne 5b, Mexico 5, D.F.
25 rue Henri Barbusse, Paris 5e
25 Ny Strandvej, Espergaerde, Denmark
Kauwlaan, 17, The Hague

First published 1957
Copyright 1957 *by Mrs. Warwick Deeping*

PRINTED IN GREAT BRITAIN
BY EBENEZER BAYLIS AND SON, LTD., THE
TRINITY PRESS, WORCESTER AND LONDON
F.157

IT happened in the spring of the year when the white thorns were in flower on the chalk hills, and the fires had been drawn from under the floors of the winter rooms. I had come from Venta, where I had been buying wine, and being in a mood for the hills and the sky I took the downland tracks which would bring me to the Great Forest, and Straight Street, and so—by a by-road—home. It was one of those golden days, so rare in this dim island, with a light breeze from the east, and the far hills hazed and shimmering, and all the young green of the year brilliant, and fresh in its greenness. The juniper trees upon the downs were like little men, cloaked and hooded, and silently watching me ride by. I looked at the land, and I loved it, for there was another love in me, and I felt at peace.

For this island was at peace. But for certain turmoils and incursions from the sea it was peaceful and prosperous with its sheep and its corn, and aloof from the storms of the Empire. Last year I had been in Gaul, where the new masters were mingling with the old, and where the old world shrugged its shoulders and talked of civilising the masterful, bearded boors. Gaul still cultivated its vineyards, and hunted, and played tennis, and read its books, and fawned, perhaps, on the new nobility, while sneering politely at the Goths and Germans. Lutetia was still Lutetia, and, in Italy, Rome was still Rome. I had been to Rome, and to me it had appeared like some perfumed courtesan, smiling upon all men, a decadent, sensual city, the dignity and greatness gone from it.

Yet, in my young strength, and on this splendid day, I saw our island as a peaceful paradise in a world of change. We had the sea between us and the Empire. Our sea fortresses were strong and secure. True, we had lost the Legions; our people were not trained to war, and the King had brought certain barbarian hirelings into Kent to chasten the Caledonian beyond the Wall.

Londinium was a city of merchants. The great pharos showed its light at Rutupiae. Calleva, city of the woods, drew the country folk of those parts to its baths and shops and country club. The rich took the waters at Aquae Sulis. Glevum and Corinium were serene towns. Viriconium I had seen, but not Deva Verulamium; and Camulodunum was prosperous and peaceful. Sorbrodium on its hill looked out upon a splendid prospect.

So I, Gerontius, rode upon my way, past the old hill forts that were mere banks of grass and flowers, feeling life good in me, and fearless of the future. I carried no weapon save a knife at my girdle, for, in my father's days no man might carry a sword, for Rome wore the sword. A boar spear had been allowed us, and bones—for the killing of deer. There were wolves in the wooded midlands and in the north, but I have never seen such a beast, or dreamed of human wolves from over the sea. The Frisian and Saxon shipmen were just pirates, freebooters and raiders, sometimes eluding our ships by sneaking shorewards at night. The King had garrisons at the castles of the Saxon Shore, and I was young and hearty.

I loved this island, and my estate lay in the hill country south of Londinium in a valley between the heaths and the downland. It was called Sweet Water, for a little stream ran through it, and there were meres and fishponds. I had my great house, and my garden and orchard, meadows and wheat-fields, a vineyard on a southern slope, my woods and wastes, my smithy and carpenter's shop, my barns, my cattle and sheep and horses. I hunted. I took a chariot to Londinium and bought all that I desired. I was lord of my land, with slaves and labourers at my service. I had my mill and my fish-ponds, and all seemed good to me. I do not blame myself for being blind, and there were many others like me.

My horse was a white beast named Cæsar, some five years old, bred by a famous breeder of horses in the high country south-west of Calleva. I was wearing a white tunic and a belt of gold, and over it a cloak of lambswool, dyed purple, and

2

my shoes were of red leather. So I, the young lord of lands, a man of might in my own measure, for I was taller than any man I had met in Britain, and I could have swung a heavier hammer than my smith, came in the glow of the evening to the great guest-house under the downs upon Straight Street. They knew me there, and a groom came out to take my horse, and fat Augustus, the keeper of the inn, met me on the portico steps. A room was vacant for me, and I took a bath, and went to the guest-hall to eat and drink. There were merchants here, and seafaring men, and travellers, but I had a table apart, and pretty Eudorcia served me. There were dishes and bowls of Samian ware, and platters of hollywood, and glass from Italy. I drank wine from Gaul, and thought of Igerna and how I would see her on the morrow. The talk among my neighbours was of wool and wheat, and trade, ships and wine, of tin and oysters, but not a word was there of war. When I had supped I sat in the portico and watched the daylight die on the downs, and talked to a man who had come from Armorica, a grizzled man with fiery eyes. He, too, was no dreamer; he had travelled through Gaul right from the southern sea, and he said that the country was settling down, and that the new men from the east were being taught manners and table-craft by the old Gallic gentry.

I slept like the strong young man I was, and heard a cock crow at dawn, and the birds beginning their song in the grey thickets and garden. Little did I think of what the day would show me. All was peace here, and no women wailed.

I said my prayers—for I was a Christian, and a holy man named Morgan lived in a cell in a wood above my valley. I broke fast, paid my bill, kissed pretty Eudorcia, partly because I thought I should be seeing my love before nightfall. I mounted Cæsar, and set forth along Straight Street with the downs and the sea behind me, and the sun and the wind on my right shoulder and cheek.

The Great Forest rolled eastwards with its mysterious green glooms, like a sea of many colours compelled to stillness by some magician. And still it was, vast in its wildness, and almost empty of man, for there was no life in it save that of woodmen and charcoal burners and the workers who smelted iron. You might skirt along the downs and so come to the great fortress of Anderida and the sea, and from these southern heights a wayfarer could distinguish in clear weather the great forest ridge and the northern downs, between which my valley lay. Trackways were few and muddy, but Straight Street flew straight as an arrow towards Londinium up yonder.

I had my eyes on this great green wilderness, and I kept Cæsar off the paving on the soft turf beside it. I saw the domes of oaks and beeches, spring pines, great yews, thorns in full flower, ash and birch—silver trunks spouting green foam. A great stillness reigned, peace that seemed limitless. The thorns smelt sweet, and so did the sheeted bluebells under the oaks and beeches. There was wonder in me, and the joy of life. I met but few other wayfarers, a waggon or two, a dame and a servant in a chariot who smiled upon me, two girls who giggled. At an old shrine by a brook a beggar sat picking his nose. He stretched out a hairy paw to me, and I felt in my wallet and threw him a coin.

Cæsar could cover his forty miles a day, but the sun was well in the west when I came to the lesser road which branched westwards from Straight Street and climbed the heaths above our valley. I saw the little old temple on what we called Burnt Heath, its portico pillars black against the sun. Down yonder lay Great Yews, the manor of Fabiscius, Igerna's father, and three miles beyond it my land touched theirs. I pulled Cæsar up by the temple and sat looking down into the valley. It was all hazed with evening sunlight, a golden trough below the downs, and infinitely peaceful, or so it seemed. But a sudden uneasiness sat with me on my horse. And why? I loved Igerna, that dark, slim girl with her lily skin and midnight eyes and hair, but her father was not an easy man. He came of pure Roman stock and was inexorably proud, while I had much British blood in me, and I had found my lord Fabiscius difficult and careful. His estate was greater than mine, and he had known me as a wild and bustling boy, mischievous, pugnacious, a little arrogant. He had caught me

4

plundering his orchard, for Fabiscius was a great grower of apples, and he had thrashed me and I had kicked his shins. Yes, my lord Fabiscius had reason to regard me with caution as a suitor, and I could understand that in his haughtiness he wished to prove me as a man who had ceased to be a lout. So, I sat there for a while by the little temple, a young man somewhat shy of an old man who had a sharp tongue and masterful eyes. I gather that it is good for the young to feel some humility in the presence of their elders. I will confess that I was a little afraid of him. Moreover, I knew that he had his eyes on another suitor, a young cock of the Correlian family, great lords in the western lands.

Then, a curious thing happened. Cæsar threw his head up and snorted, and began to fidget about on restless hoofs. Maybe animals can be fly, or perhaps smell tragedy from a distance, but I thought at the moment that the horse wanted to be back with his stall mates and a pail of water and corn. Cæsar had scented home, but he was not going home before I had stopped at Great Yews, and I took the track which led down into the valley. I saw the manor lying there in the green hollow, with the grove of ancient trees which gave it its name black upon the hillside above the orchard wall. The long house gleamed white under its red pantiles, and the thatched roofs of barns and cottages were a warm brown in the sunlight. It was a stately place, with a crypto-porticus, courtyard and porter's lodge. The round quarrels of its windows glistened. I saw it all in miniature and from above, and at a distance it looked tranquil and serene.

I saw no one in the fields, but that was understandable, for the work of the day was done. I was thinking of Igerna, and how her father would greet me. The track led down to the valley brook and followed its twistings round groves of trees. I had come to a corner where a group of old thorns scented the air, and suddenly Cæsar shied, and then stood still, head up, quivering. Surely, the horse was not scared of a bunch of sweet-smelling thorns?

I spoke to him, patted his neck, but he would not move. Puzzled and a little impatient, I rolled out of the saddle, and

5

leaving the horse, trembling and wild of eye, walked down the lane and past the white flowered thorns.

I saw a man lying on his back in the middle of the sandy road. His face, or what was left of it, and his tunic were crusted with dried blood. Nor was it good fresh blood, but dark and rusty. His head had been split like a billet of wood, and his brain was mixed with the clotted blood upon his face. This was the first dead man—violently dead—that I had ever seen, and for half a minute I just stood and stared at the ugly thing at my feet. Cæsar had scented death, and I—in regarding it—felt cold and empty in my stomach.

Who was the dead man, and how had he come to die so violently? I went nearer. He was black of beard, with that rust-red gore crusted in it; his clothes were not those of a labourer, and he wore a signet ring. And then I recognised him; the body was that of Candidus, my lord Fabiscius's steward.

I stood and stared, and felt my stomach heave. Who had slain him, and why? Outlaws from the woods, or some fellow who had borne him ill-will? Yet the dead man had been known as a just and humane steward. Moreover, how had he come to lie here undiscovered in the middle of the valley road, for, raw as I was, I knew that this was no fresh corpse.

Then I looked about me and saw that the grass had been trampled down on either side of the road. Tall weeds such as cow-parsley had been crushed, and this trodden herbage spread along the brook's bank. Not one man but many had passed this way, and there was a sudden cold fear in me. I went back for my horse, but when I got him by the bridle and led him to the place where the dead man lay, he swung away from me, squealing, with his hindquarters in the brook. My fear and forebodings were urgent, and I was fierce with the beast and smote him with my fist. With the corpse behind him he became tame and docile, though all a-quiver; I mounted and stroked his mane and spoke to him gently. His ears went up, and he gave a little neigh, and broke into a canter. So, we left the dead man lying and made for Great Yews.

Silence; emptiness; not a live soul to be seen. The deep green valley was full of the evening sunlight. I could see the yews on the steep hillside, dark and glassy, yet there was a sinister strangeness about that sacred grove, like a black frown on the forehead of fate. I felt cold, but my belly muscles had hardened. I was thinking of Igerna, and there was a gathering fierceness in me. Had some marauding and murderous band of outlaws broken into this peaceful valley? What should I find—yonder?

The road straightened out with the brook a-glitter beside it, speared with water-flags and rank growth. I saw the stone bridge and the white house. It seemed to be sunning itself in the glow from the west. I saw white pigeons on the red ridge-tiles, and they were symbols of peace, yet there was something in the silence that scared me.

I heard a cuckoo calling quite close to me, and was mocked by the bird's cry, and to remember it. The white pigeons on the red roof strutted and cooed. I came to the little stone bridge and the porter's lodge, and some instinct made me leave the horse there with his bridle over the post by the mounting-block. The gates were open, and half the court-yard in shadow, half in sunlight. I stood in the gateway and called the porter.

'Fidilis.'

Silence—silence everywhere, save for the cooing of the pigeons. I took two steps forward, and saw two feet stick-ing out of the lodge doorway. A tremor went up my spine. Another dead man? It was so. Fidilis lay with his head cleft like that of Candidus, and the lodge floor was all blood.

Then a rage of fear and of fury took hold of me. I drew my knife, it was all I had, but that blade was not to be needed. I ran across the courtyard to the portico steps and into the vestibule. The inner doors were open, and the atrium was dim, but there was light enough to see the things that lay there. Fabiscius was sprawled on his back, with a knife in his

7

chest, and the splendid mosaic pavement was darkly red. Other bodies lay there, distorted, twisted into strange postures. The place smelt like a slaughterhouse, yet in the utter silence I could hear the pigeons cooing up above. A kind of frenzy seized me. I stood for a moment, staring at the head of Bacchus in coloured tesseræ with his purple hair and red lips. The face in the pavement seemed to leer, and it had a splodge of blood on its chin. Furniture was broken, hangings torn down. These men must have fought here, helplessly, hopelessly, with stools and fire-irons and naked hands. The horror of it all flamed in my blood. I stepped over the bodies into the great corridor, and I heard myself calling in a strange, hoarse voice—'Igerna—Igerna.'

There was no answer, but more silence and more horror, for at the far end of the corridor I came upon a more dreadful sight, women and children flung into a heap, some of them upside down with their legs lying over the heads and bodies of others. A woman's face glared at me, eyes open, mouth a black circle, and about her neck were wreathed the legs of a child. I stood and shook, and my stomach heaved.

The horror stupefied me. Had all Fabiscius's folk fled into the great house for safety and been slaughtered like cattle in a cave? And who had done this dreadful thing? I remember striking my forehead thrice as though I thought myself dreaming. I closed my eyes, looked again, and saw that woman's face framed in a child's legs. And then the most stupefying thought of all came to me. Igerna might be there, dead and crushed and fouled in that tangle of corpses.

Almost my knees gave way. I felt my stomach heaving. I staggered into the winter-room, aware of a vast disorder, of open chests, and Fabiscius's iron strong-box lying overturned and empty. The place had been plundered. But what of that? I sank down on a gilded stool, my head between my knees. The face of a cherub in the great pictured floor simpered at me. I was sick upon that infant face.

I groaned. I pressed my fists into my belly. Everything seemed blurred; my head was going round. But that other anguish grew and gripped me, the thought of my love

8

crushed and fouled in that filthy corner. I ceased to vomit, and my belly tightened.

I remember crying out—'Igerna—oh, Igerna!'

Then a little sound came to me. I sat rigid, scared, fancying that something in that pile of bodies out yonder had moved. Or was it a ghost rapping? Sweat broke out of me. The setting sun was shining in, and I had one foot on the cherub's face, in the midst of my own vomit.

I heard the sound again, a dull knocking. It seemed to come from under my feet. I started up, with every muscle tense in me. The hypocaust, or furnace! There was a hollow space under the mosaic floor.

I was out of the house like a madman, for someone was alive here who could tell me how all this horror had come to be. The entrance to the furnace was in the kitchen court, and I found it, an arch of flint and tile sunk below the ground. Faggots and great logs were piled here, and I went down the steps into the stony pit. The place had an iron door, and it was shut. I knocked on the door and shouted.

'Is anyone there? I am a friend.'

A voice answered me, and when I heard it I tore that door open and plunged in. The black space under the great floor had been cleared of ash, but it was foul with soot and I saw a figure crouching there, a dim white face streaked with the soot of the place, two huge eyes, a cloud of hair.

'Igerna.'

For a moment she was mute, and then she fell forward into my arms. She gave one little cry and fainted, and I carried her out into the dying sunlight.

I stood there, holding her, looking down at her face all smeared with soot. Her blackened hands hung limp. What next? How much did she know? I could not take her into that dreadful house.

There was a water cistern in the great court, and thither I carried this slim, dark girl who was but a child. I held her in the hollow of one arm and, scooping water with the other hand, washed her face. The coldness of it revived her. Her eyes opened in a black blaze of terror. She clung to me.

9

'Oh, Geron, Geron.'

It was her child's name for me, and she clung to me like a child. I held her close, and kissed her forehead.

'I will take you home, Igerna.'

She shuddered, and with head back, looked into my face.

'Tell me—the truth.'

I put up a hand and turned her face to my shoulder. How could I tell her? And maybe my silence was sufficient, for she broke into wild weeping. Moreover, the twilight was upon us, and the horror of that house, and the silence made me remember that we might be in dire peril.

'I am taking you to my house, Igerna. You have borne enough. Leave all to me.'

As I turned towards the gate I was aware of the pigeons fluttering towards the dovecote, and the noise of their wings was strange, and unreal. I remembered the dead man in the porter's lodge. Igerna must not see that thing: I put a hand over her head and pressed her face to my shoulder, and so carried her—convulsively sobbing—across the bridge. The horse was standing patiently, and he turned great solemn eyes on us. The world was going black and grey, and suddenly there was fear in me, not craven fear alone, but fear and cold courage. I looked right and left along the road, and up at the darkening hills. My right hand went to the knife I had put back in its sheath. Oh, wild thought! If these devils were still near us, and fell upon us, the knife would be for Igerna, and then—I would fight to kill before I too became like those others.

I lifted Igerna sideways into the saddle, and bade her hold to it, and unlooped the bridle and led Cæsar along the road. I was as tense as an iron rod, looking, listening. We had three miles to go, and it would be dark before we reached Sweet Water, but there would be lights there and live people.

And suddenly a thought shocked me. Lights! Would there be lights? What if this devils' crew had sacked and slaughtered there? What if I found more death? I felt my belly go hard, and my muscles stiffen.

10

Ye gods, what a day! And what of the night that lay before us?

It grew more dark, and all my senses were as tight as harp strings. I remembered that there would be a moon, and the sky was clear. I heard the brook running, and that was the only sound I heard, together with the ring of Cæsar's shoes. I glanced at Igerna, and saw that she was sitting straighter on the horse's back. She had ceased to weep.

I hesitated, and spoke to her.

'Igerna.'

'Yes, Geron.'

'Can you tell me anything, bear to tell it?'

She was silent for a moment, and I saw her face dimly white in the gathering darkness.

'I was in the wood above the orchard when it happened, just under the edge of the beech trees. I saw a little crowd of men come along the road to the house. I thought they must be some of the King's new soldiers, and I ran down the hill——'

She paused with a catching of the breath, and I laid a hand upon one of her knees.

'And then——'

'You heard——?'

'Yes,' and suddenly she put her hands over her ears.

'No—I cannot speak of it. I had reached the garden, and oh—Geron—I was afraid. I was a coward.'

'Thank God you were,' said I; 'and so you hid in the one place where——'

I felt her hand on my shoulder.

'Must I speak of it?'

'No, Igerna. But tell me one thing. You heard those devil voices. Did they speak in British or in Roman?'

'Neither. They were loud and terrible voices, and seemed more like animal sounds.'

'From belly and the depths of the throat. You understood no words?'

'No, Geron.'

Then I think I began to divine the origin of these brutes. They were no outlaws, no mere wild men from the woods, but wolves from over the sea. Some savage band of raiders had broken in—perhaps by night—past our coast defences, and followed some river into our hinterland, as was to be their custom. And we—weaponless men untrained to war—were mere sheep for the slaughter. I was profoundly ravaged in myself, but I will confess that I did not even then foresee the bloody and dreadful future. I thought of this tragedy as a mere chance happening, a horror that might be avenged, and never recur.

But the danger was grim enough. Where were these beasts —now? Had they gone by the way they had come, carrying the plunder of our country houses, and the young girls, and such food as they needed, to some river estuary or creek where they had hidden their ship or ships? I could not say, and my ignorance was part of the pressing darkness. I looked and I listened, and now and again I held Cæsar in and stood straining my ears. The country that I knew so well had become strange, sinister, and haunted. By now I should be seeing the lights of my manor—but I saw no lights anywhere.

Well named was our manor—Sweet Water—for the brook spread here into a great mere, and from the mere a channel led water into the fosse about our house. I held Cæsar in. I could see nothing, hear nothing, not even the barking of a dog, and this darkness and silence were full of fear. A great beech tree grew beside the road, and I drew Cæsar into the black shade, and spoke in a whisper to Igerna.

'I am going to—spy out the land. My people must be asleep.'

She clutched at my shoulder.

'Don't leave me, Geron.'

I took her hand and put it to my lips.

'You will be safe here with Cæsar. If I should shout to you, ride up into the woods.'

As I turned to go I was aware of a pale light in the sky behind us. A full moon was coming up, and I saw its rim swell above the valley. Light. Yes, that was what we needed, and yet might fear, and I came back to Igerna and the shadow of the great tree. I would wait for the moon to rise.

'Here is a lamp to guide us.'

I leaned against the horse, and Igerna's knee was against my shoulder. There was silence between us, the silence of being together. Cæsar's ears were cocked and turning. The horse was as uneasy as I was, and now and again I felt a little phrenetic quiver beneath his hide. I stroked his muzzle, and he rubbed it against me, but made no sound, for which I blessed him.

A great sheet of light was now spreading across the mere, and it was like a shield of silver. The high woods glistened. I could see my house, white-walled, dark-roofed, the out-buildings, and belfry, for my father had built a little sanctuary for the good Morgan. He would come down from his cell on the Sabbath, and preach to us, and celebrate the Holy Eucharist. I had the Saint in my thoughts at that moment. Morgan might be a tower of strength and of comfort in a crisis.

But the light was good now, and I pressed Igerna's fingers, and went forward, drawing my knife as I neared the bridge across the moat. I went slowly, cautiously, every sense on the alert. What should I find here? More horror? I came to the bridge and stood listening.

There was not a sound, and I saw that the courtyard gates were open. I prowled across the bridge and into the court-yard, and just inside the gates Bran, the hound, should have been in his kennel. I saw a thing like a snake lying on the stones, the dog's chain. I stooped and looked into the kennel. The dog was gone.

I did not know what to make of this. Was the omen good or bad? I took the shadow of the eastern wall, and crept up to the portico, my knife ready. Not a sound. I saw that the doors were open. What should I find within? Step by step I slid in, and stood listening, but there was not a sound, and suddenly I got the feeling that the house was empty.

It was very dim, but I could see the tiled floor, and there were no dead things there. I crossed it into the great corridor, and again stood listening. Not a sound. I grew bolder and passed to the servants' quarters, and craning my head round a half-closed door, saw the dull embers of a fire. Light! I needed light, and I knew that a torch was kept in an iron holder on the wall. I found it there. I plunged it into the embers, and when it was alight I went back into the corridor, holding the torch aloft. No bodies here, no horrors, nothing but the play of light and shadow on the walls and floor. I passed into the summer-room. It was empty, but without disorder. I looked into my sleeping chamber. It might have been waiting for me.

I shouted, and nothing but an echo came to me. The house was empty but untouched, and I realised what had happened. News must have come to Sweet Water of the horror at Great Yews, and all my people had fled.

I stood there holding the torch, suddenly conscious of my clenched teeth, and that I was sweating. I drew in and let out a deep breath, and slipped my knife back into its sheath. My muscles seemed to go slack. I sat down on my bed, with the torch flaring in my hand and its smoke going upwards.

What next? Should I bring Igerna into the house? But we were still in danger, and this dark and silent house might give her terrors after what she had suffered already. And then I had an inspiration. There was an island in our mere, and on it a little water-house which my father had built and used when he had wished for solitude and peace; moreover, a small black barge should be lying at the mere's bank. I went striding out and down the corridor and into the portico, still carrying my torch, until it came to me that the torch glare might betray me to enemies. I beat it out against a pillar, and crossing the courtyard and bridge waded through the long grass to the mere. A black shape lay moored there, and I saw safety in that dark shell. The mere was deep, and could be crossed only by swimming.

I ran back to the great beech tree.

'All's well, Igerna.'

She gave a little cry.

'Oh, Geron, thank the Christ—for your sake.'

I took Cæsar by the bridle.

'I have a safe and pleasant place where you shall rest and sleep, Igerna.'

'Sleep! Shall I ever sleep?'

'In God's good time, yes. I am taking you to the island where there will be moonlight and still water. I will make a bed for you there. And you must eat.'

She answered with a little sighing sound, and I knew that she felt that she could neither sleep nor eat.

I fastened Cæsar's bridle to the ring by the porter's lodge. I could stable the horse later and give him water and corn, but Igerna was my first concern. I would have put my arm round her as she waded through the lush grass, but gently she put me off and in silence. She looked so slim and frail in the moonlight, but I could divine her mood and its meaning. Even caresses such as mine disturbed her in her bitter sorrow, and from that moment she was both child and woman, instinct with a young dignity, a mysterious aloofness.

'Do not touch me, Geron, now.'

'I am yours to save, Igerna.'

'There is bitterness in me, my dear, and shame. I—I should have died with my father.'

I drew a little apart from her.

'Would he have wished that, Igerna? Your father was not that kind of man.'

But she had a fine and serious spirit, had my beloved, as I was to discover to my own chastening. I was no lout, but I was to learn that a young girl may have an inwardness beyond mere man's comprehension, or rather—too fine and fastidious for the things of the flesh. Meanwhile, we had come to the water's edge. The mere was a black mirror with the moonlight upon it, and I unfastened the rope, and looked at Igerna. She stepped in the little barge, unhelped, and I took the pole and thrust off towards the island. The water was deep a few yards from the bank, and I had to bend to the work and thrust deeply to touch bottom. The sky was a great silvery dome above us, the water like glass, save for our ripples. There was no sound save the drip of the water from the pole and the 'plash' it made each time I dipped it in.

So, we came to the island, and I held the boat against the bank, and Igerna stepped out, and stood as still as a statue.

I said, 'You know where to go, Igerna. I am going back to look to the horse, and to bring over what we need.'

She bent her head to me, and with her hands folded over her bosom turned towards the island-house. Willows grew about the island, screening it, and dipping their greenness into the water. I turned and poled back, my mind full of many matters. We should need food over yonder, and bedding, platters and bowls and what-not, a pitcher and ewer, a lamp, and oil. The island-house possessed a couch, a chair and a table, and the place would be our refuge while the peril lasted. I thought of the good Morgan, and wondered if he too had fled. And had my people left us food? I tied up the boat, and going to Cæsar I led him down to the mere and let him drink, and when I brought him to the stable I found a great silence there. My people had taken the horses. It was so dark in the stable that I went and rekindled the torch, and unsaddled and unbridled Cæsar and fed him. Then I patted his neck and went back to the empty house.

Was there food in it? An abundance. I found meat, bread, milk, honey, butter and wine, and I collected my gear, and put food on a great dish, and carried it down to the mere. Then I gathered the bedding from my bed and the guests' room, and made another journey, leaving my torch in the house. I made three such journeys with a jar of oil and a lamp, tinder and steel, a stool and a chair, and other vessels. Lastly, I remembered an old sword and a boar-spear which hung on the wall of the winter-room, and I took these weapons and felt glad of them.

It must have been near midnight when I had finished all my ferrying, and the moon was high in the sky. Igerna helped me, but with a kind of stricken silence. I lit the lamp in the little house, and its light was so small that I doubted whether any prowler would have seen it with the moon at full. I put meat and bread and butter on a platter, and poured wine into a beaker, and placed them on the table.

'Sit and eat, Igerna.'

She ate but little, but I will confess that I was ravenous. She would not touch the wine, but drank some milk. The wine was for me, and I needed it. Then I spread her gear upon the floor, and carried mine into the little portico.

I heard her voice.

'It will be cold there, Geron.'

I answered her gently.

'I am going to sit and watch awhile. Seek sleep, Igerna.'

I had left my weapon in the portico, for I did not wish her to see instruments of death. So, I closed the door on her, and spread my pallet and coverings and my pillow, and unlaced my shoes and shed them. I drew the sword close to my bed, and my bed was so placed that it guarded the doorway.

I lay down, but sleep would not come to me. I was restless, and harried by the day's dreadful happenings, and challenged by what might happen on the morrow. The utter stillness of the night was like the face of a dark Sybil mouthing questions. Had my people escaped to safety? Was Morgan still up yonder? What did the future hold for Igerna, the immediate future? Had she fallen asleep? I sat up, turned and glanced at the closed door, and saw a line of light below it. The lamp was still burning.

And then the love in me flared up, with no scorching flame, but with a rich and tender radiance. I was her sentinel, her watchman, her guard. I knew that I would give my blood and life in fighting to protect her, and in knowing it knew that it was good to feel as I felt. God and beauty and mystery may be in such love, bringing mere man and God together.

From that moment a profound peace descended upon me. I picked up the old sword, and holding it like a cross, put my lips to it. I was God's man, and Igerna's man, and I would be a fighting man. I had height and strength, more so than my fellows. I felt my heart beating hard, and my belly filled with a wealth of exultation. I could prove myself to other men, and to Igerna.

So, peace came, and I placed the sword beside me, and lay down, and twisting my head saw no light beneath the door.

Igerna slept, or so I hoped, and my prayer was that she should have no evil dreams.

II

THE dawn came with a stealth that promised splendour. A little mist hung over the mere, and all the grass was drenched with dew. I saw the wooded hills catch fire, and the blueness of the sky increase. There was no sound save the singing of the birds.

The dawn seemed in my blood. I left my bed, and going to the water's edge looked about me, and then stripped and plunged and swam. I made for the further bank, and wading through the water-flags and weeds, ran naked to the house.

I thought that I had never seen it look more peaceful, yet with a poignant peacefulness. I loved the place, and to me it was a house of happy memory. The sun had topped the hills by now, and was shining along the valley, and never had I seen a more lovely valley in all Britain than this one of ours. The great downs rose to the north with their black yews and brilliant beeches, their thorns and white beams, and in the south the heaths and woodlands touched the sky. It was all dewy and still with an exquisite diversity of greenness, and so peaceful that it was not easy to believe that evil and cruel men could torture and kill. Christ's man I might be, but no flowery sap.

Sweet Water, too, had its pigeons, and they were strutting in the courtyard and on the pantiled roof. They were pets of mine and very tame, and some of them fluttered to my feet. But I had things to do: to feed and water my horse, and explore the house and buildings now that the daylight was with me. The house was my first concern, and I found it as it had been the night before, silent and empty and unravished. In the summer-room I found a table set as though my people had expected me, and that their flight had been sudden and in panic. Here were all the familiar things of my young days, the scrolls on a shelf, the great table, my father's gilded chair, the oak hutches, the paintings on the walls. It had a famous pavement in many colours depicting the four seasons of the year, and I can remember that the face of Old Man Winter had frightened me as a child.

I passed through all the house and found it clean and in order. Even the dairy retained its earthenware pan of milk and cream. Cheeses and hams hung from the rafters, and in the cellar the wine and the honey-ale had not been touched. I went out into the little courtyard at the back of the house, and heard hens clucking. My travelling chariot and the farm wains were there under their peat roof. I opened the great doors of the barn and the granary, and they were as I had left them, though I heard a rat scuttling away from the stored grain. I passed through a door in the garden wall, and saw the fruit trees and the herbs, and the yew arbour at the end of the long wall. The sunlight shone upon it, and all was peace.

I went to the stable, and led Cæsar down to the mere to drink, and, looking across the water, saw a lovely sight.

Igerna was kneeling on a little grassy shelf at the water's edge, her tunic loosened and caught below her breasts. She was washing in the mere, cleansing herself from the stains of the hypocaust chamber. Her black hair hung about her naked shoulders, and she looked as white as Parian marble against the greenness of the grass and willows. She had not seen me, and I looked and loved and felt a twinge of guilt in me for looking at her as I did.

Cæsar had his muzzle in the water, and the sucking sound he made must have floated across the mere. I saw Igerna's head go up; she turned and saw us, and her hands drew her clothes up above her breasts. I pretended to be watching Cæsar drink, and when I looked again Igerna was on her feet, her black hair clouding about her oval face.

I raised an arm in salutation.

'Peace be with you, Igerna,' and then I fled behind the horse, for, would you believe it, I had forgotten my own nakedness; though why nakedness should be shame to man or woman I cannot say. The Greeks were not troubled by it, and the Spartan young men and maidens used to run and wrestle in a state of nature. Maybe we islanders, born to clothes in the rain and the frosts have come by shy skins, but I pulled Cæsar from the water and used him to hide me to the house. I stabled him, fed him, and going in, took a clean tunic and cloak from the hutch in my sleeping-room and went back to the mere.

Then, by the grace of God, I felt a fool. Here was I—in dry clothes—with the water between me and the island, and the barge lying over yonder. Should I swim again? Ignerna had entered the island-house, but as I stood there I saw her come to the doorway.

I called to her.

'Igerna. Gerontius is a fool. I swam hither, and now I have dry clothes on me.'

She stepped out into the sunlight.

'Your clothes shall stay dry, Geron.'

She entered the boat, unfastened it, and picked up the pole, and to begin with her work was easy, but when she reached deep water I thought that she would either lose the pole or take a ducking. She did neither, but after sundry splashings and divergings she managed to bring the boat to the landward bank. In other days her tussle with the boat and pole might have been matter for laughter between us, but we were both as serious as death.

We crossed over, Igerna sitting gazing down the valley, and I handling the pole. I knew where her thoughts were, while mine were leaping hither and thither like a dog baiting a bull. What was the dog's move to be? Should I tarry on the island, or carry Igerna to Astolat or Ponter, where she would be more secure? I rubbed my chin, and remembered that I had not shaved, for it was the fashion of the men of the lordly class to use a razor. Only the labourers and serfs went hairy. Then, what of Morgan and my people? The Saint might still be in his hermitage, and my people in one of the near-by villages.

20

I poled the barge to the bank, and Igerna stepped out through the water-flags.

'Are you hungry?' I asked her.

She shook her head and was silent, and her silence made me feel that she was far away from me, and a stranger. This tragedy seemed to have set her apart, and the laughing girl had become a silent, wide-eyed woman. There was a new mystery about her, and in her wounded mood I felt that she was too sacred to be touched. But her inward aloofness was not all self. If she was woman, I was man to be fed. We passed up to the house, and I picked up my travelling pack to get my shaving gear, while she entered the little building.

Her voice came to me from within.

'Where will you break fast, Geron?'

'Oh, in the sun, but do not trouble, Igerna.'

'In the portico?'

'Well, in the portico. Leave it to me.'

She said—'It helps—to use one's hands.'

I got out my shaving-bowl, soap, mirror and razor and went down to the mere's edge. Cold water would have to serve. I hung my mirror on a willow bough, and lathered my chin and upper lip, and was on the point of setting to when a distant sound startled me. I sat listening, razor in hand. What I heard was the sound of horses coming fast along the valley road from the east, and I squirmed and lay flat behind a willow tree and called to Igerna.

'Stay in the house, Igerna. I hear horses.'

Then I saw horses and riders appear round the green elbow of a wood. There were three of them, and though they were riding fast, I judged that their horses were weary. In fact, I saw one beast stumble, to be jerked up by a pull on the bridle. One of the riders had a queer, white head stained with dark splodges, and as they came nearer I realised that his head was swathed in bloodstained linen. Another rider had his left arm lashed to his body. By their clothes and their horse-gear I knew them to be of our people.

I sprang up, and with my face all lather, waved to them. They saw me. The man with the bandaged head pulled up, but the other two rode on, and I guessed that there was fierce fear in them. I shouted—'What news?', and he of the bandaged head rode down to the water's edge. His face was deathly pale.

'Who are you, my friend?'

'I am master of that house.'

'If you are wise you will leave it.'

His voice came hoarsely, and his horse's head was drooping.

'But—what news?'

'News. Have you been blind and deaf?'

'I have been on a journey.'

His mouth was a black hole from which mocking laughter might have come.

'Sweet innocence! The King is dead.'

'Dead!'

'Yes, my friend. You seem ignorant of high matters. We and the barbarians held a feast and a great council together. When we raised our wine cups they drew their daggers. I—was one of the fortunate few. Thirty bloody corpses, the chief men of this realm. Is that sufficient news for you?'

I stood staring at him across the water.

'Is there no more?'

'More? There is. These savages whom the King had hired have broken every pledge. They are out ravaging and slaying. Londinium has shut its gates. And we have no fighting men in these parts to put against them.'

I was dumbfounded. But he of the bloody head was turning his horse.

'Go west, my young friend, and do not trouble about shaving your chin, if you value your life. These devils show no mercy.'

He raised an arm and rode off after the pair who had been too terrified to tarry.

I had asked for news, and by the Lord Christ I had got it, and as I stood watching the fellow ride away, I wondered whether Igerna had heard these dreadful tidings. She had, for when I turned about with my face all lather I saw her standing between the two white pillars of the little portico. Her eyes looked as jet black as her hair.

I could not face her for the moment and I went back to my willow tree and scraped my chin, and as I did so my eyes watched the valley road. Now I understood how Great Yews had come to its doom, and I wondered whether other of the barbarians had crossed the sea to join their fellows. The whole bloody business may have been planned. And what of Great Yews and its dead? One could not leave the dead to swell and rot and stink, and yet the task of burying all those bodies appalled me.

I was rubbing my face with a napkin.

'Evil news, Igerna, but look at the meadows.'

'Yes,' said she—'cloth of gold. Why must men shed blood?'

I could not answer her, but gazed at the grasses piled thick with buttercups, just simple flowers. But my problem was not simple. What to do with Igerna, what to do with those dead.

She walked back towards the island-house, and I followed her. I saw that a meal was spread, and I carried a stool out for Igerna. There was silence between us, for all these horrors and perils had made us mute. I knew that her father had had kinsmen in the west country, and that an uncle of Igerna's was lord of Corinium, with a great country house near that stately city, but Corinium was far away, too far for me—the lover.

I ate my bread and meat and butter, and drank honey-ale, but Igerna ate but little. There was still that mystery about her, an aloofness that baffled me. She might have passed into another world. My feelings towards her fumbled. Was it that she needed no lover with this great grief upon her, but a fatherly councillor and friend?

I had my head down when she spoke to me.

'I must see them, Geron.'

'See—whom?'

'My father and the poor dead.'

That shocked and scared me. How could she go into that dreadful house and keep her reason? I was wondering what to say to her when we heard the voice. It came from over the water, and when I heard it I sprang up and grasped my sword. I had had my back to the mere, and as I looked at Igerna I saw that there was no fear in her eyes.

'It is Morgan, Geron.'

Morgan it was, white-haired and white-robed, holding his wooden cross in his hand, and when I saw him my heart gave thanks, for here was a good and wise man with whom I could share my problems.

I poled the barge across, and as I neared the bank Morgan raised his cross and blessed me. He had been black as night in his youth, but now he was silver-grey, broad-headed and broad-faced and fresh of colour. He had the bluest eyes I have ever seen in a man, nor were they old eyes, but swift and sparkling, for though Morgan was a saint, he had the wisdom of the serpent. His presence was superb in the calmness of its dignity, and whenever I was with him I felt better and braver than myself, for when he laid his faith upon you, you hailed him as saint and father.

'Evil news, my son. I cannot wish you peace.'

I stepped out on the bank and he kissed me on one cheek.

I said: 'Igerna is with me. Have you seen the horror at Great Yews?'

He had. His eyes seemed to flash, for he was man as well as saint.

'I have, my son. I feared that the child——'

'She was the only one left alive. She had hidden in the furnace room. I found her there.'

I told him of the riders who had passed that morning, and of the terrible news they had left with me, and Morgan, leaning upon his cross, gazed steadfastly into my face.

'So—the King is dead. God rest a shameful soul.'

I understood him, for our King had been known as a weak man, and a profligate, a man who would bargain with sin and bribe the Devil himself. He had sought to compromise with these savages, and they had slain him.

'Do you know where my people are?'

He shook his head, and was silent, brooding.

24

'They may be at Astolat. I have seen other things, my son. The beacons have been blazing on the southern downs. I have seen them.'

I knew what that portended. More long ships were off our coast, ready to land another savage swarm, and what could Anderida's weak garrison do against them? But I was thinking of Igerna, and the dead at Great Yews.

'Father—she would see those dead.'

'That must not be, my son.'

'Will you speak with her?'

'I will.'

And then a sudden inspiration came to me. How could one deal with all those dead and a house that could never be cleared of dreadful memories, save by fire? Fire can cleanse, and already I had a feeling that there were times ahead of us when the torch and the sword would be our symbols.

I said: 'Would it not be better, Father, to give the house and the dead a funeral of fire?'

He looked at me and considered. Then he gave a movement of the head, his blue eyes looking across the water at the island.

'Those are good words, my son. But first I would speak with Igerna.'

I ferried him across, but did not land on the island, for I knew that Morgan's wish was to speak with her alone. I saw her kneel to him, and he raised her and kissed her upon the forehead; nor was I jealous, for that was a Christ's kiss. Some old men grow lascivious in their latter years, as though to prove their potency, but Morgan had conquered and transcended the flesh, and there was a pungent tale told about him. It was said that a certain lady with a merry heart and an ogling eye had visited Morgan in his cell, and tried to play Eve with him, and that Morgan had laid her across his knees, and chastised her with a sandal. I can well believe it, and it was a tale worth telling.

I stood and watched them, and listened to the voices, though I could not hear what they said. Morgan sat in my father's chair, and Igerna stood before him, hands clasped over her

25

bosom. Morgan did most of the speaking, and I gathered that he was telling her of Great Yews and its dead, and she listened to him as to a father. Meanwhile I kept a watch upon the valley, for now I knew that the green woods and the grey downs might be full of peril for us.

I saw Morgan rise, and again Igerna knelt to him. He blessed her, and then he must have seen my sword lying in the portico. He bent down and took it in his hand, and felt its balance, and then he swung it so that the blade flashed in the sunlight. A sudden thrill went through me. The saint had swung my sword, and I saw a symbol in that act. Then, he held it by the blade, and kissed the crossed pommel, and held it to Igerna's lips. She, too, kissed it, and our sword had become doubly sacred.

So Morgan came to me and held out the sword to me.

'That will be a new cross, my son. Take it and bear it. I am no man of blood, but men of blood must be answered with the sword.'

We passed over from the island, and Igerna came with us, to pole the boat back after we had gone. We had this great task before us, and were fearful of leaving Igerna alone on the island, but there was no other place where she could safely abide our return from Great Yews. She would hide the boat in the rushes when we had gone on our way, and put out the fire, and leave nothing visible outside the house that could betray the presence of any people on the island.

I looked into her eyes.

'Are you afraid to be alone, Igerna?'

'I fear nothing now, Geron. What is there left for me to fear?'

I wanted to take her in my arms and tell her how great my fear could be, but I had that strong feeling that she did not wish to be touched.

I left her to go back, in the boat, to the island and returned to Morgan. I harnessed Cæsar and put him at Morgan's service. My sword I carried over one shoulder, and on the other I held a sack with flint and steel and tinder and a couple

26

of torches. So we set out for Great Yews with the sun shining on our faces, and the shadows of the trees growing shorter upon the grass.

When we came in sight of Fabiscius's house I said that I would go forward alone and make sure that no enemies lurked there, but Morgan would not suffer it.

'No, my son, if any man has to die, let it be an old man. Wait while I go forward.'

I think I laughed for the first time since all these things had happened, though there was grimness in my laughter.

'The sword and the cross go together, Father.'

He smiled down at me.

'So be it, man of the sword.'

I liked that title, for it saluted the fighting man in me, but I will confess that I feared that house and its horrors. The white pigeons were there on the roof, and, when we had done our work, those birds would be homeless. I ran forward to the gate, and saw those legs and feet in the shadow of the porter's lodge. There was silence, utter silence save for the cooing and fluttering of the birds. Morgan had dismounted, and I took the horses' bridle and looped it over a hook.

'We are alone here, Father. All seems as it was when I first came here.'

Morgan had seen the dead man lying in the shadows. He raised his cross, and his voice was deep and resonant.

'Peace be with you, poor dead. May you be with the Lord Christ in Paradise.'

We crossed the courtyard together and came to the portico steps. I had seen all that horror and I had no wish to look upon it again, and Morgan must have divined my shrinking.

'Wait, my son, I will go in and look upon the dead and bless them.'

I waited, my sword over my shoulder.

It seemed to me a long time before he came back out of that dark house, and I saw his eyes smouldering in a stark white face. He stood there on the steps, silent as death, gazing at the green valley and the high woods, and I felt that some God-given wrath was working in him. He appeared to have forgotten me in some vision of passion and splendour, of righteous vengeance and ultimate salvation. His head was high, and he was breathing deeply, and pressing the cross to his body. Then his eyes took note of me, and flashed before he spoke.

'Gerontius—son of Mascius, I name you a Soldier of the Cross. My eyes have seen dreadful things: blood, death, slaughter without pity. Man may kill man in wrath or in some just cause, but those who slay little children are the Devil's disciples. Even I would bear weapons of war against them.'

His words and his manner of uttering them went through me like a rushing wind. Should I hear the trumpets cry, and see men of might go with me into battle?

I raised my sword to him.

'I will serve, Father.'

'All must serve, my son. I behold a holy war against fear and death and darkness. But now we have the poor dead to remember, you and I together.'

And what a labour of Hercules was ours! If those who read this journal may find a sound of the theatre in Morgan's declarings, let them picture us at work on that warm morning in the Spring of the Year. First we carried the dead man from the porter's lodge into the house, I taking his shoulders and Morgan his feet, and his face was blown up like some bladder of blood, and he had begun to stink. Then Morgan threw off his white robe, and we stripped to the waist for the labour before us. In the little courtyard behind the furnace-room faggots and cord wood were stacked, and we carried the wood into the house and piled it until our pyre was twice the height of a man. Also, we built another pyre in the corridor close to that heap of corpses, and every time I tossed my faggots down, I held my breath, and my stomach tightened, nor did I look at the poor dead, but I could smell them. So, we laboured for two hours or more, and the sweat ran off us, for we did not wish to bungle the job. Morgan was an old man, and I feared he might grow weary, but there was a fierceness in him that would not tire.

When our task was done we rested a while in the courtyard

and drank water from the cistern which was fed by a spring piped from the hillside. There was a great silence, and Morgan was as silent as the house. He looked haggard, and the lines on his face had deepened, and sometimes his lips moved as in prayer. Presently he rose, and bade me light a torch, and I did so. He took it from me.

'My hand shall light them into paradise, my son.'

I let him go, and went to Cæsar, and led the horse to a little group of trees above the brook and fastened him there, for I feared the flames might frighten him. When I returned to the courtyard the white pigeons were still on the roof, and I clapped my hands at them, but they paid no heed. I saw little wisps of smoke curling up from windows. Morgan had set them open to help make a draught, and I stood and watched those funeral plumes. Then I saw smoke sailing out into the portico, and a glow within the house. I heard the crackle of flames.

Morgan came forth, a torch in one hand, his cross in the other, his shoulders glistening with sweat. Together we stood by the water-cistern, and watched the smoke increase and begin to billow out. At long last the pigeons on the roof took fright and rising from the pantiles circled round and round with a whirr of wings, making me think of the spirits of the dead, become white birds, going Heavenwards. Morgan raised his cross and uttered a prayer, a valediction. Then, a sudden weariness descended upon him, and he sat down upon the stone plinth of the cistern, and laid cross and torch on the ground. I went for his cloak and laid it over his shoulders, for after all that sweat and labour an old man might catch cold.

The great doorway of the house was now like a great red mouth, and the smoke like blowing hair. The roar of the flames increased, and I could see smoke seeping through the roof tiles. Windows belched black clouds. The frightened birds were winging round and round, making a kind of white halo over the doomed mansion. Our labour had not been wasted. I stood beside Morgan and watched, and then a strange odour drifted to me, and I wondered. It was the smell of burning bodies.

29

The fire raged on and up. I saw tiles cracking with the heat, and little tongues of flame appear. Morgan was chanting a prayer in a deep monotone, but the reek of those burning bodies sickened me, and I was thinking of Igerna. This blaze might spell danger, for it would be visible for miles.

I spoke to Morgan, but he did not seem to hear me.

'Let us go, Father. Igerna is alone.'

I touched him on the shoulder, and suddenly a part of the roof fell in with a clatter of tiles and a roar of fire. Morgan's head went back. He rose, stretched out his arms, and his face was lit by the flames.

'Our work is done, my son.'

I put an arm about him, for he was shaking.

'Yes, Father. The dead have been served. I would think of the living.'

III

WE turned aside towards a little hill whose green top rose above a growth of old yews and thorns, and from this hill we watched the last death throes of the mansion of Fabiscius. The sight saddened me. The house was now a hollow shell or like a brazier full of flame, and the white birds were still circling overhead, and now there was much less smoke. Those birds were homeless and I wondered whether they would make a home with me at Sweet Water. Home? How long would it be mine to have and hold and to enjoy? That flaming mansion was a symbol, a tormenting torch, and here on this little hill with the white thorns smelling sweet and the old yews darkly glistening I felt more man than ever I had felt before.

And what of Igerna? Her picture came to me with sweet anguish and desire, but my desire was without lust. That may seem strange in a strong young man, but truth is truth, and to me that dark girl was sacred. My love was Christian, not pagan. She had suffered; she had escaped death by the grace of

God; she was alone save for her kinsfolk in the West, and as I stood there I saw her in all her pale loveliness, black of eye and black of hair, tender as some young flower, full and red of lip, with her beautiful brow and virgin bosom. An infinite tenderness consumed me. I felt that I could give my blood and strength for her, and die happily at her feet. All that I would ask her to do and say would be to kneel by me and look in my dimming eyes—and whisper—'Geron, I love you.'

Morgan's voice roused me.

'*Explicit:* the spirits of the dead rise to Heaven.'

His eyes were smouldering in his tired face, and yet there was peace upon his brow. We had done a great deed, and done it well.

'Father.'

'Yes, my son.'

'I am troubled for Igerna.'

He looked at me with a sudden, benign smile.

'That is as it should be.'

The simple words came to my lips.

'I love her, I shall love her until death. I could love her in dying. I love her more than I love myself.'

He laid a hand upon my shoulder.

'Such love is of God, my son. It gives that which God would give. Such love forbids mere lust, the greediness of the flesh; and in its consummation it will be—a sacred act.'

I stood looking at the burning house.

'All—that was her's—is gone. What now? I am troubled. What will she desire?'

Again he smiled at me.

'Ask her, my son.'

'I? Would not it be better for you to speak with her?'

'That's as it may be. Youth goes to youth.'

I turned my eyes from the burning house.

'What she wishes—that I will do, even if it goes against my love for her.'

So we passed on and came to the mere, and all was as we had left it. The water was full of sky and cloud shadows, and the yellow water-flags were reflected in it, and I saw Igerna standing under a willow tree, her black hair falling over her bosom. She brought the boat across to us, from its hiding place in the rushes.

'Go, my son. I will stay and keep watch.'

Then I, a strong man, suddenly felt afraid and strangely shy of that young girl. How would she look at me; what would she say? Had she seen the smoke of her burning home? I poled the boat back to the island, keeping my eyes on the water and the ripples my pole made. I did not look at Igerna till the boat's prow touched the further bank. She was silent, with a deep and baffling silence, and I felt that there was some spirit in her which I did not understand. I saw her above me in more senses than one, cold in her loveliness, and ineffably chaste. I might have said that these tragic happenings had turned her into white marble, save that her lips were red, and her eyes and hair black as the night.

I stood, holding the pole, and feeling dumb and confounded.

Her lips moved. She was gazing down the valley.

'Is it—finished, Geron?'

I bent my head to her.

'Forgive us for what we did, Igerna. But it was good and right and seemly.'

She was silent, and her silence troubled me. How should I begin to ask her what she desired to do, how I could save her? Whither did she wish to go, and with whom to dwell? I fastened the boat to a willow tree, and stepped up and out.

'There must be talk between us, Igerna.'

She did not look at me, but across the water.

'Of what, Geron?'

'The future. There is no home for you here, no safety. Even my house is not secure.'

Her eyes met mine, and they chilled me with their dark and mysterious steadfastness.

'I would speak with Morgan.'

'With Morgan?'

'Yes.'

Those simple words of hers ravaged me. So, she would

speak of herself to an old man, and I—a young man—was not to be the recipient of her intimate thoughts and wishes. Well, was that not right and natural? Morgan could play the father and the confessor, and I—the lover—might seem too young and urgent.

'It shall be so, Igerna.'

'Bring him to me.'

'I will bring him.'

So I had to undo the lashings and pole the boat back across the water, and to me it had become bitter water. There seemed to be an inexorable and dark mood between me and the girl I loved.

Morgan was waiting for me, and my solemn face must have been a mirror to him.

'She would speak with you, Father.'

He entered the boat and I ferried him across, and when he had landed I poled back across the mere. I thought it just that they should be alone together and that Igerna should be able to speak as she pleased to Morgan without my being within hearing. But I was restless and troubled about my love, and I harnessed Cæsar, and rode out westwards along the valley road towards a village that lay under the shadow of the downs. I came to it and found it smokeless, silent and empty. Even the cattle had gone from the fields, and no dogs barked.

Then, if you please, an impudent thing happened. Sudden sounds came from a bosky lane leading from the woods, and I saw a man running with his mouth agape. It was Gildas, my steward, a fat fellow with ponderous legs; his eyes were bulging, and my instant thought was that some of these savages were chasing him. But it was not so. After him came a wild boar, tusks gleaming, little eyes evil. I had my boar-spear with me, and I dug my heels into Cæsar, and calling to Gildas I met the beast's charge. He was young and fierce and lacked cunning, and my spear caught him cleanly in the flank and rolled him over. He lay kicking and squealing, and I turned about and finished him off.

Gildas's fat legs had failed him now that the urgency had gone out of the game. He had flopped into a shallow ditch among the herbage, eyes bulging, belly and chest heaving, mouth agape. I might have laughed, had there been any laughing mood in me, which there was not. Gildas's red and sweating face had surprised me as much as the wild boar had surprised Gildas.

'Well,' said I, 'and well met. I was wondering what had befallen you all.'

He sat up, holding his belly.

'Thanks, Master, for you and your boar-spear. The beast would have trampled me down and ripped me.'

I nodded, and looked at the black brute twitching and oozing blood.

'I came to see if I could find any of you. What happened?'

Gildas groaned.

'Have you seen Great Yews, Master?'

'I have.'

'A fellow fled from there and brought us tidings, and I feared greatly—that——'

Again I nodded at him.

'Yes—you were wise. But these savages did not come to our house. Where are my people?'

'At Astolat, with many others.'

'Good. And you——?'

'I am not a man of great courage, Master, but I was moved to come and see how things were with the house.'

'Where is your horse?'

'I had no horse, Master. I felt more safe on my own feet, and I kept to the woodshaw.'

'Easy cover, Gildas, till you met the boar.'

He had recovered his breath by now and he came up out of the ditch and put his clothes in order, and I, looking at his flabby legs and fat belly and soft pink face, saw no fighting man in Gildas or in the thousands like him. What, indeed, had we to put up against these fierce invaders but tame serfs and comfortable townsmen who knew nought of arms and war.

I began to question him.

'Are there any fighting men at Astolat?'

34

'A few old colossi, Master.'

'Veterans. And the rest a rabble. Well, go back to Astolat, Gildas, and tell the people there to keep good watch. There are smiths at Astolat?'

'Yes, Master.'

'Bid them forge spearheads and swords, if they can use such craft. Ploughshares will be out of favour.'

I saw that he was loath to leave me, but I was thinking of Igerna and of Morgan and of what might be passing between them, and I sent him off along the valley road, and watched his fat legs wagging and his head turning this way and that. The wild boar had scared the soul out of him, and he looked right and left for other perils.

I turned back along the valley, nor had I gone a mile before I saw that the weather was changing. The wind had been in the east, with a clear sky and cold dawns, but up yonder over the downs I saw a mass of blue-black cloud. Thunder was in the air, and one of our island's incalculable moods was setting a frown on the face of the morning. And yet that ominous sky had a sinister beauty, and the woods and water, still sunlit, seemed to dissolve in mystery. Were the heavens in sympathy with these dark and tragic happenings? I saw the sky rent in the distance and heard the rumble of thunder, and it seemed to tremble in my belly. Oh, strange, deathly year! I came to our fields of young corn, lushing up and gleaming under the stormy glow, and I wondered who would reap that corn, we or the barbarians. What problems were upon us? Food and house cover, the home fires and the saving of our cattle. I saw another jagged rent in the sky and heard thunder as I came through the meadows to the mere.

I passed a little grove of thorns, all white and scented, and thought of the rain upon them, and the falling petals. The light had become a strange and brilliant glare from under the edge of the black canopy up yonder. I made haste to stable Cæsar, and plucked an old horse-cover from a hook and laid it upon my shoulders. Then I went down to the mere's bank and stepped into the barge.

I saw Morgan but no Igerna. He raised an arm to me and

35

I poled across, watching his face as he came down to meet me. The storm light was on his countenance, and upon the grass and upon the willows, and I felt that he had unhappy news for me, tidings that might be bitter to a lover.

He looked at the sky.

'Let us go to your house, my son.'

Why to my house? And what of Igerna? But I was the disciple, he the master, and I held the boat to the grass bank while he stepped down and in. The first raindrops fell upon us as we passed over, and I had a feeling that the heavens were weeping for the woes that might afflict our island. By the time we had reached the white pillars of the portico the storm had broken and hailstones were bouncing in the courtyard. A sudden wind wailed in the house, and it might have been the voices of Igerna's dead.

I fetched a stool for Morgan, and another for myself. The hail had ceased, and drenching rain was falling, and running from the roof and across the courtyard. The heavens crackled above us, and the island and its willows were blotted out by the deluge. Morgan sat silent on his stool, watching the storm, while I watched the master's face.

At last he spoke to me.

'You love Igerna, my son.'

'Better than I love myself.'

'Then it will be your lot to love her in that way.'

Lightning struck a tree in the valley and I saw a great limb crash, and I felt that something in me was to be struck in that way.

'Igerna would take the veil, my son.'

I was dumb, and I listened to the storm and Morgan's voice, and to another voice in me that cried out in protest. He spoke calmly, kindly, and yet I felt that he blessed Igerna's choice. Lightning and thunder and rattling rain, and my young desire crucified in a world of tragedy! I knew that of late years sister-hoods of holy women had grown up in our island, women who had withdrawn themselves from life and the lusts of the flesh, and served Christ and the poor, but that Igerna should become such ravaged my soul. She was but a child to make so desperate a choice. I felt that sorrow had so shocked her that she did not know what she was choosing.

There was no living man for whom I had more affection than Morgan, but at this moment in my life I rebelled against him. I had left my stool and the shelter of the portico, and I stood there in the rain with my face to the heavens. Young Ajax defying the lightning! A Christian I might be, but there are urges in man that are part of nature, and the sudden storm was in my blood.

I said: 'She is too young, Master, to make such a choice. Is she not to know love and the exultation thereof, and all the beauty of life and of loving? I have a right to ask her.'

He answered me gently.

'I did not press this choice upon her, my son. It was of her own choosing.'

'But she is too young.'

'Souls may grow old in a night.'

I raged up and down in the rain, and then came and stood before him.

'Do you grudge me a man's right, Father?'

'No, my son. I am an old man and my blood is calm and cool. But——'

I waited.

'But, my son, the world is both old and young. I have before me visions of storm and of terror, the young and the ruthless destroying the old. Igerna may see the world as I see it. Her spirit is naked and crucified, and it may be that she has been so shocked by these vile happenings that there is a child's horror within her.'

'Of man—the beast?'

He bent his head to me.

'Think of the women, my son, who followed Christ.'

'I am no Christ,' I said to him, 'but a lover. I have a lover's right to reason with her.'

He smiled at me kindly.

'The soul of man, my son, may transcend reason.'

The storm passed with strange swiftness, and gouts of

sudden sunlight fell upon the grasses and the trees and upon the still water. The whole world was wet and gleaming as I went down to the mere, with the black clouds in flight and the sun shining like a great, victorious hero with a golden shield. All nature sang in me, and my heart beat hard and fast. I was the lover, with the mayflower smelling sweet, and the green earth steaming and fragrant. I would speak as a lover to my love, and with infinite tenderness turn her from the dark doors of a pious prison.

I sang as I poled the barge across, and triumphant youth exulted in me. What was a dead Christ to a young lover, for my mood was for all time and godless in its passion. I would take Igerna in my arms, and with a man's kisses bring her back to life and loving. So I came to the island's bank and the wet willows, but I saw no sign of Igerna. She was in the little house and hidden from me.

Mea culpa, other things also were hidden from me.

So I came to the little house, and saw that the door was shut against me, but I was not troubled by that closed door. I stood outside the portico and called to her.

'Igerna—Igerna.'

There was no answer, and still I did not fear that closed door. I called to her again, and perhaps with more passion in my voice:

'Igerna—Igerna.'

Again there was no answer, and I stepped forward and put my hand to the latch. The door was bolted against me, and I beat gently on it with my knuckles.

'Igerna, I would speak with you.'

Still—silence, and the man in me grew urgent.

'Igerna, come forth to me. I love you.'

Then I heard a little sound as of someone rising from a chair. Igerna may have been on her knees, praying; I thought of that afterwards. I heard a bolt withdrawn and the lifting of the latch. The door opened, and Igerna stood before me.

I drew back and gazed at her. She was in the shadow, but somehow she seemed a figure of light. Igerna it was, but not the Igerna of my world. Her face had a white radiance, mystery, and her dark eyes looked at me as though I had no substance. And suddenly I was filled with fear, and dumb anguish, for something in me knew that my love was beyond the mere importunities of man.

I saw her lips move, and as I listened to her the reality of her unreality amazed me. Here was a creature who but yesterday had been a child, speaking of strange sublunary things as though they were as actual as the trees and the grasses. I stood and stared and listened like an oaf.

'I dreamed a dream, Geron, but it was no dream. The Lord Christ came to me in the night, and laid a charge upon me. I—who was a coward and afraid—am to be brave and sanctify myself. My father is dead, and all his people, and I—must live for Christ.'

Religious jargon? So it might have sounded to me had I not looked upon her face. God had laid His hand upon her, and claimed her as His own. She had put a spell upon me, and I was voiceless.

'I have spoken with Morgan, Geron. He is a saint, and knows all that is in my heart.'

And what was in mine? I felt myself trembling. I let out those poignant words:

'Igerna—I love you.'

I put out my hands, and stepped towards her, but she stood straight and slim and still, looking me in the face.

'Do not touch me, Geron.'

I knew that I could not touch her. My hands fell, and suddenly she came close and kissed me on the forehead. And what a kiss was that; cold, chaste, revealing, a farewell!

I hung my head. I said: 'No other woman shall ever kiss me.'

She stood back, and for a moment she smiled.

'Make no vows, my brother. I have the vow upon me. Morgan has given me counsel. I go to Corinium, to a holy house there. It is God's will.'

I looked at her slim white hands folded over her bosom.

'Grant me one thing, Igerna.'

'What do you ask of me?'

'That I may go with you to Corinium to guard you. That is all I ask.'

'It shall be as you wish, Geron.'

IV

YE gods, how I was to laugh and mock at myself in the days that were to come! I—Gerontius—the fighting man —a silly saint! I had gone soft; I was a squelch, like an overripe pumpkin under fat pig's snout. So fatuous was I that instead of ravishing my love I offered myself as a kind of pious young pimp to conduct her to a sacred brothel. And what a pilgrimage I had chosen! But this child woman had cast a kind of spell upon me, a Circe spell, save that she was a virgin, and would be so. Maybe I loved her better than I knew, and that the quality of my love was to be remembered and rewarded.

The strange thing about it all was that as the days went by I grew more and more bewitched, and a fanatic in my self-martyrdom. The more forlorn my desire, and the more acute its sweet anguish, the more did I become the slave of this child's infatuation. In being wounded hour by hour, the more I seemed to hunger to be hurt. I was like one of those pious creatures who gash themselves with sharp flints or knives, and rub in verjuice, or thrust a hand into the fire, or sit naked in the snow. Igerna was God's virgin. I would keep her so, and cut the throat of any man who mocked me.

Assuredly we are created of strange stuff that is not a mere manifestation of the flesh. Igerna was for setting out instanter, and I filled wallets with food, and saddled Cæsar. He would serve her as far as Astolat, and there I proposed to pick up one of my own horses for her use, and I would see Gildas and my people, and bid them return to Sweet Water and take courage. I was to find them a very craven crowd, all save Lob, the smith, who was to become a mighty man of valour.

But to the action itself. Only old men indulge in too much lucubration; young men either crow or sneer, and on this spring day after the storm I did neither. I was not such a forlorn fool as not to comprehend the tragic temper of the age, or the horrors Igerna had suffered, and that her urge was to flee from the world of men and clasp God's feet. Had I not seen the dead, and a great house go up in flames, and smelt the reek of burning bodies? Even the friendly woods warned us, dark-mouthed, of infinite perils.

I said farewell to my silent house, and wondered whether I should see it again—save as a charred ruin. I mounted Saint Igerna on my white horse, and for a mile or more Morgan walked with us. I have never known a man so utterly calm and without fear, and determined to tarry where he dwelt in the sandstone cell upon the forest ridge. We met no one. The countryside was a lonely desolation, and brooding with fear. Morgan came with us as far as the deserted village, and there he blessed us and bade us God's speed.

I looked him in the eyes.

'That which fate has laid upon me, Master, I will suffer.'

'Not fate, my son,' said he, 'but the living God.'

So we came to Astolat and the river, and found the place crowded as for a festival, but a festival of fear. Whole villages had fled hither and were camped in the wet meadows and on the hillsides. There was no order, no discipline, though in one or two streets the people had thrown up barricades. A few veterans had donned cast-off harness, but they were no more than a few rusty spearheads in a field of quaking wheat.

I found my people camped on the hillside just above the river. They had brought wains with them, and they were packed with women and children. They flocked round me like a lot of goggling geese, but I was in no temper to suffer babble and panic. I found fat Gildas asleep in a waggon he had made his own, and I pulled him out by the legs, and bade him get busy. There was no lodging for Igerna in the town, but the waggon Gildas had assigned himself had a cover and bedding, and would serve Igerna for the night. I lifted her off Cæsar and carried her on my shoulder like a child. The people kept crowding round us, crying and gabbling, and waving their hands in the air, and when I had placed Igerna in the waggon I turned upon my own rabble. What sorry stuff was this with which to face the fierce men from over the sea!

I raised my arm.

'Silence, you fools and children. This is no time for bleating and wailing.'

I bade Gildas move the other waggon further from Igerna's, but they would pay no heed to Gildas, and seeing Lob standing apart with his arms folded, I beckoned to him.

'Lob, take charge of these sheep. You are a man of muscle and of metal.'

He grinned at me, and his white teeth flashed in his black beard.

'True, O Master. We need men, not a flock of cackling hens.'

'Deal with them,' said I. 'My lady would have sleep and peace, for she has suffered dreadful things.'

Lob was the man for such an occasion. I saw him go about cuffing the men, and alone he drove this frightened flock further down the hill and made them move the waggon and the horses. I turned back to Igerna and found her sitting mute and strange-eyed on the pallet.

'First you shall eat,' said I, 'and then sleep. We have a long journey on the morrow.'

She looked at me as though she did not see me.

'Be gentle with these poor people, Geron.'

'Gentle?'

I did not say to her that gentleness had gone out of our world.

I gave her food and drink, and called to one of the women of my household to make up the bed. Then, feeling moved by a bitter restlessness I went down into the town, and spoke to two veterans who were watching by a barricade. One was a Spaniard, the other from Gaul, and it was the Spaniard who cast some of the planet lore at me. His blackness was grizzled, and his face was as dark and as creased as a walnut shell.

'Lord,' said he, 'what would you? Mars and Saturn are in

conjunction with Cancer, and all the affairs of men have dropped bellies and go ill.'

I could not argue with him about the stars and their influence upon the human scene, but I asked him what he thought of the town's chances should the barbarians come this way.

He spat.

'Lord, have you seen what a fox can do in a hen roost?'

I had. The Gaul was pulling at his long moustachios, and gazing blue-eyed at the hill above.

'There is no one to make a fight of it save we old fellows, and we are as rusty as our swords.'

I said: 'I wish I had a legion of you, rust or no rust. This country has been castrated by too much peace and ease.'

The Spaniard laughed in his beard.

'You look a man of sinews, lord. Whither go you?'

'Into the west, my friend, but I shall return.'

He saluted me.

'Come back with a thousand Silures, lord, and we may make a showing.'

'That is a good saying. I will remember it.'

I slept but little that night, partly because I feared for Igerna, and partly because the town and the people about it kept up a constant cackling. The fools had lit fires, as though to scare the wolves away, or warm their shivering souls. I walked about among the waggons, wondering what would happen if the barbarians fell upon us. I knew what my urge would be: to take Igerna and put her upon a horse, and cut my way out, or die with her, and make a brave business of dying.

At last I wrapped myself in my cloak and lay down on the grass under Igerna's waggon. It cast its shadow over me, though the moonlight patterned the wheels and their little triangles of light beside me. For a long while I could not sleep, but felt Igerna above me, and there was no sound from her, but only the cackle of the camp. It caused me to think furiously of the happenings of the last few days and of their bitter significance. In Britain we had been a clean and a comfortable people, with our baths and our heated houses and our

43   SC—D

cornfields and our flocks. Our cities had their theatres and their arenas, libraries, hostels, churches. We had lived smoothly and peacefully save for occasional rivalries and raids, and we had grown soft, and thought ourselves safe and secure. We had combined a placid acceptance of the Cross with the nice filling of our bellies; we had washed and anointed ourselves, and felt warm in winter, not fearing—as we should have done—these wild and hairy men who took the sea spray and the wind into their bosoms. Astolat and its clattering crowd of fugitives was a picture in miniature of what this island was and might be.

I was on the point of falling asleep when a sudden uproar roused me. A man's voice was shouting. I heard screams, wailings, the puling of children. The voice kept on shouting like the voice of a madman.

'The barbarians are upon us. Fly, fly.'

I sprang up, cursing, and looking over the tailboard of the waggon saw a white figure, kneeling. So Igerna had not found sleep. I stretched out my arms to her.

'Come. You must go.'

But she remained quite still, like one in a dream.

'What must be—must be, Geron.'

And then that frightened fool with the bawling voice came running close to us, spreading panic among the people. I stepped aside and waylaid him, and smote him upon the mouth. I took him by the throat and held him.

'Silence, you fool. What frightened you?'

He choked and gabbled at me.

'Let me be. I saw men crossing the river.'

I shook him. Assuredly, I was growing fierce.

'What men? Ghosts of your own making.'

Lob came lumbering up on his great, bowed legs.

'What is amiss, Master?'

'A fool and his own fear. Take him and go down to the river and see if you can see what he says that he has seen.'

The fellow squirmed and struggled, and I tossed him to Lob, and went back to the waggon. Igerna was still kneeling there, her hands together, her face lit by the moon.

44

'Can you not sleep, Igerna?'

'I sleep while I am awake. I have visions, Geron.'

I sat down on the grass, and waited for Lob to bring me news, and all the while I seemed to see that kneeling figure lit by the moon. Had the Lord Christ appeared to her as He had appeared to Saul of Tarsus? Had she been visited by some holy spirit? Or had the happenings at Great Yews taken away her reason? My love strove bitterly in me, and I was filled with yearning and compassion. If I had lost Igerna I owed it to those devils who had slain her father and all his people, and there was grimness in me. I, too, wanted to kill.

Lob came lumbering back, minus his companion.

'Two asses had broken loose, Master, and had gone to the river to drink.'

'What did you do with your ass?'

'Pitched him into the river.'

V

DAWN came, and for a little while the camp had been still, and I had slept. I sat up and saw a serene sky, and mist in the valley. What of the day, and what would it bring to us? I crawled out from under the waggon and stood up, and was astonished by what I saw. Igerna was on her knees. She seemed to be in a trance, eyes wide open, the whole of her utterly still. I did not speak to her. She was in some other world than mine.

We broke fast early, though Igerna's meal was nothing but a bowl of milk fresh from one of the cows my people had brought with them. She looked like milk, mute and wide-eyed and asleep in being awake. I will confess that I ate fiercely, for there were other hungers in me, and maybe I had a vague fore-feeling of the frustration and the mystery that were before me. I know that women can lie, just for the love of lying, and men also, and pose and play a part, but

Igerna was no such creature. I would have said, with Morgan, that the Holy Ghost had entered into her, and that my live and lovely love was to become a saint.

While I ate, sitting in the sun beside the waggon, I called Lob to me and spoke to him. It was plain to me that Gildas was poor, flabby flesh, and that I needed a man of muscle and red blood, and I chose Lob for that man. I said that peace had passed from us, and that fate willed it that we should be fighting men, and that I chose him as my second. He was to go to Sweet Water, taking any fellow who had guts, and watch and defend the place while I was absent.

Would he do this for me?

His teeth gleamed in his beard.

'I will, Master. I have my smithy there, and there is work to do.'

'Good man, Lob. Put watchers on the hills, and if the barbarians should come again, and in too great a strength, march back to Astolat.'

I could see that he was feeling full of swagger at my trust in him, and my trust was not misplaced. I told him to speak with Morgan, for Morgan was as wise as God. And I needed a quiet horse for Igerna, and he should see to it. And had we a lady's saddle?—We had. Fat Gildas's wife had come from our place on such a saddle, for her father had been a breeder of horses, and she could ride. Well, Madam Gildas, if she returned to Sweet Water, could use a waggon or her own good flat feet.

Some of my people watched us with sullen faces as we set off upon our journey. I believe that they thought we were deserting them and leaving them to the danger, for those who are poor in spirit are poor in their opinions. I heard one woman say: 'My lord goes to Aquæ Sulis to take the waters, while we drink danger.' It did not much concern me what these people thought or said, for I had begun to realise that they were soft trash, and that too much peace and easy living had made them cheap in spirit.

I took to the high downs beyond the river, and it was my plan to strike the road from Penter to Colleva, and I knew of a great house on the edge of the heath country where I had friends who could lodge us for the night. And what a ride this was to be, a strange and silent pilgrimage, with Igerna beside me on her quiet old horse, an Igerna who seemed to dream with open eyes. Verily, some strange and mysterious ever-spirit had entered into my love and possessed her. I was not man or lover, but a God-given guardian of a maid in some holy trance. There was compassion in me, and a great yearning, and my desire was sleeping like my love. I kept watch upon the landscape, and looked at her from time to time, but her eyes saw nothing of reality. They were the eyes of a woman walking in her sleep.

We met but few people on that upland road, for our world was going west, not east, but one small party caused me to smile with inward and sardonic laughter. Three porters with six packhorses carrying kegs passed us on the grass trackway. They were cheerful fellows and they saluted me.

'What merchandise is that,' said I, 'wine from Gaul?'

'No, oysters, lord, for the gentry.'

Oysters! So our world still peddled oysters, though Londinium might be burning.

By noon we were off the chalk ridge and going north-west past a chequer of woods and fields and heaths. We came to a farm where a woman was hanging out washing, and I rode up and asked her if we might rest and eat in her house. She was a red-head, cheerful and bouncing, and she bade us enter, and then her face changed suddenly. She was looking at Igerna, and I saw her cross her first two fingers and mutter something to herself.

'Lord,' said she, 'I fear my food and drink would not please such as you.'

I glanced at Igerna. She seemed to have seen nothing, but sat on her horse gazing at the little white house. There were pigeons on the roof. Did she remember?

I drew the woman aside.

'Sister,' said I, 'the lady has no evil eye. Have you not heard the news?'

Her green-grey eyes were sullen.

'What news?'

'That the King is dead, and many of his notables, and that the barbarians are burning and slaying.'

'I have heard no such news, lord.'

'Be thankful. You live apart. The lady yonder has had her father and all her people butchered. Can you wonder that she is not as other women?'

Her face softened, but the words she uttered shocked me.

'Poor lady, she has lost her reason.'

I let the question pass, and the woman bade us enter. I lifted Igerna off her horse, and led her by the hand into the house. Her hand was limp and lifeless in mine, and as she walked she looked neither to the right nor left, nor up nor down. Her eyes were two dark pools of mystery.

The place was clean, and the woman set bread and meat and milk before us on a table. I caught her casting curious glances at Igerna, and I shook my head at her, and she left us alone to eat.

I set food and a bowl of milk before Igerna.

'Eat, sister,' said I, 'it is a long way to Corinium.'

She humoured me, but the manner of her doing it shocked my soul. She crumbled bread—she would not touch the meat —and put it to her lips as though her body was some mechanism, and she did not know what she was doing. She drank the milk in the same strange way, her eyes looking over the rim of the bowl—at nothing—or at some projected inward vision. She ate and drank as though the live self in her was asleep, and I thought of the woman's words and felt sorrowful.

Was my love mad?

I would not have it so.

I paid the woman and thanked her. The good soul had watered and fed our horses, and she stood and watched me lift Igerna into the saddle. Her eyes were pitying, and I hated the pity in her eyes. Did she see that which I—the lover— would not see? I mounted Cæsar and we rode off.

Towards evening we came to my friend's house which stood on a green hill not far from the Colleva road. A lovely valley sloped from it towards the south, and a great pool gleamed in the valley bottom. The mansion itself was not as most houses were in our island, for it was of three stories, with many windows, and a little domed pavilion on the roof from which Eugenius could watch the stars or all the land about him. The road led up to a spacious terrace with urns and statues and a fountain, and beds of herbs and flowers edged with clipped box.

The sleek peacefulness of the place and its smiling richness were to me very strange and disturbing after what I had seen and suffered. A servant had come out to hold our horses, and he was a stranger to me, and tempted to be insolent.

'Is your master at home?'

'My master has guests, and is at supper.'

'Go, tell your master I would speak with him.'

He leered at me.

'What name shall I say?'

'Gerontius—of Sweet Water.'

I believe the fellow thought that we were impostors, and were trying to force ourselves upon the house, but he went, for I was growing grim, and in a little while Eugenius came out to us. He looked flushed, as with wine, and someone had crowned him with a wreath of roses.

'Well, well, well,' said he, 'welcome,' and he looked at Igerna, for Eugenius was a lady's man.

I dismounted and beckoned him aside, and he winked at me. I was beginning to think Eugenius a fool and a fop.

'Who is the pretty lady?'

I laid my hand upon his shoulder, and so roughly that he winced.

'My dear fellow! Why this thusness?'

'Are you deaf and blind like the rest, my friend?'

'What's in the wind?'

I told him, and he looked incredulous and just a little scared, but when I described Igerna's tragedy and all that had followed, no man could have been kinder. He was kind but weak; a volatile soul whose chin ran away from his mouth and whose hands were the hands of a woman. Dear, dear, the whole bloody business was incredible! Assuredly, the poor child should have every consideration, a quiet room apart and a good woman to attend her.

And then he shrugged.

'I have guests.'

I said I could join them, and he looked dubious, but my great concern was Igerna.

'Send for a woman, Eugenius. The child is not fit to face people.'

Very shortly I was to realise that my friend's guests were not fit to look upon a saint.

Eugenius went into the house and I stood beside Igerna and spoke to her as to a child to whom simple words had to be used. I said that she would find the house of Eugenius more peaceful than a hostelry, and that a woman was coming to attend her, and she must sleep and eat. She heard me and understood, and for a moment she seemed to become woman to me, and to show the face of the old Igerna through the veil of her sanctification.

'Thank you, brother Geron, for all your kindness to me.'

Brother, and kindness! What words for the ears of a lover!

Then Eugenius returned with a serving-woman, and I helped Igerna off her horse. I liked the look of the woman. She curtseyed to Igerna, and her eyes were kind. Igerna turned for a moment to my friend.

'Thank you, sir. May the blessing of God be upon this house.'

Eugenius took my arm, and we watched the two women enter the house.

'What a lovely,' said he, 'and how sad and wasteful.'

I turned on him sharply. Eugenius's face had an appreciative shimmer.

'She is a saint,' said I, 'and the Holy Spirit has visited her.'

Eugenius was not to be sobered when wine and women were in the picture.

'Bad luck for you, my friend, to be enamoured of a saint. Go to the bath and then join us at the table.'

For, in those days, we bathed twice a day, and it was not

50

considered seemly for a gentleman to come hot and sweating from the saddle and seat himself among the elect, but Eugenius and his sleek inanity were getting under my skin. I said that there had been too much silk and scented water in this island, and that men would have to become tough and hairy if they were to face the new terror.

He pressed my arms.

'Ah, my friend, you are a little—er—upset.'

Upset! If he had had to do what Morgan and I had had to do, his stomach would have been no more than a flaccid, queasy bag.

The house of Eugenius was very much the house of a great gentleman who revered the Arts. It possessed an atrium with a water-cistern, and a splendid floor and painted walls. The supper table had been set in the atrium, and when I entered it with Eugenius his guests did not rise but stared at me somewhat impudently. I was travel-stained and unshaven, and doubtless my face was not that of a Ganymede. There were five of these guests, three women and two men, and when I looked at the women I gathered that this was no dovecot. The ladies were luxurious, painted harpies.

Eugenius introduced me.

'My friend, the lord Gerontius. He is upon a journey.'

He gave me the names of his guests, and a bold-faced wench with copper-coloured hair moved aside on a carved bench and made room for me. I was young and lusty, and perhaps to her liking. She flashed a smile at me, and her lips were ripe fruit.

I sat down beside her.

'And how, sir, are heifers?' said a supercilious young man who sat opposite, twiddling his wine-glass.

If this was humour I was not for it, and I was blunt with him. Did he take me for a bumpkin and a farmer?

'Bulls should be more in the picture,' said I.

He simpered.

'Every man to his taste, sir. Do you keep prize bulls?'

I had my sword girded to me, and I unbuckled it and laid it on the table. All of them stared.

51

'That is the new symbol. I gather that you have no news here.'

'News, sir, news?'

And then I told it to them, and never have I seen faces go more slack and shocked. They looked askance at me, and even the painted faces on the walls seemed to become masks of fear. I saw my supercilious young friend staring at that piece of steel, as though I had thrown a venomous snake upon the table. He had one of those pert, girlish faces that are narrow between the eyes and between the cheekbones. Maybe he was trying to think of something pert and clever to say to me, but, in the old parlance, his tongue clove to the roof of his mouth.

A servant set oysters before me, and filled my glass with red wine, and I drank, conscious of the eyes of all of them upon me. Then Eugenius spoke; he had been a stammerer, and when in emotion he stammered, and his chin would quake.

'You tell a good story, my friend. How much is romance, how much is truth?'

I said: 'I think you once dined with me in the house of Fabiscius. You may remember it.'

'I d–do. A l–lordly mansion.'

'There were more than twenty corpses in it when Morgan and I set it alight, a death-roast that you could smell until your dying day.'

I will confess that I was brutal to them in my candour, for I saw them as frivolous parasites, the product of too much riches. My copper-headed neighbour edged away from me, and her eyes had narrowed and lost their easy glamour. It was Eugenius who rose, and proposed that they should leave me to eat in peace. They did so, and they trailed out to the great terrace, and presently I heard the music of harps and of flutes. Eugenius and his like would fiddle while our world went up in smoke and flame.

I was finishing my supper when the man who had served me came and bent over my shoulder. He must have overheard what I had told Eugenius and his guests.

'Is it true, lord, that these things have happened?'

'Only too true.'

I heard him sigh, and caught a glimpse of his scared white face. He would have slipped away with some dishes, but I called him back.

'Show me my sleeping chamber. I have much to do to-morrow.'

'Yes, lord.'

I picked up my sword and followed him to a room in an upper corridor, and at the end of the passage I saw a woman seated on a stool, the woman who had been assigned to serve Igerna. I spoke to her softly.

'Is the lady sleeping?'

'I cannot say, lord.'

But I was well content. I was near Igerna, and in case of peril I could serve her. I left the door of my room open, and I slept.

VI

I WOKE to a strange and silent house, and, the day being very young, I gave no great thought to the silence. I washed and dressed, and passing along the corridor saw the woman's stool outside Igerna's door. I knocked gently on the door.

'Igerna, are you awake?'

Her voice answered me.

'Yes, my brother.'

'We must take the road early. I will go and have our wallets filled.'

I passed down the stairs into silence and emptiness. The remains of the supper were still upon the table, and I supposed that in this luxurious house the world rose late. I walked down a corridor which led to the servants' quarters, and I clapped my hands and shouted.

'Hullo, there! Is all the world asleep?'

Silence. Open doors mouthed at me and were dumb. The

house was empty, and all these loyal souls had fled in the night. I had my wallets with me and I found all that I needed, food and wine and milk. I wondered whether Eugenius and his guests had gone with the servants, and whither? There was bitter scorn in me, and yet how could one blame these poor fools who had been pampered in a rich man's house? I was returning to the great staircase when I heard Eugenius's voice. He was calling for his body-servant, and his thin voice sounded querulous in the empty mansion.

I saw him on the stairs above me, tousle-headed, bleary of eye, and I gathered that he had drunk himself silly. He put a lock of sandy hair out of his eyes, and his weak chin gobbled.

'Satan take these slug-a-beds. I can make no one hear.'

'Nor will you, my friend,' said I. 'Your valiant people have fled.'

Then he fell to scolding at me like a frightened woman. All this was my doing. If I had not spun such preposterous stories, Eugenius's bath would have been warm and scented, and his breakfast carried up to him. I will confess that I was a candid friend.

'Eugenius,' said I, 'if you can find a horse in your stables, mount him and ride west. And where are your guests?'

'Gone,' said he. 'Your bloody rumours sent them home.'

'Good. Then I have rid you of some parasites.'

But my own words prompted other thoughts. What if these frightened fools had taken Cæsar and Igerna's horse? I left my wallets on the stairs and raced for the stables, to find the horses safe and Cæsar demanding corn and water. What befell Eugenius I do not know, for I had other matters to attend to. It was my hope to reach Calleva that same day, and Calleva, with its great walls would be a secure refuge. I carried up food for Igerna and placed the jug and platters outside her door, and wondered if the same strange dream-state possessed her. I heard a horse's hoofs as I descended the stairs, and I supposed it was little Eugenius making for safety.

But our adventures here were not ended, or rather—we were to see another end to them. I had led out the horses, and mounted Igerna when I saw a little crowd of figures streaming up the valley, and for a moment my heart beat hard, and my belly tightened. I pulled the horses quickly under cover of a wall, and creeping to the terrace, looked down the great green slope. No, these impetuous gentry were not enemies, but a mob of slaves making for the mansion. I guessed what their purpose was, plunder, and as we rode away we heard their howls and shouts, and I feared that these animal noises might bring terror and evil memories to Igerna. It was not so. She did not seem to hear those voices.

We were well away on the Calleva road, when, happening to look back I saw smoke rising above the trees. Eugenius's house had gone up in flames, and the hate and envy and malice of the common people had been satisfied.

The road ran straight as a spear shaft across the heathy wastes, with blue hills in the distance, and the sky cloudless.

Nature was in no mood to match the malice and madness of men. We rode in silence with the sun behind us, and this silence had become less strange to me, for it was like the silence of some sacred place into which the soul of my love had withdrawn itself. And yet when I stole glances at her, and saw her young loveliness of skin and hair and eyes, I was smitten with secret anguish, for this white flower would never flush in my arms. Strange that I who could be rough and fierce with men should feel so utterly gentle towards her, but some love is like that.

I think we had covered some fifteen miles, and the sun was warm upon our backs, when we came to the wooded country, great oaks and beeches, birches and old yews. It was time to eat, and I was about to tell her so when she stopped her horse, and her words astonished me. She pointed to a great thorn that was in flower.

'Let us rest here, Geron.'

I looked at her wide-eyed, and she turned and looked at me, steadfastly and with eyes that had lost their sleeping haze.

'You are a good man, Geron, and I love you, but I am given to God.'

I would have gone down in the dirt at her feet. We drew aside, and dismounted, and she took the wallets from me

55

while I tethered the horses where they could graze among the buttercups. I had put a clean white cloth into one of the wallets, and when I returned from tethering the horses I saw Igerna on her knees, spreading the cloth under the thorn tree. I stood and watched her for a moment, her hands busy as she put out the food; the smell of the mayblossom will always be part of that picture. It seemed to me that Igerna had come back to the world of matter and of men, and with a sweet sanity that yet belonged to another world, and that our meal under the thorn tree was to be a love-feast, but not of pagan love.

Kneeling, she looked up at me.

'Come, Geron. Here—I serve, for you have served me so greatly.'

I sat down on the grass opposite her, and she poured milk from a flask, and set bread and meat upon a platter.

'Eat and drink, Geron, and be at peace.'

'Not till you have——'

'But I serve. For once my hands are yours, my dear.'

I wanted to kiss those hands, and as I looked at her, white petals fell from the tree upon her black hair like sacred manna out of heaven.

I saw her smile, and again her lips moved.

'Be patient with me, Geron. What must be must be. I was away somewhere, and I am here again. I have had visions. I must obey that which my eyes have seen.'

I bent my head to her. Strange, that I, a young man in the force of my years, should have renounced for her sake all that I desired, but it was so. She had suffered much, and all my soul felt gentle to her.

I said: 'I love you, Igerna, and I shall always love you.'

So we sat and ate our simple meal under the flowering thorn, and Igerna's hunger was that of a young girl, but her words to me were all of mystery. She told me how her spirit had passed out of her body and walked through dark and dangerous places until it had seen a light, and an angel with spread wings glowing like a sunset. The angel had spoken to her: 'Have no fear, Igerna. God has set his seal upon you and

chosen you for His own. Follow the voice that is within you.'
She told me that this voice had been speaking to her all
through the hours of darkness and of daylight, and that it was
like the voice of her dead father. She was to go to Corinium
and join the sacred Sisterhood in that city, and wait until
other mysteries were revealed to her.

I listened and was sad, and oppressed by a feeling of utter
helplessness. How could I contend with such a voice, or dare
to doubt it or to flout it. Had not the Lord Christ shown
Himself to faithful women, and might He not still reveal
Himself in dreams and visions? It would be blasphemy for
me to question the voice of God.

I looked up into the heart of the tree, as though God might
be there.

'He has laid a bitter duty upon me, Igerna, but I will not
fail you.'

'I shall think of you—always, Geron. You will be the first
in all my prayers.'

And that, it seemed, was all I should be to her, a shadow-
man shut out of her world, and to be prayed for!

Once more we mounted, and rode on through the forest
country, for Colleva was known as the city in the woods, and
towards evening we saw the gilded roof of Colleva's basilica,
and a golden figure on a high pillar above the dark walls of
that secret city. The figure, on its pillar, was like a great
finger held up in warning, and when Igerna saw it she pressed
her hands to her breasts and cried out that she had seen this
very symbol in a dream. Even Colleva looked like a dream
city, for the woods about it were of oak, all in spring leaf with
the sunlight shining upon them about and beyond those grim
dark walls. I could see that the gate was open, and people
were passing out to tend their gardens and their little fields
beyond the town's pancrium.

There were tombs beside the road, as was the custom in
those days, and as we rode on we saw people carrying flowers
and green branches with which to decorate these memorials
to the dead. Then a bell tolled somewhere in the city, a peaceful sound, and to me the whole scene was unbelievably peace-

ful after the grim things I had seen. Had Colleva heard no rumours, or cast them aside as mere rumours? I saw no sentinels upon the gate towers, and no armed men upon the walls.

So we passed in to the ringing of that bell, and found Colleva at its evening leisure, the little wine-shops open, people strolling or gossiping at doors. I saw no frightened faces nor any shadows of alarm. The white-walled houses sunned themselves, and children played in the alleys. I knew of a quiet guest-house beyond the forum, and thither we rode. The keeper of the guest-house knew me, and she came forth to greet me in its little courtyard. She was a fine old dame with white hair and a serene and ruddy face, and I dismounted and drew her aside, and spoke to her of Igerna.

Her blue eyes looked incredulous. Almost I felt that she did not believe me. Like Colleva itself she had heard no tidings of blood and tears, but she believed me before I had done with her, and was ready to be gentle to Igerna. She had an empty room, a quiet room with a window opening upon the garden, and to that room she led Igerna.

Now, on the opposite side of the street stood Colleva's fashionable wine-shop, and men's hostelry, a place which would serve me for the night, but I had been so concerned with Igerna that I had not cast a glance across the way. I had the horses by their bridles, and as I led them out of the gate I saw the white pillared portico of the inn packed with little tables and Colleva's young 'Elegants' enjoying their wine and their wit. These town fops belonged to the fraternity of scented fools who supposed that it was clever to be impudent, and singular to be supercilious. Moreover, their tongues were apt to be as unclean as their minds, and I gather that I was fair game to them.

I clapped my hands for a servant to come and take the two horses, and the little 'Community of Impudents' clapped with me, an ironic, smirking chorus.

Said one sallow young man whose hair was crimped and larded, and who wore half a dozen rings on his fingers:

'Your Excellency has taste.'

I was beckoning to a servant and I ignored the fellow.

58

'Take these horses, and see them well looked to. I need a bath and a supper table.'

The man knew me and touched his forehead.

'Your servant, Master.'

I heard a high-pitched voice say: 'Did you hear, sirs? His Excellency will take a bath.'

'Brother, he may need it. Pretty ladies do not welcome sweating lovers.'

They laughed, and I began to take notice.

'You choose to be facetious, gentlemen.'

'Holy Gemini, His Excellency wears a sword!'

The sallow fop giggled.

'Do you open Venus like an oyster, sir?'

I stood and looked at him, and he simpered.

'You are playful,' said I.

'Go and wash, brother, before you go to trouble the girl. I applaud your taste in ladies.'

There was silly, lewd laughter, and my temper flared. Was Igerna to be soiled by the tongues of these idle fools? I went and stood close to the sallow young man.

'Get on your feet. I do not hit a man when he is sitting.'

'Sir—sir—you take offence too easily.'

He lolled there, grinning at me, and suddenly I caught him by the collar of his tunic and heaved him up, and then smote him. He fell across a table and cups and wine flagons crashed, but he had more spunk than I had expected. He scrambled up and rushed at me, but I stopped his wild blows and taking him by the middle threw him across another table into the thick of his fellow fops.

For a moment or so I thought the whole fraternity would show its courage by falling on me in chorus, and I laid my hand on my sword.

'Gentlemen, I think you are a little ignorant of what is happening not so very far away. Swords will be more important than pomade pots.'

I looked from one to the other, and their eyes shirked mine, and I righted Sallow Face's table, and sat down at it, and unbuckled my sword and laid it on the board.

59   SC—E

'That is my mark or signature. Our friend with the bloody face should know that the lady over yonder had her father and all her people put to the sword. Have none of you heard that the King and his notables have been slain by the sea-rovers?'

There was a glum dumbness around me. So they had not heard—which seemed to me incredible.

'Sir,' said one youth who looked more of a man than his fellows, 'is this true or are you jesting?'

'It is much too true,' said I, 'and your city may be glad of its walls.'

The fop-party broke up and drifted away. My tidings had taken the stomach out of their impudence.

If I came as the first bearer of bad news, it must have spread swiftly through the city, for I, a restless and unhappy lover, felt a restlessness about me as I wandered. Colleva had become a city of ghosts whispering in dark alleyways and doorways, yet there were more lights burning in windows, and these lights were lit by fear. I passed through the gate of the colonnade about the forum, and saw that the windows of the basilica were lit from within; and I heard a murmur of voices. The city fathers were in conclave. There were lights, too, in the temples that had become Christ's, and in the new little church I heard a priest's voice speaking to the people, and I turned into the narthex porch to listen.

'A judgement has come upon us, my children, woe and wounds and peril. I would say to you that this island and this city have suffered from pleasure, and too much ease. Buying and selling, buying and selling, merchandise, rich living, and too little fear of God.'

It was a candid and a gloomy voice, but it was telling the truth to the people, and the little church was brittle with silence, the silence of souls to whom fear had come in the night. I turned away, and was passing the labrum when I heard a voice calling, the voice of a town crier.

'I seek the lord Gerontius. It is the lord Gerontius I seek.' I hailed him.

'I am Gerontius. What do you want with me?'

60

'Lord, the fathers of the city are in session. They would hear the news you bear.'

I followed him back to the forum and the basilica, and entering the council chamber, found the city worthies squabbling among themselves. It would appear that one member of the council, Colleva's demagogue, was pouring scorn on the whole business, and when the doorkeeper announced me, this voluble fellow addressed me.

'Ha, here is the gentleman who has run away from a few bandits. Let him confess to his cowardice.'

I looked at this swarthy moneylender with his large nose, and red and gabbling mouth, and knew him for what he was. I said: 'Gentlemen, I am here in Colleva with a sacred duty to perform. Tomorrow I go to Corinium. I shall return to Colleva. Then, if my friend has the stomach for it, he can go with me towards Kent. He may have his throat cut, but that will be his affair, not mine.'

Clean shook his fist at me.

'Ha, the words of a boastful fellow. I do not boast.'

'That is excellent,' said I. 'Has the gentleman ever worn armour?'

An old fellow chuckled.

'No, sir. Nothing but a belly-band, I gather.'

Then there was uproar and shouting until the president's bell brought silence.

'We would hear what the lord Gerontius has to tell us.'

I have never been a man for the tribune or the pulpit, and in my young strength I was for deeds not words, and maybe I did not respect these civic elders as I should have done, and I told them curtly of what was happening within ten miles of Londinium. It astonished me that no news had come to Colleva, but I suppose the treacherous attack had been so sudden that people who were threatened by it had thought of nothing but their own homes and safety. I got the impression that the council chamber grew darker and faces more dim and solemn as I told them of the King's death and the slaughter of the notables. And I had seen such slaughter. These old

61

men seemed to sink in their chairs. My words struck no spark from their old and rusty souls. I could feel a common terror lying heavy in their slack bellies. Even my swarthy Clean looked down his immense proboscis and was dumb.

One voice asked a question.

'What would a young man—like your excellency—suggest?'

Almost, I laughed. Was not the problem as plain as a pikestaff?

'Forge swords and spears, my friends. Arm your young men; man your gates and walls. Set watchers in the woods. And if you fear greatly for your city, send the women and children and the old folk elsewhere.'

Then my Clean found his tongue and his swagger.

'I am the man for that, though—like our young lord—I am not a man of acres.'

I turned to go, for I had had enough of Clean.

'You will pardon me, sirs, but I have a long journey on the morrow, and would sleep.'

I left that circle of fuddled, frightened faces, for Igerna's face had come between me and them. Was she sleeping, was she awake, was she grieving?—for an ache in one of my love's fingers mattered more than the anguish of a city. Young men should love like that, and women wish to be loved thus, but my love was desperate and forlorn, and while being gentle to Igerna, I lusted to take life by the throat and crush it. Men who have some secret wound in them can be fierce fighters, and love and war are strangely complimentary. Meanwhile I walked back to the hostelry, and climbing the wall of the garden, sat astride it, looking for lighted windows. There was but one upper chamber in which a lamp was burning, and I had more than a feeling that it was Igerna's. Indeed, even as I sat there under the stars I saw a figure in white come to the window, and I knew it to be Igerna.

I sprang down from the wall, and walked between beds of herbs to the house. There was a wild tenderness in me that would out. My feet must have crushed the herbs, for I smelt the sweet savour of them.

'Igerna.'

She leaned out to me.

'Oh, Geron.'

'Can you not sleep, my love?'

'No, Geron.'

'Nor can I sleep. I feel that I can never sleep again. Igerna, fate has been bitter to me.'

She answered me very gently. ...

'Geron, I love you, but not as a woman may love. Be patient with me—oh, be patient!'

I put up my hand to her.

'In loving you, my love, I am other than myself. There is no evil in my heart. I would die for you—with joy and gladness.'

She seemed to sigh.

'Go now, Geron. God has laid this duty upon us. I shall think of you always—yes, always.'

I left her. I trampled across the herb beds, and climbed the wall. She was still at her window, white and motionless, like a saint in a picture. I leaped down into the lane, but sleep and the urge for it seemed far from me. I wandered about the dim streets most of the night.

We set forth early next morning, but we were not to be alone. We had turned to look back at Colleva with the slanting sunlight shining upon it. We could see the gilded roof of the basilica, and the golden figure on its column, the pillars and pediments of temples, red roofs and coloured walls, some were white, some yellow, others brown and rose. The pomerium was deserted, but before we turned upon our way I saw a little crowd of people pouring from the western gate, some on foot, some mounted. Colleva was vomiting its fugitives.

We rode on towards Spinæ. I was in no mood to be one of a crowd, and I felt that Igerna would wish to be alone with herself, but before we had gone two miles I heard a horse cantering behind us. It carried a fat old man with a bald head, and a persistent and amorous smile, one of those old fools who never grow old with dignity. He joined us; he saluted Igerna, and placed himself beside her.

'Well, pretty lady, what of the morning?'

I pulled Cæsar in and laid a hand on the bridle of Igerna's horse. The old fellow stopped with us, and gave me a leer.

'Ha, ha, young man—I'm only a fatherly fellow.'

I looked him straight in the eyes.

'Pass on, sir. Neither I nor the lady like patter.'

He reddened up and scowled at me. I suppose he thought me a jealous lout, but he rode on, the sun shining upon his pink bald pate.

We took our midday meal in a little grove of oaks beside the road. I spread the cloth and served Igerna on my knees. I fell on my knees to her, for, in a little while I should see her no more. She gave me gentle glances, and few words; fate lay between us, and I knew that I was losing that which I loved more than life.

People passed upon the road, people who seemed to be hastening from some storm. I saw a woman with a child at her bosom pause and look at us. Then, she came across the grass. She was an oldish woman with a tired, sad face.

'Of your mercy—can you give me milk? I have had no milk for the child. My daughter died in bearing him.'

Igerna was on her feet. She took the child into her own arms.

'Sit down, mother, and eat.'

We had a flask of milk, and Igerna gave the babe suck from it, and I—watching—was rent by the thought that but for those sea-savages Igerna might have held a child of ours like that. The woman seemed famished; she devoured bread and meat, and looked upon Igerna with hungry and grateful eyes.

'Blessings on you, lady. Some day you and the gentleman will have a babe to care for.'

I could have smitten the poor wretch, but Igerna smiled as in her sleep.

'That may not be, mother. I am to be a virgin given to God.'

And the woman looked at me as though she thought me a fool.

We saw her again later on the road to Spinæ, for a passing wain had taken her up. She was sitting bent on the floor of the waggon, holding the child, and looking with blind misery at her own feet. Her head rose as we went by, and she looked at us, but did not appear to know us again, and she must have been stupid with weariness and woe.

I have nought to say of Spinæ. It was a dull and dusty place, and crowded with dusty people, and I chose not to tarry here, but to try our fortune further along the road. We came to richer country, high hills and deep valleys, great grassy hills and beech woods, and in many a valley there was a farm or a mansion. I chose one such place, a great white house at the head of a wooded valley, as stately as a white swan on a nest. There were men working in the peaceful fields, and in the park about the house I saw deer grazing. I pulled up and called to one of the labourers and asked him who dwelt here. He was a fresh-faced, pleasant fellow, and he smiled at me.

'I thought all the world knew that, Master.'

'I am a stranger to these parts.'

'The lady Julia is the mistress here.'

'Old or young?' said I.

'Both, sir, if you get my meaning.'

I did. He was a merry fellow, and I supposed that Dame Julia was one of those who are determined to cherish perpetual youth, but I was short of subtlety. The woman who was to be our most beneficent hostess was sixty-five years old with the eyes of a laughing girl.

We met Dame Julia driving out in her chariot as we neared the house, and she herself was handling the reins. I saluted her, and she stopped her horses and looked with those bright black eyes at each of us, and how shrewd and penetrating were those eyes. I asked her if I might speak with her alone. I had dismounted and she stepped out of her chariot, leaving the reins in the hands of her groom.

'Well, young man, you have a very serious face.'

'I carry serious news.'

65

She glanced meaningly at Igerna.

'It is very lovely news. And your name?'

'Gerontius, your ladyship, but my news is less lovely than the maiden.'

I told her what I had to tell, and she listened with complete calmness, her eyes never leaving my face. In fact, I had a curious feeling that she had foreseen much of the news I had to tell her, and that like some prophetess she had divined the terrors that would afflict this island. I saw no fear on her face, but an austere courage.

'Yes, young man, I can give you lodging. Igerna has suffered much. You say you go to Corinium.'

I bent my head to her, and suddenly she smiled, and there was compassion in her smile.

'The devout lover. Some devoutness goes against the flesh. And afterwards—Gerontius?'

'I go back as a fighting man.'

She bent her head to me.

'Would that I were young and a man like you.'

VII

DAME JULIA and her great house could give us all the kindness and comfort that man could desire, but it and its mistress gave us other things. Igerna was weary, and went to her bed, but I sat late, with wine before me, talking with this great old lady. She had lost both husband and sons, and though there was a gaiety about her, it had the tragic gleam of a tired but valiant spirit. Sitting there in her great gilded chair, the lamps lit and the servants dismissed, she spoke to me like some stately Sybil, and her words were of deep meaning. She could remember the Legions, she had watched a spurious peacefulness emasculate this island; she had foreseen these tragic happenings.

She said: 'Maybe blood and fire may make men of our

people. If not—it will be the end. And you are a man, Gerontius.'

Yes, I confessed that I was fierce to fight, but that we had no arms or harness. I had my sword .... And then she looked at me with a mysterious smile.

'You would have harness, my son?'

'I would.'

Therewith she rose and beckoned to me, and led me to what had been the mansion's armoury. Hanging there were a corselet, arm-pieces, a shield, and a gilded helmet with cheek pieces. It was a gorgeous armour, inlaid with silver and gold.

'There, my son, is your gear. It should serve a hero instead of hanging useless.'

For a moment I was dumb.

'Take it,' said she.

I raised her hand and kissed it.

'May I wear it as it should be worn.'

She said: 'You will.'

The Romans had a saying that a man was made by his toga, and I will confess that the fighting man in me was heartened by this harness. Dame Julia told me that it had belonged to her great-grandfather who had been a notable captain in the wars against the Caledonians and the pirates from Hibernia, and one shoulder-piece bore the cut of a sword. A sign of honour that. It would have pleased me to have donned the armour that very night, and even to sleep in it, for I was raw to harness, and a man must learn to carry it. I think Dame Julia read what was in my heart.

'Tomorrow, my son, my old fingers shall fasten the buckles for you.'

I saluted her.

'Why should you so honour me?'

She laughed, and gave me a merry look.

'Even an old woman may like the looks of a man.'

Was I a vain fellow?

Yet, without vanity where is youth's panache?

I took my bath that morning, and was shaved, and I lay on a marble couch and was rubbed with some sweet-smelling unguent. If this was to be my last day with my love, she should see me in harness, and if the vestal gown was to be hers, my gear should be that of a fighting man. I had been taught to wrestle and to box, but sword-play would be new to me, and yet young fierceness may be more potent than a veteran's cunning, none the less I vowed that some old sword-master should give me lessons.

I found Dame Julia in the surma-room, with the table laid, and that splendid armour lying ready for me on a couch. Would I be armed before my love came to us? I would. The Dame's eyes were jocund and maternal.

'It is wise to leave a good portrait in the mind of a maid, my son.'

I could not smile with her, and my foreseeing of the future was not hers.

'It might have been otherwise,' said I. 'I have a debt to wipe off with these sea-savages.'

'You are bloody-minded, Gerontius.'

'I am.'

I stood while she took the corselet and laid it upon me and fastened the straps and buckles. Then came the shoulder-pieces and the arm-pieces. The baldric and sword could wait a while, but the Dame crowned me with the helmet. Then she stood back with folded arms and surveyed me.

'Fine feathers, my son. You carry harness—as it should be carried.'

'Fine feathers do not——'

'Cha,' said she, 'that old tag! Fine feathers help to make a man.'

Then Igerna came in through the curtains and saw me, and for a moment I think she took me for a stranger. Strange stranger—I. And yet I might have felt like a dressed-up boy had I not seen in her eyes that which a man may desire to see.

The Dame kissed Igerna.

'Behold your hero, my dear.'

Times were too grim for teasing, and I was feeling no hero, nor was there any laughter in me. Igerna was looking at me over the old lady's shoulder, and there was something like fear in her eyes, or so it seemed to me. Was the woman in her seeing me as a lover whose fine feathers might end in a trampled and bloody mess upon some stricken field? Her lips were pale, her face full of sudden yearning.

I blurted at her: 'Dame Julia has made a wonderful and gracious gift.'

'Yes,' said the lady, standing off, 'a man should be able to carry harness. Look well at him, my dear. Women may weep, but men must ride to battle.'

Igerna did not appear to hear her. She stood gazing at me, and then with upraised hands she came and lifted the helmet from my head, kissed it, and re-helmed me. That casque was to suffer many fierce blows, and to turn them, but never a blow that moved me more than the touch of a girl's lips.

When we set off that morning from Great Beeches, for such was the name of the Dame's mansion, she gave me a letter to a very notable lord who dwelt a few miles from Corinium. In the Roman days this place had been the home of Corinium's Præfect, and the present lord, Artorius, was the son of the last of the Roman Præfects. His house stood close to the White Way and was known as Collis Alba, and Artorius was not only a man of great possessions but of singular reputation.

'This letter will commend you to him.'

I thanked her, and kissed her hand, and she looked with jocund eyes at Igerna.

'May not an old woman be kissed otherwise, my dear?'

So I kissed her otherwise.

'Tarry here on your return, my son.'

'I will,' said I.

The weather grew grey and blustery that day, as British weather will, and in spite of my new panoply the drear day was heavy upon me. Trees tossed green and tragic hands, and the meadows were like little restless seas, and towards

69

noon the wind blew a soft drizzle into our faces. I had a cloak strapped to my saddle, and I unfastened it, and putting Cæsar close to Igerna's horse, spread the cloak over her shoulders.

She gave me a deep, dark look.

'You give everything, I—nothing, Geron.'

I would have taken her into my arms, for I felt a great sadness in her. She was going to live among strangers, and all her past had gone up in flames, but I was strangely shy of her, more shy of her I think than she was of me.

'No,' I said, 'you give me everything—to fight for.'

She answered with a little shudder.

'I am afraid, Geron, I am afraid. The world is like the wind and the rain and that grey sky.'

Did she fear for me? That would have made me happy. But her sadness moved me.

'You will be safe in Corinium, Igerna. No one can harm you there.'

She gave me yet another deep, dark look.

'Shall I wish to be safe when there is horror in the mouth of each morning?'

From a little hill we saw Corinium in the valley, a grey city smudged by the rain, with wind-blown clouds above it, and yet I had seen Corinium in the sunlight, colourful and gay and flashing its many windows like jocund eyes. There was no colour here on this sad and moaning day, and the place looked like a dim ghost city. Even the fields and woods and the great hills in the distance had a mournful greyness.

I turned my gaze upon Igerna, and even her face had gone small and dim, and the light of her vision seemed to have vanished from her eyes.

So we came past the tombs to the East gate, and for the first time our journey I saw armed men upon the walls, and there were sentries at the gate. Corinium had heard the news, and though the terror was far from its walls, Corinium had taken it to heart. It was the second city as to size in the whole island, and maybe it held pride of place.

A sentry stopped us at the gate, his spear held slantwise, and this interference seemed to me mere fuss and foolishness, but the man was a veteran who had been called from his farm, and his grey beard cocked itself at duty. Moreover, it may have surprised him to see a man in harness, and curiosity prompted this formal challenge.

'Whence came you, sir?'

I liked the look of the old fellow. He was a tough country-man, and not city scum.

'We have come a long way, my friend, and from troubled country.'

'You bear arms, sir.'

'And why not?'

I drew him aside, and told him of Igerna's tragedy, and his old eyes grew kind.

'You will pardon me, sir, but I have orders. All comers from the east are to report to the city council.'

'That I will do, when I have seen the lady to the house of the holy women. Maybe you can direct me.'

'It is in South Street, sir, just beyond the old temple.'

I thanked him, and he saluted me.

'It is good to see such harness, sir.'

'It is good harness.'

'And you can carry it.'

We passed through to grey cobbles that were wet, and houses that had melancholy eyes. Corinium was within doors, and the streets were very empty. Even the wine-shops were closed, and I had a feeling that the city felt as gloomy as the sky. Or was it the stern silence and vigil of a place that had been shocked into prophetic grimness? We passed round the forum and the great basilica, and I saw the grey pillars of an old portico, and here three beggars were sheltering from the rain. They tumbled up and held out dirty paws to me.

'Pity the poor, lord.'

I was not feeling pity for such wastrels, and I gave them nothing, and they cursed me.

So, with the curses of these wretches in our ears and the rain on our faces, we came to a high white wall and an oaken gate, and I knew in my heart that this was our journey's end. I could see nothing but the red roof of the house above the

71

wall, and to me the place had a forbidding look. Was my love to end her life in a sepulchre such as this? An iron cross was fastened to the gate, with the Chi Rho above it, and I had no doubt but that this was the house of the most Holy Women.

A fellow with a sheepskin over his shoulders came up the street, and I hailed him. He had a heavy, stupid face, and his eyes stared like glass pebbles in a window. He nodded at me when I asked him if this was the house we sought, and then he stared at Igerna, and so lewd and lustful was the look he gave her that I felt like smiting his evil face.

'They won't let 'er in there, Master,' and he giggled.

So much for city manners.

I dismounted, walked to the gate, looked up and down the empty street and saw the fellow watching us from the portico of the grey old temple. He and the beggars were of the same fraternity. Need I confess that I was loath to knock upon that forbidding gate. It might have been a coffin lid let into the wall. And then, when my fist was raised I heard a little cry from Igerna.

'Geron—oh, Geron!'

I turned and saw her face suddenly wild and anguished, and for a moment I stood dumb. Had her heart failed her; had her vision faded? And then she spoke again in a strange, still voice.

'Knock, Geron, knock, and leave me.'

My love seemed to burst like blood from a wound. I went to her; I stood by her, looking up. She was as pale as death and as silent. And then, suddenly, she bent and kissed me upon the forehead.

'Christ be with you, Geron.'

She was off her horse before I could speak, and running wildly to the gate. I saw her knock, and then press her face to the iron cross, and many times have I wondered how things would have fared had I laid a lover's hands upon her, and not fumbled like a devout fool. Here was I, holding the bridles of two dumb creatures, and as dumb as they were, watching that gate, that fatal gate. I saw it open, and a cowled figure appear; I could not see the creature's face.

Would they take Igerna in? What if the house was full, or not open to unheralded neophytes? I had a moment of almost savage hope, but it was no more than hope. The portress stood aside and beckoned Igerna in, but that was not my last glimpse of her or the final gesture. The rain had increased from a drizzle to a deluge, and Igerna must have remembered my cloak, for she came running back to me and swinging the thing from her shoulders. She did not look into my face or utter a word, but laid the cloak over Cæsar's neck.

I saw the door close on her, and there was nothing but silence and the rattle of the rain upon the cobbles and upon my helmet and harness. I turned the two horses, and rode back past the old temple. The beggars and my sheepskin friend were sheltering in the portico. They mocked me.

'Fine feathers and a fool, Master.'

'Hee-hee, you be no man to handle a maid.'

I rode by, brittle with anger, but head in air. Was I to be moved by the mockery of such wretches?

And yet I wondered whether these lewd fellows were not right, and that I had played the devout fool, and lost that which I loved in honouring a fatal promise.

VIII

THERE were guards stationed at the gate of the Forum and I stopped there to speak with them. They were young and well-grown men, but—I gathered—as fresh to arms as I was. I told them I was from the east, and that the sentry at the gate had warned me that the city fathers wished to speak with anyone who brought news.

One of the young men laughed, and there was scorn in his laughter, and a fierceness about him that matched my own feeling.

'There is much cackle, sir, if you care to hear it.'

I confessed that I had no great wish to listen to the prattling of old men, and I asked him his name, for I liked the look of him.

'Caradoc.'

'That is a good name,' said I; 'my name is Gerontius.'

He laughed, and eyed the two horses.

'Saddles for two, brother. Whither go you, or do you tarry here?'

'I have a letter to Artorius of Collis Alba.'

His face lit up.

'Ha—there is a man! Is the news true, that the King is dead?'

'True.'

'A land without a leader, and the bleating of old sheep. And after Collis Alba, brother?'

'I go east—to fight.'

He laid a hand upon Cæsar's neck.

'Gerontius of the White Horse—that might be a symbol. Would you take me with you, brother?'

I stretched out my hand to him.

'A brother-in-arms—why—yes. Come with me to Collis Alba, and ride this horse.'

We had got thus far with each other when a bald old man in a blue toga came blustering to the gate.

'What's this—what's this? A stranger here. Who are you, sir?'

I smiled at him.

'And who are you, sir?'

He spluttered at me.

'I—am—the clerk to the City Council, young man. You will answer my question.'

'With pleasure,' said I. 'I am a certain Gerontius from a county that has been stricken by the sea-savages.'

'Ha, is that so? Thus you will come before my Council. Have not these young men given you our orders?'

'They have—but young men may ask for deeds—not cackle.'

He spluttered at me.

'Young men lack manners. You will come with me, sir.'

I caught Caradoc's eye, and I laughed.

'You may be glad of your young men, sir, before this business is over. Certainly I will come with you. I can give your Council tidings that are true.'

I will confess that I was not loving life, man, or myself at the moment, and to be screamed at by this old blatherskite was the last thorn in my shoe. I left the horses with Caradoc, and followed Bald Pate to the basilica, savage with a balked love which seemed to mock at me like those mangy beggars. Was I man to have suffered Igerna to pass through that oaken door? Had I been man to her the ending might have been more to my liking, and perhaps to hers. Her little anguished face seemed to float before me reproachfully.

But we had come to the great hall with its rows of pillars and coffered roof coloured gold and blue, and its frescoed walls, and pavement in black and white marble. A grey light filled it, and I was conscious of a mysterious gloom. The colours were dim, and so were the half circle of faces, the faces of old men seated in their gilded chairs. There was a pregnant silence here, fear, vacillation, a sense of old blood running cold.

The voice of Bald Pate prompted me.

'Uncover your head, young man, before your elders.'

I did not do so. I looked at those dim old faces with their staring eyes, and I felt no fear of them. A young man I might be, but I was a living torch in this pillared gloom. I raised my arm in a salute, and spoke to the old man who sat in the highest chair. He had a halo of grey hair, and a grey face, but there was a smoulder in his eyes.

'Sir,' I said, 'I have come from the east. I hear that you welcome tidings. I can give them.'

There was not a murmur from the council. Those old faces might have been mute paintings on the wall. The palsy of fear was upon them.

The old man with the grey halo leaned forward. His eyes were the only bright eyes in that dim place.

SC—F

'Who are you, young man?'

'My name is Gerontius, and I am lord of lands in the country below Londinium.'

'What has brought you to our city?'

'Sir, that is a private matter of my own, nor does it concern you. I do not tarry here. If you would hear what I have to tell, let it be told, for I go to Collis Alba.'

He bent his head to me, and I told them all that I had to tell, as I had done at Colleva. The King was dead, many notables slaughtered, and the sea-wolves raiding and burning. The half circle of old faces seemed to grow more ghostly and grey. I felt the chill of this gloomy hall. A wind had sprung up, driving the rain against the windows, and making a hollow moaning like the voices of the unhappy dead.

When I had finished, I saw these old men looking at each other in dumb consternation, like sheep who had lost their shepherd. There was no hope for our island here. I saluted them, and turned to go, and no voice bade me stay. The sound of my footsteps echoed under the great, coffered roof.

I found Caradoc and the horses at the fore gate. He smiled at me. In the wild days that were to come he was a man who smiled, even in the face of death, while I was grim and bitter.

'How are the dear patriarchs, brother?'

'Like bladders of lard, my friend. Let us go from here.'

'I am with you.'

But I had a more passionate urge to satisfy. I wanted to look again upon that forbidding wall and the fatal door, so I rode down South Street, and Caradoc went with me. The beggars had gone from the temple portico, and the wet and weeping street was empty. I dismounted, tossed my bridle to Caradoc, and going to the oak door, laid my hand upon the iron cross.

'Peace be with you, my dear love. For me there is no peace.'

When I returned I found Caradoc looking at me curiously, but he asked me no questions, for which I blessed him.

Caradoc knew the way.

He was one of those whipcord men, lean and dark and freckled, with a curl in his black hair, and eyes that flashed at you suddenly. His strength was extraordinary, and though I was a far bigger man his strength was nearly as great as mine. It seemed strange to see this stranger on Igerna's horse, but I was to find that in losing my love I had found a good and valiant comrade.

We took the White Way, and about us rose green hills and great beech woods. The sky had emptied itself, and we had been riding less than an hour when the sun rent the clouds and poured down upon us.

'Good omen,' said Caradoc. 'Look yonder. There is Collis Alba.'

I shaded my eyes and looked. Westwards ran a steep green valley glistening in the sunlight, and at the head of this secret valley and sheltered by high woods stood a vast white mansion. Never had I seen a country house of such stature, dignity and splendour. The slanting sunlight cast a mantle of gold over it, and all about it the world was green and flowery.

'My lord has a lordly house.'

'He is as lordly as his house, brother.'

We took a road branching from the White Way, and as we drew nearer the gracious calm of this great house grew more and more apparent to me. It was the colour of fresh milk, and the pantiles of its many roofs were rust-red brown. A gate-house guarded the great court, and there were many courtyards, or so I gathered, with buildings about them, baths, stables, the servants' quarters, barns, granaries, and a well-house. A spacious garden was spread below the house, and orchards, and a vineyard, and high woods sheltered it, but threw no shadow upon it, nor kept off the sun. So splendid and stately was Collis Alba that it gave me to feel that while such noble mansions stood our island world could not go down in flame and ruin.

We were less than a furlong from the gate-house when we beheld a strange sight, or so it seemed to two lone men who knew that fear and peril were abroad. The gates stood open, and from them belched a sudden stream of colour. It flowed out and down to a great grassy space, led by a red-robed figure on a huge black horse. So astonished were we that we both drew rein and watched these armed men march out in perfect order.

I looked at Caradoc, and he looked at me.

'A good sight, brother.'

'Ha,' said I. 'I have seen nothing like it in a hundred miles or more. Fighting men. Is that Artorius on the black horse?'

'It is, brother.'

'We have come at a good moment.'

The sunlight shimmered on spearpoints, shields and helmets, and I gathered that the smiths of Collis Alba had not been idle. The column halted on the grassy space, and then ordered itself in line, four deep. Artorius sat on his black horse, and his deep voice came to us as he spoke to those armed men.

Then he gave an order, and spears sloped and shields flashed. The front rank advanced two paces. More spears were sloped. We sat and watched the war drill, and my heart felt big in me. Here—at last—was an answer to the terror from over the sea. I could mark that the men carried swords at their belts, and the old stabbing sword of the Romans. When the spears had thrust their damnedest, those swords would rip up bellies.

There came a pause and spears were grounded. I saw Artorius looking towards us, and I nudged Cæsar with my heels.

'Let us go to them, Caradoc.'

'I am with you, brother.'

So we rode to where Artorius sat on his black horse. I saluted him, dismounted, and went forward with my letter.

'Lord—greetings. This letter is from Dame Julia. May I give it into your hands.'

He looked at me and I at him. He had a great broad head, grizzled hair that flowed upon his shoulders, a ruddy face and splendid eyes. Here was a man, and as I stood before him I felt his power and all the potency of a man among men. Yes, and I and others could follow such a leader.

'Who are you, my friend?'

'Sir—I came from the east, and here I find that which I have yearned to see.'

'And that——?'

'Fighting men.'

He smiled at me, and he had a smile that made all men his servants.

'Your name, my son?'

'Gerontius.'

'Yes, Caradoc, I know,' and he opened the Dame's letter and sat reading it.

Even his manner of reading a letter made me feel that this man would never be flustered or made to hurry, though his deliberation was utterly without sluggishness. He had a measured rhythm of his own, profundity, a capacity for confronting a problem with leisured strength and shrewdness. Not that he lacked impetuosity or fierceness when such flares of the blood are needed. He could sit like Jove above smaller men, and consider all things that should be foreseen and considered before launching his thunderbolt.

What the Dame had written in her letter to him I do not know. She had sealed it with her signet, and Artorius had broken the seal. I watched him refold her letter and slip it under his girdle.

'You will favour me by being my guest, Gerontius.'

I thanked him.

'Perhaps—I may be more than that, sir.'

'Your wish?'

'To be one of your fighting men.'

He gave me a searching, steadfast look.

'This island will be glad of her young men. Stand beside me, Gerontius, while we finish our work.'

I stood and watched Artorius put his company through their battle drill, and even in his handling of these two hundred men proved to me that he had tactics of his own. Each shield carried a cross in red or blue, and the red shields formed a solid phalanx in the centre, while the blues spread out like two scythe blades on chariot wheels. For many years the peacefulness of this island had been broken by storms of raiders: Scots, Picts, Irish, Saxon, but the great Theodosius and Itilicho had dealt with them, and there had been peace. Then, when the Legions had left us these raids had fallen upon us like spasms of

79

pain, but a pain that had passed. The fighting had had no plan or order, no continuity, no settled purpose. The savages who had afflicted us had come for plunder, and each part of our island had had to beat the raiders off as best it could. But this new peril was different; it was to be an invasion, a slaughter and a seizing of the land and townships which had been ours. The blond beasts had come to stay, and I was to realise that Artorius had foreseen these happenings. A few, raw, local levies would not suffice. Britain needed legions of her own, trained fighting men, not mobs, who could take the field with discipline, and, in ordered battle, rout these wolf-packs.

I watched the red shields charge, and the blue shields sweep round in the flanks, and Artorius's tactics were plain to me. The solid centre would crash into a marauding mob, and the wings encircle that which the centre had broken into fragments. And as I stood with Caradoc beside Artorius's great black horse, the young blood whimpered in me.

Artorius looked down at me.

'There must be cunning in battle, my son.'

'I see your cunning, sir.'

'A soldier must learn his place as part of the master plan.'

The mock fight was over, and Artorius spoke to his men, praised them, and sent them to their suppers. I gathered that they were lodged in tents and bivvies on the hillside. Leading Cæsar I went with Artorius into the great courtyard, and there a groom took our horses.

His courtesy to me was splendid.

'Would you wash before eating, Gerontius?'

'I would, sir.'

So this great man led me in person to the baths, and showed me my chamber.

'We are a clean people, Gerontius, and cleanliness need not make one soft.'

'Yes,' said I, 'a stinking shirt is the symbol of a savage.'

I bathed, was rubbed with sweet ointment, and handed a clean white tunic. The servant bowed me from the bath, and I gave him money, and he led me down the great corridor to the dining-room. The walls of the corridor were covered with fine frescoes, and its windows set with little circles of glass. So we came to that most noble room, and I found myself alone in it with the great oak table and gilded chairs, the coffers and cabinets, the painted vases and glowing walls. That which was pagan had passed, and upon one wall I saw a picture of the Christ stretching out blessed hands to me, hands that bore the wound prints of the cross.

And suddenly a great sadness fell upon me, a yearning for my own home and all the things I knew and loved, my garden and my fields, my dogs and cattle and the familiar faces of my servants. It had been a bitter day for me, and heart-pangs can weary a man and bring him low, and as I looked at the Christ I felt like a sorrowful child.

I did not hear the curtain drawn back, but I felt a presence, someone's eyes upon me, and turning I saw Artorius. He had come from the bath, and had put on a white robe with a golden girdle. I remember the way he looked at me, and at the Christ upon the wall, and I knew that I could tell this great man all things, even as I could tell them to Saint Morgan.

'Be seated, Gerontius. We will eat.'

He clapped his hands and three silent servants glided in and laid dishes and bowls and plates upon the table. I took a chair on Artorius's right hand, and saw by the platters that we were to be alone. Caradoc, my smiling comrade, was supping with the steward and the house-mistress. Hot broth and bread were placed before me, and red wine poured into my cup. Then, the servants glided out as silently as they had come. We were alone together.

'Eat, my son, for often you and this island may go hungry.'

'Hungry, sir?'

'Look into the future, Gerontius. War breeds famine. What of your crops, should your enemies burn or reap them?'

I was silent, spooning broth. I had to confess to myself that I had not foreseen this part of the problem. Yes, what of my corn and my kine if these invaders despoiled me of them? And what of my people? Nuts and wild fruit cannot fill men's bellies. Moreover, my lot might be that of half the country.

'You have great vision, sir.'

He broke bread with those strong white hands of his.

'Vision is to the few, Gerontius. A slave has the soul of a slave, and he must be thought for and cared for.'

I nodded at him. I had a feeling that he liked the young when they were not spotty and arrogant, and that he was speaking to me as a man, and not to some unripe boy. The broth was warming me, and I warmed to him.

'There are things I would ask you, sir.'

'Ask them, my son.'

I hesitated. How much had the Dame told him in her letter?

'Sir, I had a reason for riding here. Maybe you know it.'

He smiled at me very kindly.

'Some letters are privileged, Gerontius.'

I understood him, and so I knew that I must speak to him of Igerna. He listened to me attentively, and I gathered that he did not think me a devout fool. My love had not been greedy, as most men's love is greedy, and when I had finished my story I waited for him to speak.

'You did well, Gerontius.'

I told him how the young men and the beggars had mocked me, and he said: 'My son, look at the Christ.'

I turned my glance to the picture on the wall, and it seemed to me that the eyes of our Lord looked upon me with strange tenderness. Could pictures speak? I bowed my head and made the sign of the Cross. I was crucified in the body of my love.

'Sir,' said I, 'you comfort me—at a bitter time. What of the house where she has taken refuge?'

'It is a good house, my son, a kind house, and no prison. I should know, for its Matron is my sister.'

Ye gods, what blessed news! I put the wine cup to my lips.

'That more than comforts me, sir. Tell me, if you will, whether a young man can enter there. Not now, when my love's wound is fresh—but——'

I caught him smiling, and there was some subtle meaning in his smile.

82

'Assuredly. That which you have done and suffered gives you—privilege. That house is not a prison.'

I drank more wine.

'So—some day—I may see her.'

He too drank wine.

'The blood of our Lord was merciful and human. I will speak to my sister, Placida. Igerna shall come here at times, and shall be treated as my daughter.'

So moved was that I rose and took his hand and kissed it.

'Sir, I shall bless Dame Julia for sending me to you.'

He laid his hand upon my head.

'I—who lost my love, can love lovers, Gerontius, and love that is not of the belly. But now, sit you down. There are other things to speak of.'

I returned to my wine and my victuals, and I had more stomach for both of them.

'What next, Gerontius?'

I told him of my hunger for home, and my urge to save my house and corn and flocks and people.

'I would go east, sir, and fight against all hazards. Maybe I shall find ruin, but go I must.'

'Have you men who can bear arms?'

I shook my head.

'They are tame creatures, but I may find one or two. And yet I would go.'

Then he said a thing that heartened me.

'My son, you may be a smith to temper the courage of men. Be brave and you may find men brave with you. Go and dare the hazard. Everywhere in this island those who can lead must do so. Every manor and village must give stout men. Then we can gather our strength together, and give battle as we should.'

I raised my wine cup to him.

'And you, great sir, will lead us?'

IX

CARADOC chose to come with me, and my blood being restless we saddled soon after dawn. Artorius was still abed, but I went to thank him and to take leave of him.

'Pardon my forwardness, sir.'

'It is a good virtue, Gerontius. Youth should be served.'

'If I should not return, I would commend Igerna to you.'

'You will return,' said he—'of that I am assured.'

So, we rode east and with such forcefulness on my part that Caradoc, who was less saddle-hardened than I was, had sore buttocks before we reached Colleva. I had left a letter with Artorius for Dame Julia, and he had promised to send a rider with it. My urgency was such that I would not turn a hand's-breadth from the way before me.

At Colleva we lodged at the same hostel, and Caradoc took his supper standing, and was abed early after rubbing unguent into his chafed skin, while I went wandering round the city to get the feel of its mood of destiny. A few people were gossiping in doorways, and about the farm gate, but I did not come upon my bright young friends. Maybe they had taken their waggery elsewhere.

One of the city 'Worthies' happened to come through the gate as I was loitering there. I recognised him, but he did not know me from Adam, for he had the aloofness and the dead eyes of age. I spoke to him, and he gave me a beady and suspicious look.

'Who are you, young man?'

I was a little weary of being called 'young man' by these old buffoons and official wiseacres.

'You have a short memory, sir.'

He looked me over, for I was in harness, and advertising Mars to an old man's world.

'By what right do you carry arms in our city?'

I laughed.

'May I ask you a question, sir councillor? Has Colleva set

its smiths to work, and are your young men practising sword-play?'

He sniffed.

'You are a swaggerer, I gather. In Colleva we are not alarmists. There have been foolish rumours——'

'Ah, very foolish,' said I, 'and your memory is strangely short. It was I who brought you news a few days ago.'

Then he remembered me.

'Ah, to be sure, the young man who had been frightened. Those rumours——'

'Are dead men and women and children rumours, sir?'

Once again he sniffed.

'You will excuse me, young man, but I am late for supper.'

There was a sadness about the city which kept me on edge and on restless feet. The lights went out and the stars shone overhead, and I was seeing the eyes of Igerna in those stars. Not a shadow, not a sound, though as I passed one gate a dog barked. Yes, there was a sadness here, and a feeling of doom, of ghosts passing me by on noiseless feet. No moon tonight, no watchmen on the walls or in the streets. So, I happened to come to the little church, and saw a faint glow in the narthex porch. I passed in and found two lamps burning, and the nave full of kneeling figures. There was no priest at the altar. These people had come to pray, and I too knelt down and prayed, as a man will, not in the clever jargon of the philosophers but for a few simple things, my love, my home, this green island, my corn crops and my people. My restlessness passed, and I was comforted, for there is comfort in prayer when other simple souls are on their knees about one. So, I arose and walked back through the silent streets and under the stars to my bed, to hear Caradoc snoring in the cubicle next to me.

Strange—that a man's sore buttocks should play the part of destiny, but after five miles Caradoc got off his horse and with a wry grin bade me ride on alone. He would follow on foot, and since my mood was fierce and urgent I rode on, and bade him make for Astolat.

What should I find there and at Sweet Water? I met few people on the road, and they had no news for me, and in the days to come I was to discover the reason for this lack of tidings. Moreover, the weather had once again changed its temper, and a wet wind blew grey clouds over my head. The trees tossed sad green heads, and the wet grasses trembled. If the summer was in it had a sorrowful and shabby face, and I was moved to remember that sparkling day when I had ridden from Venta and the white thorn had scented the warm air.

I rode along the chalk ridge, and towards evening I saw Astolat in its valley. It looked quiet and peaceful, but as I drew nearer I saw that people were still camped about the place, and I wondered whether my people were with them.

It was so. I found fat Gildas seated on the tail-board of a waggon with a bowl of soup between his knees. His eyes goggled at me. I was new to him in battle harness.

'Greetings, Master.'

I was curt with Gildas, so curt that he flopped to mother earth, slopping his soup over the rim of the bowl.

'Why are you here?'

'It is not safe over yonder, Master.'

'Safe!' said I. 'Is "safety first" to be the motto of this island? Are all my people here?'

He looked scared.

'No, Master, Lob is at Sweet Water, with the shepherd and two woodmen.'

'Good. So I have some men with spunk in them.'

'If I were a younger man, Master——'

I turned away from him, for my people were crowding round me, and I found myself surrounded by dumb, sheeplike faces. But they were unfriendly faces, sore with a strange and secret hostility, for I had yet to experience the malice of men and to confront the jealousy of the common fellow. Maybe they were moved to envy by the splendour of my harness, and my power to go when and where I pleased. In my innocence I had thought that my people were my friends; I had treated them generously and never played the master-bully. My

86

father had been sterner than I, and I was to learn that such just severity is needed; especially so when violence and war are in the air.

In fact, so strongly did I feel the unfriendliness of their stupid countenances that I was conscious of slow anger and a self-questioning pride. Why these stolid, staring eyes, and sullen faces? I looked at them, and they at me, but whenever I looked steadfastly at one particular face its eyes slid away and avoided mine. Had these fools some grievance?

I sat on my horse and spoke to them.

'There is trouble among you. Speak out, someone.'

A voice at the back of the small crowd answered me.

'Gentlemen can wear fine gear. Gentlemen can ride away on horses.'

That angered me.

'Who is it that speaks thus to me? Come forth and let me see your face.'

The little crowd glared and fidgeted, but my challenger would not come out into the open.

'Good,' said I, 'there is a coward among you, and this island has no use for cowards. I am your master, and, if any man wishes me to prove it, I will prove it.'

There was silence, the silence of the incalculable little people who make life mean with their poor, patchwork souls.

There was still much daylight left me, and my urge was to ride on and find Lob and his men at Sweet Water. I had no stomach for this sour crowd, and with a wave of the hand I rode through them. Maybe my scorn was too apparent, for hot young blood can be scornful, but blood and battle and suffering were to teach me many things: compassion for the weak, pride in the strong, and the knowledge that a leader of men must be their master and prove it in courage, wisdom, and force of arms. Be too gentle to the common man, and he will assume that you fear him, or he may over-value his importance. An implacable severity tempered with justice, praise when praise is due, a jest and a laugh when things look grim, the quiet voice of he who knows himself and the mastery that is in him; these are the qualities I came to cherish.

I had been too gentle with these grumbling fools. They needed the whip of a Roman will.

So, I rode on, leaving Astolat and sour faces behind me, under a hurrying sky, a sky that seemed grey with woe and tragedy. Wet harness and a wailing wind, and a brittle hardness within men. No welcome had I had from my people, but did I ask for a welcome from such bleating sheep? I saw the familiar hills and woods, the deep valleys, the meres and meadows. I was coming to my own house, a house which had not been violated, and I should find big, buxom Lob there, Lob of the stout muscles and the mighty heart.

Yet there was a strangeness in my homecoming. Only a few days had passed, but the familiar scene had a newness even on this dreary day. No dogs welcomed me, and I heard no lowing of kine; the fields were empty, and the wet woods wild and ruffled by the wind. There were puddles in the road, and the brook was running high and rustling among the reeds and water-flags. I saw no human figure, and heard no voices, and there was no smoke rising. The gate stood open. The mere was ruffled silver, and the willows waving in the wind. I dismounted at the bridge and led Cæsar into the courtyard, and saw wet windows blinking at me.

Silence, a most strange silence. Where were Lob and his men? I slung Cæsar's bridle over the post by the mounting block, and walked to the portico steps. The door was open, and it was like a dumb mouth welcoming me with wordless mystery. I entered; I stood listening. Then, from somewhere, came the sound of voices. Were they the voices of enemies or friends?

I went slowly and noiselessly along the great corridor with my sword drawn. One of the voices broke into song, drunkenly and with hiccoughs. It was a British voice, and that of a common man.

I came to the door of the summer-room and looked in. I saw a man sprawling on a couch, and holding a wine cup so that the wine was spilling from it; a second fellow sat astride a chair. They were bawling in each other's faces; they had not heard me, or seen me yet. I knew them for a couple of charcoal burners who journeyed around working in the woods of our countryside.

I walked into the room, and there was sudden silence. I laid my sword upon a table, and stood with folded arms. The maudlin fellow on the couch raised his cup to me.

'Why, if it ain't young Gerontius. Hic—greetings—old lad.'

Now, ours was a clean country, and these fellows had the dirt of weeks and of their craft upon them, and they were fouling my furniture and drinking my wine, and treating my house as though it was common property. And I was young Gerontius to them, and the world was upside down, and these fools were drunk and insolent.

I said: 'Did Lob, my smith, invite you to take wine in my house, gentlemen?'

The man straddling the chair turned and guffawed at me.

'Lob? Ain't seen the fellow. 'Ave a drink, young cock. Coo, what fine feathers!'

I was moved to fierce laughter.

'So my house is yours, and at your service?'

'True, old lad. Times 'ave changed. We workers are going to be—hic—the cat's whiskers.'

'Nice clean whiskers, gentlemen. Why did you not use the bath before fouling my furniture?'

He on the couch flared at me.

' 'Ere, you keep a civil tongue in yer mouth. Dirty, are we? Let me—hic—tell you it be honest dirt. We work—we do.'

I could not help laughing, and my laughter angered them. The man on the chair staggered up and displayed a fist.

'Like to feel that, young cock? A bloody nose—hic— what?'

'Gentlemen,' I said, 'will you kindly remove yourselves. I prefer to occupy my house in peace.'

The fellow lurched towards me. I did not strike him, but thrust him off and he fell over the chair. I heard footsteps in the corridor, and turning, saw big Lob in the doorway.

'Lob, these gentlemen claim to own this place. I fear they have had too much of our wine.'

89

Lob's teeth showed in his beard. The fellow who had fallen, staggered up and made another rush at me. Laughing, I hurled him backwards, and Lob completed the eviction. He gathered these new aristocrats one under each mighty arm, and carried them out like a couple of screaming and struggling pigs and pitched them into the brook beyond the gate.

I had followed Lob, and I had watched the immersion. The cold water of the brook sobered our friends, and chastened their arrogance.

'A good clean baptism, Lob.'

He grinned at me. The charcoal burners were standing waist deep in water, and clawing waterweed out of their eyes and hair. They glowered at us, but there was no more impudence left in them, for they found a new master in Lob the Smith.

So we left them there in the wind and the rain, and I went back with Lob to stable and feed Cæsar. Lob told me that he had been up on the hills on the look-out for raiders, and that he had posted the two woodmen on the downs to watch the Green Way and the road in the valley.

'They will be back at nightfall, Master.'

I caught him looking with a smith's eyes at my harness and my helmet.

'Brave gear, lord. The man who made that was a master of craft.'

I told Lob how I had come by my armour, and I had other things to tell him. Meanwhile, both of us were hungry and would eat, and I bade Lob find food, and share it with me in the summer-room.

'I will serve you, Master.'

'No, sit down with me, Lob,' said I, 'for you and I are to be fighting men and comrades.'

We sat down to what the house could give us, dry meat and bread that was ready to go mouldy, and wine of the best, and I remembered the words of Artorius. War can mean no crops, no grain in the granary, no milk or meat, but the need of the moment was to put the big fellow at his ease. He was like a great shy boy sitting with me at the table, and his big hands seemed to fumble, and his voice was lost to him. Men are curious creatures, and this tough giant who could be terrible in battle, was ever sensitive to me, and courteous and loyal, qualities that are supremely rare and precious in that puzzle-box called man. So I talked to Lob of Artorius and Artorius's forecastings of the future, and after a little wine and wisdom the smith lost his clumsiness. That is to say he had the essential wisdom in him, and a feeling for the fitness of things which so few common men possess. I was to see Lob grow in pride and manners, and become a notable captain and shepherd of men. There were to be good faith and great affection between us, and Lob's sword and valour were to carve out glory and honour for himself in this troubled island.

It was good to be back in my own house, and when we had broken our fast I saw the setting sun shining upon the windows of the great room. Once again the day had changed its temper, and, like a woman, was smiling after storms and tears. Leaving Lob to the household cares, I passed out into the walled garden behind the house with its herbs and roses and box-edged borders, and its vines and fruit trees trained to the walls. The place was smelling sweet, and the setting sun threw a sheet of light across it. A red rose tempted me and I plucked it and set it in my girdle with the fancy that it had touched my love's lips. I would think of her, and as I passed up the path to the seat under the clipped yews the box edging shed moisture upon my feet. I sat down with the sun upon my knees, and suddenly—I know not why—I felt this peaceful place fill with fear. It was not that I was afraid, but when the sun sank suddenly and a darkness fell upon the garden I seemed to sense peril, shadowy shapes amid the woods up yonder. So strong and sinister was the feeling that I stood up, listening and looking about me at the darkening hills and sky.

Then from somewhere far away a human cry came to me, a wild cry of terror and of anguish. It held for a moment or two in a long drawn scream, to break with a suddenness that made me think of a windpipe cut with a knife. A shiver went down my spine, for there was a dreadful horror in that cry,

91   SC—G

and human flesh was chilled by it. I stood rigid, listening, conscious of the failing light.

I saw Lob in the garden doorway. He too had heard that death-cry, and his white teeth gleamed in his beard. He came to me, and we stood looking in each other's faces, and I guessed that we were thinking the same thoughts.

Lob spat.

'That was a cut throat, Master.'

Yes, like the throat of some frightened beast.

'Your fellows should be in by now.'

Again Lob spat. Some men might have vomited.

'They should. Ha—what's that?'

I heard what sounded like men running and with desperate haste. There were breathless voices. I had left my sword in the summer-room, but I had my knife at my girdle, and as I drew it the red rose fell at my feet, like a gout of blood on the stones.

'Hist, Master.'

Lob's great fists were clenched.

Men were scrambling over the lower wall nearer the house. I saw two dark heads, and Lob turned swiftly towards them.

'Owain, is it you, man?'

'God—yes.'

They were the two woodmen with hatchets in their girdles, and their faces blanched.

'A dozen of the sea-devils. Did you hear?'

They were panting, and they stared at me.

'Who was at——?'

'God knows!'

I thought of the two charcoal burners, but we had other things to think of.

'Into the house. Shut the gates. Were they coming this way?'

'Yes, lord.'

'Well, we are four. Wait. We will leave the gates open. The surprise may be with us.'

We tumbled into the darkening house, and I raced for my sword and shield. Lob had a great axe, the two woodmen

92

their hatchets. I bade them come close, and I spoke in a grim whisper.

'Not a sound. If they come let them think the house is empty. We will wait just within the portico doors, where they cannot see us. Then, if they come, the first blows will be ours.'

Silently we moved along the great corridor, and took our posts within the open doorway. I stood on the left, Lob on the right. I bade the two woodmen keep back in the shadows. I could just see the mere and the island from where I stood, and the willows were going grey and the still water looked like lead. Also, I could see the open gateway, and being on the left my sword arm was free.

I spoke to Lob in a whisper.

'If they come leave me the first man, and be ready with your axe. Owain and Paulus, if any break past us, hew at them.'

'Yes, lord.'

There was utter stillness, save for a little whimpering wind, and I could swear that we heard the beating of each other's hearts. I was to know fear in the future and the shame of it, but on this night fear was outside me. Yonder was Igerna's island, a ghost island like my love, and the stone gate-pillar and the paving of the courtyard. Every feature had a strained distinctiveness in spite of the failing light.

Then a sound came to us, men's voices, laughter, singing. I remember looking at Lob and he at me. He nodded. His axe was on his shoulder.

'Not ours, Master.'

The voices were other than ours.

Then I saw them. They came to the gate and stood looking in, hairy men with great moustachios and beards, with round shields painted red or blue. Their faces were dim to me. They stood staring at the house, and gabbling to each other. One big fellow held something in his right hand, and hanging by a dark cord. For a moment it puzzled me, and then I knew it to be a human head.

He laughed and flung it into the courtyard and it bounced

and rolled across the stones. There was loud laughter from the others. The man who had thrown the head shouted and pointed at it. I did not understand his lingo, but to me his words might have been: 'Follow the bloody head, my friends. That is our visiting card if anybody is at home.'

I counted ten of them, and the odds were against us, nor was I sure how the two woodmen would behave as fighting men, but we had surprise in our favour, for I saw that our enemies thought the place deserted. They carried long knives at their girdles, and ugly looking axes slung over their shoulders, but they were not ready with their weapons. Moreover, by the way they walked and rubbed against each other, and laughed, I gathered that they had found liquor somewhere.

It was very dark in the house now, and they had not seen us. I felt my belly as tight as a drum, and my muscles quivering. I looked at Lob and saw his teeth gleaming. Then I caught myself doing a queer thing, counting to myself as though ticking off time before a race. 'One, two, three——' I held back, my sword up, listening to the shuffling feet and those animal voices. They were coming up the steps, and their bodies darkened the doorway.

In that one tense moment I decided how to strike. It might be more deadly to stab than to slash, and I shortened my sword. I had counted up to seven when the first man came to the doorway. It was the fellow who had tossed the severed head into the courtyard. I stabbed at his throat, and my sword was in luck. It caught him cleanly, and he went down on his knees. Lob's axe crashed on his head.

Shouts, savage turmoil. For a second or two the rest hung back, crowding together, and then they rushed the doorway. Lob and I laid two of them low, but two others blundered through and were met by our woodmen. We had the better light, for our enemies had the twilight behind them, and both Paulus and Owain brought down their men. Now we were four to five.

Bodies cumbered the doorway, and the tiles were slippery with blood. I shouted to Lob and the others:

'Fall on them—out—out—kill.'

And then I slipped, with a sea-wolf axe in the air above me, but Lob struck as the axe-edge slid off my helmet and gashed me on the shoulder. That blow of Lob's saved me. Four to four, and it was we who had the upper hand. Lob and I pushed through the doorway and over the dead or dying men, and the remnant of that raiding party flinched from us. They had not time for flight, and I struck down one of them, and Lob's whirling axe brought down two others. The last man fled and we let him go.

I was breathing hard and fast, and there was a scorching pain in my shoulder. I held out my hand to Lob.

'Well done, brother.'

He grinned at me. I saw one of the sea-wolves trying to rise, and I pointed. Lob's axe severed his head from his body.

Then I remembered that other head, and finding it I turned it over with my foot. The head belonged to one of the charcoal burners.

I heard Lob's voice.

'Master, you are wounded.'

Blood was running down my shield arm.

'Shut the gates now,' said I, and sat down with sudden faintness on a portico step. There was blood on it, and Lob bent over me. He laid his axe down and lifted me up, and carrying me to the summer-room laid me upon a couch.

He bellowed.

'Owain, Paulus, lights. Find wine and oil and linen.'

I lay on the couch with my head swimming.

X

I WAS astonished at the gentleness of Lob's great hands. He unstrapped my harness and uncovered the wound. The sea-wolf's axe had cut through the joint where my shoulder-piece joined breastplate and backplate, but it seemed to be no more than a flesh wound. Blood was still flowing; the first blood I had shed in battle.

Owain and Paulus had brought lamps, oil, wine and linen. I sent Paulus to watch at the main gate, and Owain held the lamp for Lob. He washed the wound with wine, making me cringe and curse, and poured in oil, and bound a linen pad over the wound.

I looked up into his face. It was benign and gentle, and so different from his battle face.

'That's a good job done, Master.'

'But for you, Lob, I might have lost more than blood.'

He grinned at me, and bade Owain set the lamp on a stool beside me.

'Wine in the belly, Master, as well as wine in a wound.'

'Good medicine,' said I, drinking from the cup he gave me.

And then I remembered Morgan, and wondered if any harm had befallen him.

'Lob.'

'Yes, Master.'

'Have you seen the Saint? He should be with us for his safety.'

'He was here but yesterday, Master.'

'Go to him tomorrow and bring him here.'

Lob left me and I lay with my shoulder twingeing, but my heart was in great fettle. Night had fallen, and I could see the stars through the open window, and I thought of the eyes of Igerna. Would she hear of my wound? Would it move her? I lay relaxed, in a kind of love-dream. Sounds came to me from the other part of the house, and I wondered vaguely about them, until I heard the wheels of a hand-truck clattering over the courtyard stones. I lay and listened and then I understood. Lob and the two woodmen were dragging out the dead men, laying them on the truck, and trundling them down to the brook side for burial. Four times I heard the wheels go to and fro, and then there was silence. Only one thing vexed me: that we had not slain the whole ten of them, and that one had escaped, for he might bring trouble upon us.

My sore shoulder was likely to keep me awake, and as we were setting a watch, each man taking his turn, I took the first watch by the great gate. As I have said, the sky had cleared and the stars were shining, which so often happens in this island, the sun seeming to bring cloud; and as I walked up and down I thought of those nine dead men lying by the brook for burial. How much less terrible did they seem to me now that we had met and vanquished them, yet they were but a bloody corner of the great scroll that was to be history. I was hungry for news, the news that mattered. Were more of these heathens landing from their long ships; what was Londinium planning; were any fighting men gathering in the eastern provinces, or was there nothing but chaos and fear? Could we hold this house of mine until the crops were in, and would help come from the west and Artorius be our hero?

I had watched for an hour when I heard footsteps and a knocking at the gate and a hoarse voice calling.

'For the love of Christ take me in.'

I went to the gate.

'Who is there?'

It was the other charcoal burner who had escaped the fate of his fellow. I opened the gate and let him in, and so scared was he that he fell on his knees and clasped my legs.

'Lord, they have slain my brother.'

'That is no news to me,' said I. 'Get up, man, and be a man.'

The pain in my shoulder passed away and left a numb ache behind it, and when Lob came to take his turn at watching I went in and lay down and slept. I must have slept for hours, and when I opened my eyes the sun was slanting in, and beside my bed sat Saint Morgan.

Never was I more glad to see any man. I sat up, and my shoulder hurt me, and there was a heart pang in me as I looked into this fine, familiar face.

'All went well, Father,' said I. 'Igerna is where she wished to be.'

The crowsfeet crinkled up about his compassionate eyes. He raised his hand and made the sign of the Cross.

97

'For that I bless you, my son. Those who are brave in loving are brave in battle.'

I was not feeling very brave at the moment. I had suffered seven strenuous days, and there was a strange weariness within me. I lay down and looked at Morgan. He told me that my men had buried the dead Saxons, and that he had said a prayer over them.

'Would I could bring the Cross to them in place of the sword.'

I was not feeling merciful to these butchers of women and children.

'The sword first, Father, and then—perhaps—the Cross. What news have you?'

He spread his hands.

'Nothing—save that all the country about us has become desolate. Our enemies go where they please.'

'What of Londinium?'

He shrugged.

'I hear that they talk much behind their walls. We have no leader.'

'I know of one.' And then I told him of Artorius, and his eyes began to glow.

'I would see that man, and speak with him.'

'Why not, Father? I can find you a horse for the journey.'

I saw that Morgan was eager to go, for our need was desperate. The sea-fortresses were either taken or besieged, and no man had the courage to come into the open field and fight.

'I will go straightway,' he said, 'as God's messenger. I am a man of vision, my son. Stand up and let me bless you.'

I stood and he signed me with the cross.

'Gerontius, I see you as the man who shall lead other men to battle. I hail you as our Dux.'

Then he kissed me, and suddenly I remembered that he might see Igerna. Would he tell her of my wound? I kissed him as I would have kissed my father.

'Pass that to Igerna, if you may.'

His eyes gleamed at me.
'I will, my son.'

So Morgan set forth to preach a crusade against the heathen,
and this was no time for kisses. The smart of my wound had
quickened my wits and my temper, and Lob and I took
counsel together. He was wearing the helm and the corselet
and dagger of one of the slain Saxons, and he had stripped the
rest of them of their gear, but I bade him leave them unburied
until our men from Astolat had seen them in the cause of a
good example. The fellows who would not fight should dig
the grave of those whom we had vanquished.

Food, arms, men. Lob and I sat in council, and I named
him my captain. Our needs were urgent, for though there
was grain in the granary and our water-mill could grind it,
my people had driven all the cattle and sheep to Astolat, and
we needed milk and meat. Moreover, if we gathered fighting
men together we should need all the food we could come by,
and our scythes and our axes should become weapons. We
had the hay crop to reap and carry, and Lob would need help
in the smithy.

So we talked together and made our plans. Lob should
go to Astolat and bring back the horses and waggons and
some cattle and such of the younger and more lusty men
who could labour. The women and children and the older
fellows could be left in peace at Astolat. We might make
fighting men of some of the youngsters, but Lob had not
much faith in their courage. I also bade him seek out Coel,
my body-servant, who had fled with the rest of them, and
send him to me. Lob could take my horse, while I and the
two woodmen kept watch and ward.

So Lob set forth, and I went to gaze upon the Saxon dead
whom Lob and the woodmen had laid out on the brook's
edge. They had been stripped of their harness, and they lay
cheek by jowl, bleached and bloodstained, with glazed eyes
and gaping mouths, and I—remembering the horror of Great
Yews—had no pity for them. I remember how one man's
nose hung down on his chin, and another's head was in halves

99

with the white brain bulging—both tributes to Lob's axe.

Yet Morgan had said a prayer over these poor corpses, and with my shoulder smarting I could tell myself that Morgan might be wiser than I in his compassion, and yet I could not pity these blond brutes who would have slain us all without mercy. Yes, and if Igerna had been with us——! I turned away, both from the unlovely dead and the unlovely thought, and saw a live man on a horse, comrade Caradoc.

I was glad of him and his smiling, galliard face, and I dared to hope that his buttocks were less tender. He grinned at me as he got off his horse, and then he saw those dead, and his face went stiff and grey. Such butcherly shows were new to him.

'Christ—brother!—What's this?'

'Dead heathen. The luck was with us.'

'I thought they were some of ours.'

His eyes stared and he held a hand to his belly.

'They came on us last night, thinking the house was empty. Only one of them got away.'

'And how many were you?'

'Four.'

Then his eyes came to me, and he saw my bandaged shoulder.

'Four against ten. That was good going. And you are hurt.'

'Just flesh, thanks to Lob and his axe.'

'Was that the big black bear I met on your white horse?'

'It would be.'

'He put me on the way. By the blood of our Lord, I would rather be with him than against him.'

I took Caradoc with me into the house, past our charcoal burner who was down on his knees swabbing the tiled floor where we had done our killing. All the insolence was out of him since he had buried his dead brother's head, and looked upon those other dead. I was indeed the master. I showed Caradoc where he could bathe and sleep, and I told him of all our plans. He was a farmer as well as a would-be fighting man, and he could be of great help to us.

'Look at our hay, Caradoc, and say whether you think it is ripe.'

'I can swing a scythe,' said he. 'Put me at the head of the reapers. I'll set the pace for them.'

He had got his colour back and was smiling, and a man who can smile in the face of coming perils was to be a comrade of a comforting spirit.

Owain was watching on the downs, and Paulus in the valley. I had told Lob to return quickly, for that tenth man who had escaped might bring swift vengeance upon us. Caradoc went to the bath, and I—moved by bitter-sweet memories—waded down through the meadow hay to the mere. A little wind was blowing, and the grasses waved about my feet, gossamer-headed and golden-spiked or plumed like barley. There was red sorrel among them and white daisies, and my wound had ceased from smarting, but I had the smart of my last love within me. I stepped into the barge, unlashed it, and poled across to the island, and wished in my heart that I could see Igerna kneeling there by the island-house. There was a great yearning in me, and never had I thought to see sadder trees than those waving willows. I made the boat fast to a bough, and climbed out, and went and stood in the little portico. The shadowy inwardness of the house was like my soul, poignant with deep, unforgettable things, a dim white face, mysterious eyes, and the clouding of a young girl's midnight hair.

Sorrowful I might be, but after the bloody business of the night it helped me to think of Igerna in a peaceful house among good women. If Mother Placida was Artorius's sister, then Igerna had a friend who should be serene and wise. Deep verities may come—even to a young man—in times of stress and terror, and maybe I saw with Saint Morgan's eyes the world that lay before me, a world of fear and cruelty and disorder, in which a man's fate might be to strive and battle against all that was black and evil. It is a fact that young men are less afraid of death than are the old, if some faith sustains them and calls to their young and generous blood.

I had walked to the edge of the mere, and was looking up

the valley when I saw dust rising and guessed that Lob had wasted no time. Horsemen and waggons, I saw them round the corner of a wood: Lob on my white horse and another man walking beside him. There were beasts and sheep; and the noise of the wheels and of hoofs filled the valley. The sight was good for the eyes, and I entered the barge and poled across. Then I saw that the man walking beside Lob's horse was Coel, my body servant.

I was glad of Coel, for I had always thought him a man to be trusted, and even if he had fled with the others that could not be held against him. He was a red-head, suave, smiling, with queer, green-blue eyes, quick of tongue, and perhaps too fond of women, but he had always served me well, and had been at hand whenever I needed him. Yes, Coel was a comely fellow, save for a curious mouth with a prominent and everted lower lip, of a vivid redness and deeply lined so that it had a ribbed look, and from the angles of his mouth sharp clefts curved up towards his nose. I should have called it a cruel and insolent mouth, but I had had no insolence from Coel.

He came running down to the water's edge to meet me, and for the first time I seemed to notice the red hair on his legs. And he looked better barbered and sleeker than I was.

'Greetings, Master.'

He laid his hands on the prow of the boat and drew it into the bank.

'Greetings, Coel,' said I, 'I thought I had lost you.'

He smiled at me, fawningly.

'*Mea culpa*, Master. All of us were afraid——'

I stepped out and smote him playfully on the crown of his red head.

'We shall have to make a soldier of you, Coel.'

'As you please, Master.'

Lob had come down towards the mere, and was standing watching us, and his great hairy face made me wonder. Was Lob jealous of my body-servant? He was looking at Coel rather like a great black bull watching a sleek fat hound. I beckoned to him, and sent Coel off to find hot water and a razor, for my chin was bristling.

I saw Lob and Coel look hard at each other as they passed. The big fellow came lumbering towards me with a frown on his face and I wondered if Coel had been using his quick tongue on Lob. Lob in his Saxon harness was no longer Lob the smith.

'Not much time wasted,' said I.

He nodded at me.

'Where did you find Coel?'

Lob fingered his beard.

'Prancing round with a woman, Master. I caught them going into a wine-shop.'

'Coel is something of a lady's man.'

Lob grunted and I gathered that he and Coel were not loving each other, but we had other and more serious matters to concern us, the cattle and sheep to deal with, and our waggon to be put to use. The beasts would be safe in our great cattle-house, and the sheep could graze in one of the meadows, with a shepherd in charge.

'How many men have you, Lob?'

'A baker's dozen, but poor stuff. I had to clout some of them into leaving the petticoats.'

'Well, we will try and clout some courage into them.'

So we planned to make a sweep of the countryside and gather in the grain and the beasts that had been left by the gentry and farmers who had fled. Plunder it might be, but it would be better with us than with our enemies. Our miller and our baker had come with Lob, and their work would be to grind corn and bake bread for our people. A sheep could be killed for meat, and we should have milk from our kine. Lob, Caradoc, and I would ride out with the rest of the men and the waggons, leaving Owain, Paulus and the others to watch the house and the cattle.

I left Lob to get things going and went in to be shaved and barbered, but while Coel was busy with me, I heard sullen voices, and Lob shouting. Was he having trouble with the men? My face was all lather, but I did not wait for the razor but went out to the portico steps, and saw our labourers bunched together like a herd of stubborn beasts who would not be driven.

I spoke to Lob.

'What is the trouble here?'

'No guts, Master. The fools are afraid of their silly skins.'

One fellow, bolder than the rest, cawed at me.

'You go and wash the soap off your face, Gerontius. We ben't soldiers nor slaves any longer. We stay or go where we please.'

The fellows stood with arms akimbo, and the rest of them growled applause. I looked at Lob and smiled. I walked down to those surly fools, and I smote the ringleader full in the face, and he went flat and lay flat like a felled tree.

'Call Paulus and Owain and Caradoc. Bring horse-whips, Lob. We will whip these cowards as they should be whipped.'

And whip them we did, until they all cringed in a corner, and put up their hands. Then I went back to be shaved.

I wondered how Lob felt when we set forth upon this strange business of plundering our neighbours, and to look upon familiar scenes that now spoke of desolation and danger. Our first call was at Great Yews, and I will confess that the blackened, roofless house was still a horror to me. The poor place was a crematorium in which all my young desires had gone up in smoke and flame, and I thought of Igerna crouching in the furnace-room or among the pillars of a hypocaust, her lovely face fouled with soot.

I saw Lob chewing his beard and Caradoc's eyes smileless and staring, and our little crowd of labouring heroes stood bunched together like beasts ready to bolt. They had climbed into the waggons when we had left Sweet Water, but Lob had ordered them out.

'March, you beggars. We will harden your flat feet.'

Yet the manor of Fabiscius was no mere blackened and empty prize. The farm buildings had escaped the flames, and we found grain in the great granary, and hams and cheeses hanging in the cold storehouse. I sent a man into the columbary and he came down with a dozen squabs. There were hens scratching in the stackyard, and we found some starved pigs in a pound. The poor beasts squealed and scuffled feebly against the fencing, and I was astonished to find them alive, so we fed and watered them, and never have I heard such gruntings and gobblings over the meal we mixed for them. We found a bin half full of meal in the granary, also a swarm of brown rats. Moreover, in one of the meadows Lob sighted some sheep grazing, and so full of plunder was the place that we loaded our waggons and set out for home.

Leaving Lob in charge I rode on ahead, and when I saw the mere and the island house I thought of it as a safe storage place for much of our grain, secure from plunderers, if the barge was moored by the island. I believed that Coel could swim and he could be put to use as a ferryman. And as neared the house I heard a familiar sound, the plash of the mill-wheel where our miller was grinding corn, and I could see the wheel turning, and the water gleaming as it spurted from the paddles. Owain was on guard at the gate, and I asked him if he had seen Coel.

'No, Master.'

Coel had a surprise in store for me, and I was a surprise to Coel. I caught him very much at his ease on my couch in the great saloon, wearing a blue cloak of mine, drinking wine, and polishing a Saxon helmet which he had purloined. I gathered that Coel had not thought to see me home so soon.

'Ha,' said I, 'you take life gracefully, Coel, but not on my couch. Get up, man, and work.'

I was not pleased with Coel, nor was he pleased at the way I had caught him. He did not rise as quickly as he should have done, and his propitiary smirk had a sullen edge to it.

'Pardon, Master—but the weather has given me rheumatics.'

'Is that so, Coel. I see that you are a little slow in moving. Work is good for stiff joints.'

He was holding the helmet, and I took it from him, and laid it aside.

'I have a job for you, Coel. Take the barge across to the island and swim back.'

'Swim, Master. Me—with my——'

'Yes,' said I, 'and be brisk, my lad. And put my cloak back where you found it.'

'Of course, sir. I only took it because of my rheumatics, and weather is cold for June.'

I can suppose that a gentleman's body-servant may feel himself somewhat of a gentleman, and be tempted to play the little gentleman behind his master's back, but this impudence was new to me and I chose to chasten it. I watched Coel fold up my cloak and lay it over the couch, and his movements exaggerated a pert deliberation. 'Oh, very well, my lad,' thought I, 'we will be upon our dignity,' and I walked with him to the mere's edge, and pointed to the barge. He was about to step into it when I reminded him that he would have to come back naked or in wet clothes.

He looked sullen and injured, but he shed his clothes, and got into the boat, and now that he was naked I could dub him a fine figure of a man, well shaped and with good muscles.

'We will make a soldier of you, Coel. You should be a lusty fellow.'

He gave me a curious smirk and a gliding glance, but I did not then suspect all that was in his heart.

I stood and watched him pole the boat across, and though the job was new to him he did it not too badly and with a certain grace. He moored it to a willow, poised himself and took a plunge, and I saw his red head like a flower amid the broken water. He came swimming across to me with quick and powerful strokes, and on his floating face there was something like arrogant malice.

'Well, Coel,' said I, 'swimming seems good for the rheumatics.'

He got to his feet and waded out, but he did not look at me.

'Yes, Master. Cold water may be as warming as women and wine.'

We made two more such journeys to deserted farms and manors, and brought back so great a store of grain, beasts and birds, with some wine and honey-ale that we were hard put to find room and storage. We filled the barge with sacks of corn and piled them in the little island-house, and Coel did more swimming, and it was a chastened Coel who spoke to me as a servant should and was always and suavely at my service. He polished my harness and my sword, and looked at me proudly as though he saw in me a fine figure of a man. Moreover, we had gathered on our foraging expeditions lone and desperate men, a score or so of them whom we had found living like vagabonds in the deserted villas. Some of them had come from the sea-coast through the great forest of Anderida, and to the stouter fellows among them we gave Saxon arms. They too had seen bloody happenings and brought us news, and rumour had it that Rutupia, Lemanis, and Durovesum were all in heathen hands, and that the Saxons had made Rutupia their port of landing, and that newcomers had brought even their women with them.

At Sweet Water Lob was sweating at the forge, with men to help him with the furnace and bellows, and though the craft of sword and spear-making was new to him, his skill was such that weapons came to us. We had hides in store, and I found a man who could fashion coats of leather and face them with bosses and ribs of iron, and make us shields. We sent out patrols daily, but the green country about us seemed empty of our enemies, and this very emptiness troubled me. What was happening between us and the sea?

I had had no news of Morgan and no message from Artorius, but I guessed what Artorius would be planning were he in my shoes. If the eastern ports and fortresses had fallen, Londinium was the strong centre from which a counter-thrust might be made. Yes, what of Londinium? Of the great city the bitter men who had joined us could tell me nothing.

Well, I would ride to Londinium and find out for myself, and take Caradoc and Coel with me, leaving Lob in charge, but when I spoke of it to Lob he would not be prevented from riding with me. So I shed Coel, and early one dawn we set forth, with the woods green and still, and the grass silvered with dew, and the early sunlight slanting upon the downs. Our safest way would have been by Panter, for there were no heathens north of the Thames, but I chose to ride by way of Stone Street. The risk was greater, but we might learn much more. Climbing the downs we came through the woods and thickets to the river gap by the White Bridge and scouted towards it, keeping cover. There was an inn for wayfarers by the White Bridge, but we could see no sign of life in the valley. The place was deserted, and silent as the grave.

So we climbed the great bald brow of the further down, and sat awhile on our horses, scanning the countryside under our hands. I saw a column of smoke rising in the distance, but of our enemies there was no sign, though the smoke might be their symbol. Some farm or mansion had gone up in flames. Lob was chewing his beard, which suggested that he was chewing the cud of thought.

'I guess, Master, that if they come west—it may be by way of the White Bridge.'

I said yes to that. Stone Street was open to us for the moment, but it might be overrun before we could return.

Now it happened that we fell in with a solitary horseman who told us that the heathens were swarming south of Londinium. These were grave tidings, and we turned off the great road, and bearing north, crossed Father Thames by a ford which was paved and marked with stakes. A causeway through the marshes brought us to the great highway between Panter and Londinium, and this highway was as empty and as silent as the marshes, and because it should have been alive, more sinister and strange.

So we came to the tombs along the great West Road, and the suburbs, and not a soul did we see until we came to

Lud's Gate. It was shut and waggons and stones and bulks of timber had been piled in front of it. Lob and I looked at each other. No smile of fortune this, with the gate barricaded so that no one could pass in or out. There were guards on the gate towers and we hailed them.

Now, it may sound incredible, but these fellows would not let us in. They shouted to us that all the gates were barricaded, and that the City Council had given orders that not even a postern should be opened. Londinium was expecting an attack by the heathen, and the City's Old Men were wetting their breeches.

Lob, who could roar like a lion, shouted at the guards on the towers.

'Where's your spunk, you she-men? The first city in the land is afraid to let in so much as a flea.'

'Be you fleas?' said a voice.

Lob shook his fist at the gate.

'We are fighting men. We have fought these beasts, and had the best of it. May you rot inside your walls.'

All we got were rude gestures, and still ruder answers, and I turned my horse, and laughed at these fools.

'We have seen enough. The street crowd has no stomach for fighting.'

In fact we had discovered all that we needed to know. No flaming torch of hope would be brandished by the fat hand of this most opulent city.

We rode homewards by the same way, joking grimly among ourselves, and perhaps feeling that we were fine fellows compared with those walled-in heroes, but the day was not to be without good fortune. We saw no Saxons, but on the downs above the White Bridge we chanced upon a body of bitter and battered men trailing their way wearily towards the west. I hailed them, and saw them close up and handle their poor weapons, scythes, poles and axes, but when they realised that I was no enemy they came crowding round me, their eyes fierce in their starved faces.

'Who are you, my friends?'

A big fellow who was their leader told how they had

fought with others at a river ford to try and halt the heathen and keep them from their homes, but they had been worsted, and this was the remnant.

'Where are your women and children?'

There was grim silence, and then a voice said: 'In Durovesum—for their safety.'

That was a pitiful answer, for Durovesum had fallen, and I suspected that these men knew it.

'Brother,' said I, 'we are of those who would gather our strength and drive these savages into the sea. Help is coming from the west. We have food, and shall have arms. Why not join with us.'

I saw some of their faces light up, and there came a murmur from them.

'That is the stuff for us, captain. Give us food and arms. We would have blood on our hands.'

They cheered the speaker, and they cheered me, and so it came about that our little company was strengthened by some forty desperate men who had bitter happenings to avenge.

More men, more food.

Now that we were stronger I felt that we could be more daring, for the men who had joined us had been toughened by battle and suffering, and were ready to accept discipline. I found two smiths among them, and set them to work with Lob. The hay was ripe and the weather fair, and Caradoc led the scythemen and set the pace. My own fellows, who now were more meek than sullen, were given the homely jobs and were twitted by my new men who called them the petticoat legion; irony that might persuade them towards becoming soldiers, but I did not put great trust in them, and set them upon menial jobs and carrying hay. Two of them served as our butchers. They could slay sheep if they would not slay Saxons.

So we sent our waggons further afield, guarded by armed men, and I went with them, taking Mascius—the big fellow—as my second-in-command. Max had a grimly cheerful countenance, and was scenting blood, for he had a wife and three children lost to him. Our plundering itinerary covered much country. We found stray horses and cattle, grain, poultry, honey-ale and wine; also empty waggons, and we filled these as well as our own. My new men had built breweries, and were feeding on the fat of the land, for a fighting man needs a full belly. Also, we collected all the tools and implements and metal we could lay our hands on, for Lob needed such stuff for his smithy.

I now had some seventy men with me bearing arms, a dozen of them mounted, and we drilled twice a day in a meadow, as I had seen Artorius drill his men. As for our enemies, we saw no sign of them, which led me to wonder what they were preparing to do.

XI

WE had had no news of Morgan, and I was becoming troubled about him, though—God knows—we had sufficient trouble of our own. We had a watch posted by day on the hills, men with horns, and orders to blow them should they see anything that promised peril, and at night we set a guard about the place. I, Lob, and Mascius took our turns in charge of the guard, sharing out the night in three watches. What with all our labour and our journeyings and our business of becoming soldiers, and our false alarms by day and by night, I—for one—lay down dead tired and slept like one of the dead.

I was thinking of Igerna as much as ever, but with less of a lover's anguish, not because my love was less, but because my days were so full of happenings, and I was a man in charge of men. I had to plan, and issue orders, and hold council with Lob, Mascius and Caradoc, and the burden was—like my heavy harness—a little new to me. I wore it always, and made my men wear theirs, both for the sake of hardening them and emphasising our need to be ever on the alert. We were like men in a fort on the frontier, overlooking enemy country, and never knowing when or how or whence an attack might come.

And then, on a summer evening, Morgan came riding out of the sunset on the hills, carrying a white cross, with two armed men behind him. I happened to be on the island, counting the sacks of corn stored there, with Coel serving as scribe with a set of tablets. When I saw the Saint riding down the hill my heart leaped in me, and I bade Coel take the boat, kiss Morgan's hands and bring him to me.

I met Morgan under the willows, and reached out my hands to him to help him up the bank. He looked in great heart, did Morgan, in spite of his long journey, for his eyes were bright. I would have kissed his hands, but he put his lips to my forehead.

'Blessings, my son.'

'It is good to be blessed by you, Father.'

'My old eyes have seen a transformation.'

'We have not been idle.'

For Mascius had the men out in the meadow, and was putting them through spear-drill, and for a moment we stood and watched them.

Then, Morgan took my arm and we walked to the island-house and I laughed as I said: 'We shall have to sit on corn sacks, Father. This is one of our granaries.'

So we sat on sacks of corn and I waited, not for news of Artorius, though that would be precious, but for some word of Igerna, and Morgan's eyes were crinkled with light and shrewd old wrinkles.

'Beautiful weather, my son. The crops in the west are promising well. I see you have the hay in.'

I looked at him and saw the kindly mischief in his eyes.

'Yes, Father, and I have a new pair of shoes, and one of our cows calved last night.'

He smiled at me.

'Patience is a great virtue, my son—but I have news of a sort for you. Doubtless you would like to hear it.'

I nodded at him, and suddenly I heard a little sound, and

cocked my head, and went quickly into the portico, and there at a corner of the wall I caught Coel waiting to use his ears. That angered me. I took him by the shoulders and sent him staggering.

'Go down to the boat and stay there. The words of your betters are not for you.'

For a moment he looked sheepish, and then he gave me an innocent and reproachful smirk.

'Pardon, Master, but my ears are at my country's service. A man may hunger for news.'

I watched him go, and then went back to Morgan and sat down on my sack.

'A man with the long ears of an ass, Father.'

'One must suffer asses, my son.'

'Always and everywhere?'

'That may depend upon the temper of the ass. Some beasts need the stick.'

He lay back on the sacks and looked through the doorway at the sunlight shining down the valley.

'What would you hear from me, Geron?'

'I think you know.'

'Igerna is well—and—happy.'

'You have seen her?'

'Yes, with Mother Placida. A most wise woman—that.'

'You saw her at Corinium?'

'No, at the house of Artorius. You see, my son, good women need not be shut up in cellars. One should not fly from humanity, but be with it—to savour it.'

I sat silent—thinking.

'Did you tell her of my—wound?'

Morgan seemed to hesitate.

'I did, my son, and she . . . A maid may be proud of a man, and can pray for him.'

I felt that he was keeping something back from me, but I did not press him further, and then he began to speak about Artorius and his plans.

'Artorius has a thousand men with him, men from the west, and more are coming. He would be strong before he marches, but march he will. His words to you are: "Hold fast, if you can, until we come." '

This was great news, but I was thinking more of Igerna and how she knew that I had been wounded, and a young man in love must have his dreams and his vanities. God forbid that Igerna should be unhappy, but I did wish her to be troubled about me, and to give me more than a virgin's prayer. Maybe my face betrayed me, but Morgan was a wizard in reading both souls and faces, and he gave me words that were like wine to a man who was faint.

'There are two loves, my son, and I would bless either, the love of God, and the love of man. Igerna may choose the white rose or the red. I talked of that matter with Dame Placida.'

A great hope stirred in me.

'You mean, Father——?'

'Patience, my son. That which you did was good and generous, and not of the flesh. Placida is your friend. She would not deny you the right to love. She is wise in wishing the choice to be Igerna's.'

'She would not turn her against me?'

He sat up and put out a hand to me.

'I believe that lovely people should wed and bear lovely children for the grace of God and the blessing of this dear island. Have patience, my son.'

'I will,' said I.

So moved was I by this news that when Coel had ferried us back from the island I felt the urge to be alone on some high hill, for, in these strenuous days I was but rarely alone. Men are simple souls save when they play the peacock as philosophers, and as I climbed the downs my heart seemed to be saying: 'She loves me, she loves me.' I blessed Dame Placida for her woman's wisdom, and for not being jealous of ardent youth. So many women turn sour and shrivelled when their faces are not pleasing to men. I climbed to Snow Hill, a white mound on the crown of the great ridge which served as a mark for those travelling from the south, and I sat down on the cap of turf that topped the burrow. Not only did I see all the loveliness of our hills and woods and valleys, but my vision seemed to cover all this precious island, the cliffs and the sea, Father Thames, the towers of Corinium, the great pharos of Rutupiæ, the cliffs of Gaul, the western mountains, Snowdon, Uriconium and its strange hill, the City of the Legions. How lovely was the land, even when skies were grey and trees leafless! For I was in love with a maid, and to my strong young love all the world was lovely.

I must have been in a kind of dream, but I came back to earth to see Coel at the foot of the mound. He was smiling up at me as though in his cunning he knew my thoughts. I saw too that he was girded with a belt to which hung one of Lob's new swords. I was not pleased at seeing him. The fellow seemed too busy about me.

'Do you bring some message, Coel?'

'No, Master.'

'How did you know I was here?'

'I followed you, Master. Am I not your body servant, and there is danger in wild places.'

I looked at him steadfastly, but his face seemed open and honest, and I could not quarrel with his faithfulness, but my day-dream had been broken, and I rose and returned with him to my house.

I was at supper with Morgan in the summer-salon, and I will confess that I had had the very pagan pictures in the mosaic floor covered with rugs. My grandfather had been a man of broad humour, and I can remember crawling about the floor as a very small child and becoming interested in Venus, a sufficiently nude Venus. I had asked my grandfather a question, and he had bellowed with laughter. 'Why has not the lady got what I have got?' But prudery or no prudery I had had those pictures covered, nor—by the honest truth— had I ever thought of Igerna as Venus.

I saw Morgan glancing at the floor with a certain droll shrewdness.

'Is my modesty so frail, my son?'

I laughed, and was about to put another point to him

when we heard one of our horns braying in the distance. An alarm!

I sprang up and reached for my sword and helmet. I could hear men shouting and the clatter of feet, and Lob's face appeared at the window.

'Enemies, Master.'

We had prepared our plans to meet a sudden attack, and it centred round the defence of the house, courtyard and buildings, and our men knew their posts, but our defence was not to be wholly passive. Mounted men were always ready to ride out and make contact with the watchman who had given the alarm, and I mounted one of the horses and led the patrol. The horn blast had come from the downs above us, and as we pushed our horses up the hill we met the horn-blower running down. It was Owain.

'Armed men, Master, coming along the Green Way.'

'On horse or foot?'

'Both, Master.'

'From yonder?'

'No, from the west.'

This puzzled me, and I bade the others stay where they were, and I rode on alone until I reached the crest. There was a broad grassy space here between the yews and thorns, and not a hundred paces from me I saw a little column tramping along with the setting sun behind them. Moreover, one of the mounted men carried a standard like the legions of old, and its sign was the sign of the Cross.

No enemies—these. For the moment I wondered whether it was the advance guard of Artorius's host, and I rode a few paces towards them. They halted when they saw me, as though wondering whether I was friend or foe, and I hailed them.

'I am Gerontius, captain in these parts. Whence come you?'

Then they cheered and came on, waving their fists, and I saw that many of them were oldish men. A veritable patriarch with a grey beard appeared to be their Dux.

'Hail, Gerontius. You are the man we seek.'

'Well, here am I, my friends. Have you come to join our company?'

'We have, lord. We are men or the sons of men who served Rome. We grew sick of the slovens and the cowards who had no guts for fighting. Your name has been noised abroad. "That is the man for us," said we.'

'And you are the men for me, my friends. We have food and shelter and a strong company. How many of you are there?'

'Three and thirty, counting Tobias the boy. He blows a trumpet and would not stay behind.'

'Welcome, all of you, especially Tobias the boy.'

Grey Beard's name was Mabon, and he and I clasped hands and swore faith to each other, and then I called for Tobias, and Tobias was very ready to be noticed, a smiling, wheat-haired boy with mischievous blue eyes. He had his horn slung to him, and he carried at his girdle a fierce and pro-digious dagger.

'Welcome, Tobias, horn-blower and hero.'

He looked up at me as though I in my harness could be his hero.

'Welcome, lord.'

So, with Mabon riding beside me and Tobias walking close to my horse, we joined our patrol and led our reinforce-ment down the hill to Sweet Water. The sun had set, and with the darkness upon us I bestowed these men for the night in the portico and the main corridor, bedding them with some of our hay, and being country fellows they seemed well content after a supper of bread and meat and honey-ale.

I now had some hundred fighting men behind me, and might feel that we had the strength to fall upon our enemies should they venture into our country.

XII

THE hazard of battle was to be ours sooner than I had expected.

It had become our custom to send out a dawn patrol along the chalk hills as far as the bluff overlooking the White Bridge, where the Green Way sloped down to the water-meadows and Stone Street. This track way was as old as time, and gave passage westwards to any enemy whom an embattled Londinium shut off from the great highway north of the river.

Mascius was in charge of the patrol that morning, ten mounted men, and I am not likely to forget that dawn. The birds were still in song, though with less lustiness, and their singing came to me with the grey stillness of daybreak. I lay and listened, but there were other sounds, other smells. My new company were snoring in the corridor, and the scent of hay and of strong bodies permeated the house. Such human sounds and odours might have been unwelcome to some who had become the luxurious parasites of peace, but they were consoling to a captain who would lead men into battle.

I was lying relaxed and listening, and thinking of Igerna when I saw Morgan in my doorway. Even in the grey light of the dawn his face had a prophetic and luminous look.

'My son—I have had a vision. Arise; we must be ready.'

I sat up, gazing at him.

'News, Father?'

'I have seen blood on the arms of the Cross.'

Whatever his dream had been, or whether it had been a waking vision, it was to prove Morgan a veritable prophet. I rose, and went to the bath, stepping over the bodies of men who were still asleep.

'Let them sleep awhile,' said Morgan, 'for it may be the last sleep for some of them, this side of Heaven.'

A bronze bell hung inside the bathing room, and it was

my custom to ring it for Coel who slept in a cubicle close by, but this morning I did not ring it, but took my cold plunge, and stood on the marble bench and towelled myself. Morgan had left me, to rouse Lob, Caradoc, and Mabon, and I was putting on my clothes when Coel came to me yawning behind his hand.

'You are early, Master.'

I bade him fetch my harness and help me into it, and again he yawned and not noiselessly so.

'Wake up, man. This may be a day of doom for some of us. Get the sleep out of your bones.'

He gave me a pert look.

'Are you a prophet, Master?'

I was leaping upon the bench and swinging my arms to feel the strength and the suppleness of them.

'We have a prophet in our midst, Coel, a man who is wiser than you or I.'

I was out in the courtyard with Lob, looking at a horse that had gone lame, when we heard a horn blowing and saw Mascius and his men coming helter-skelter down from the chalk hills. At first we thought that they were being chased by the heathens, and I ordered the trumpeter to blow the alarm. It was then that I found Tobias beside me, bright of eye and eager to take up my order. His pink cheeks swelled as he blew, and his blue eyes smiled at me.

The place was in a turmoil, men running to arms. My new friends came tumbling out of the house, Mabon blowing out his beard in his excitement. I bade them form up in the courtyard, and I sent Caradoc to meet Mascius and his men, and to tell their horn-blower to blow three blasts on his horn if our enemies were upon us. Every moment of time might be precious. We had the gates open ready for them to ride in, and now that the garrison was gathered I ordered every man to his post.

We had not long to wait before Mascius and Caradoc rode in, and Mascius gave me the news while he was still on his horse.

'Our enemies are at the White Bridge.'

'In strength, Max?'

'No, lord, an advance guard, or so I judged. They have crossed the river and are camped on our side of it in the old hostelry.'

'You are sure, Mascius?'

'Sure, lord. I crawled along a ditch to within a hundred paces of them.'

'How many are they?'

'I should say four-score or so, more or less. I reckon that they are there to hold the bridge. They were washing in the river when I saw them.'

I called Morgan, Lob, and Mabon to me, and ordered food to be served to all, and while we ate in the great salon I put my plan to the others. Our enemies had sent this advance guard to seize and hold the White Bridge, not suspecting that there was much danger from our side, and it might be easy for us to surprise them and deal them a blow that would give us the breathing space we needed. Moreover, even a minor victory would be precious to us, all the more so since the sea-wolves might have come to despise us. If we trounced them and beat them from the White Bridge, we could wait more confidently on the coming of Artorius. I did not propose to hold the bridge, but maybe to destroy it.

I watched the faces of my friends, and I gathered that they were with me, and it was Morgan who answered.

'To dare is half the victory, Gerontius. I shall be with you, carrying the cross as your standard.'

Lob growled in his beard, and I saw Mascius' eyes gleaming. He had horrors to avenge.

'Let us go, lord, and speedily, and fall upon them before more come.'

So it was agreed between us, and accepting the hazard we left Sweet Water to the servants, and climbing the downs, took the Green Way. There were a hundred of us, and I and Mascius rode on ahead with the horsemen, leaving Lob and Mabon to bring on the foot. Morgan came with us, carrying his cross.

Now, fortune was with us on that summer morning. We

came to the wood-end high above the White Bridge and saw our enemies scattered about the meadow, some taking their ease, others grooming horses, or gossiping in little groups. They had set no watch and suspected no surprise. Their painted shields lay on the grass like great round flowers.

While we waited in the wood-shade I made my plan of battle. Out foot-soldiers should go charging down the hill, but we horsemen would make a half circuit, and crash in on a flank when the battle was joined. I put my plan to Morgan and Mascius and they applauded it. We should inflict a double surprise upon our enemies, and surprise would be much in our favour.

The very day itself was with us, for the morning continued grey, and had the sky been clear we should have had the sun in our eyes and shining upon our weapons. Mascius besought me to let him lead the charge down the hill, with the men who had come with him, for, as he put it, 'We would have blood on our hands, and our swords in the bellies of the sea-devils.' I nodded to him. There would be no flinching about Mascius. So we put our two parties in array, bidding no man speak, and that there should be no cheering until they were close upon the Saxons. Morgan, Lob, Caradoc and I, with our horsemen, rode down behind a long finger of wood which pointed towards the valley, and would bring us on the left flank of our foes. It was a wood of beeches, and we could ride to the edge of the wood-shade and be screened by the great grey trunks and yet command the scene of battle.

This was to be my first set field in which a captain has to wait upon the clock of circumstance, but I do not remember feeling any fear, only an excessive clarity of mind, and a tightness in my belly. Morgan sat beside me. I had bidden Mascius wait until we had time to take up our position, and I saw that the ground lay open before us without a single hazard. Our enemies had seen and heard nothing. I saw two of them start a wrestling match, while others gathered round and made a circle.

'Praise God, we have them,' I said to Morgan.

He smiled at me.

'You are a veritable captain of Christ, my son. Man must sometimes kill to save.'

I could see the edge of the wood from which Mascius and his men would pour, and I sat and watched it, and while waiting, I let my thoughts go to Igerna. I felt that I was fighting my love's battle, and that I was to be the avenger of all that she had suffered. Lob had edged his horse close to mine, and his teeth gleamed in his black beard. His beloved axe lay couchant upon his right shoulder.

Then I saw our footmen break from the wood above and flow down the grassy slope in a close column, for I had taught them Artorius's plan of battle. It was the old phalanx picture over again. I drew my sword, and put my shield forward and bade my men be ready. My eyes were on our enemies down by the bridge. I saw some of them shout and point towards our charging foot, and instantly there was turmoil and confusion. A horn blared, and scores of men rushed for their shields and arms. I saw Mascius close upon them, and they were in no proper order, but bunched in groups, yet very ready to fight. Our time had come and we were cantering over the grass, and drawing close before our enemies saw us. Some of them made to turn our way, but Mascius and his men were in the midst of them and the fighting was fierce. I saw the wild faces of our foes as we crashed in. One fellow slashed at my horse's head, but I turned the blow, and thrust my sword-point into his throat. We trampled them and hewed them down, and Lob's axe was a weapon of dreadful power. Yet, I will say that these sea-wolves fought it out and did not fly, even when he had them broken and in disorder. Our charge took us into the very centre of the battle; we and the foot were pushing the scrimmage steadily towards the bridge.

The end came quickly, and perhaps a dozen of our enemies escaped from the slaughter we made, for no quarter was given. A few fled across the bridge, others swam the river, but we too had suffered. I was unwounded, but Lob had lost an ear, and Caradoc had had a spear through his sword arm. I looked for Mascius and could not see him, for Mascius lay dead in a welter of bloody bodies, but when I looked upon him I understood that he had died as he would have wished to die. He lay on his back with two Saxon corpses under him, and there was a smile on his face. I saluted the dead Mascius, and grieved for him, for his loss would be bitter to us.

I saw Morgan on his knees, in prayer. He had planted his cross before him, and going to him I heard his words:

'Oh, Lord Christ, forgive them that which they have done in wrath.'

For, before Morgan could intervene, our men had finished off all the Saxon wounded, and I will confess that to me it seemed the better way. We had no use for Saxon wounded, for we had wounded of our own, ten of them, and seven dead. Some of the wounded could walk, but four of them we had to lay across our horses, and three had to be placed on litters of branches cut from the wood. We found some mattocks and spades in the hostel, and we buried our dead, but tossed the Saxons into the river.

Morgan prayed over our dead, and suddenly the sun shone through the clouds upon our victory. We had found linen, too, in the hostelry, and Mabon was bandaging Lob's head while he sat grinning. As for the White Bridge we left it whole, for the river had no great depth of water and was easily forded.

I had forgotten Tobias the boy until I saw him standing beside me with a Saxon spear over his shoulder and a Saxon casque on his head.

'Well, Tobias, where were you?'

He smiled at me.

'In the thick of it, lord. I got one of them with this spear.'

XIII

DAYS can vary in their quality, be jejune and grey, or spacious and vivid, and there are dawns that are glamoured with unexplainable mystery. Maybe the curtains are drawn back from the windows of one's secret soul, and eyes that are more than eyes look out upon the handiwork of God. The wrath of battle passes, and a man may bow his head in humility and compassion, and ask the poor dead to forgive him for their loss of life.

Some such pity was born in me when I looked upon the fresh earth that covered Mascius and his fellows, and with Morgan standing beside me I remembered that all men are men. Hunger and the lust for power and possessions are the Devil's disciples, and I thought of the Saxon dead whom we had thrown into the river.

I spoke to Morgan.

'Father, I am not happy about those poor bodies.'

'Which, my son?'

'The bodies of our enemies. They are men—as we are.'

He turned benign eyes upon me.

'Wrath has passed, Gerontius. What would you do?'

I told him what was in my mind, and I saw that my madness was his. So, we did this mad thing, for my men must have thought me crazy. I set a guard upon the bridge, and I waded into the river with Morgan, and bade the rest follow me, and there we recovered such poor bodies as we could find, and dug a grave and buried them beside our own. I remember the queer, mute way in which my fellows looked at me, and humoured my madness, and yet in the eyes of some of them I seemed to see a silent, human acquiescence.

I had lost all count of time, and when we beheld Sweet Water lying below us in the valley I was astonished to see the sun well down in the west. Moreover, I was weary and hungry, and so were all of us, nor had our victory crowned us with arrogance. We had left dead comrades behind us, and some of our wounded were groaning.

I stopped my horse on the brow of the hill and sat gazing at the peaceful landscape, my house and its garden and farm buildings, the mere and the island, the soft green valley, the silent woods. No wind blew, and the stillness was utter. Not a grass head moved, and there were yellow flowers staring placidly at the sun. I, too, felt voiceless, wondering at the madness of men who could not be content with God's good earth and husbandry, and still and starry nights. I thought of Igerna, and my love yearned in me. I, who had dragged bloody and bleached dead men out of a river, hungered to hold beauty in my arms.

It was Morgan who broke the silence.

'May it ever be as peaceful, my son.'

I echoed that prayer, and doubted it.

'We have won a fight, Father, but—maybe—my home will have to pay a price for it.'

'Not if Artorius comes, as come he will.'

'God speed him,' said I.

I supped alone with Morgan in the summer-room, after I had washed myself; and Coel served us, a Coel who had not known battle. He was suave and courteous, but somehow his smooth service irked me. I heard a man groaning in the courtyard, and getting up to look saw one of Mascius's men walking up and down and holding a bandaged head. To and fro he went like a suffering animal in a cage, and I wondered what could be done for him, or how we could assuage his pain.

'Coel.'

'Yes, Master.'

'There is poppy seed in my cabinet. Take that man a small spoonful of seed and some wine.'

He did not hasten to obey me, but began cleaning some dishes, and his procrastinating angered me.

'Did you hear my order?'

'Yes, Master.'

'Go and do what I bade you do.'

God gave us peace for a period, though I counted such respite not in weeks but in days. Our wounded needed time to heal their wounds, and not one of them died, thanks to Morgan and his medicine-craft, for Morgan was a veritable Æsculapius. Moreover, his spirit was such that it put new heart into our men, and wounds heal the better for a cheerful temper. Morgan was no magic-monger, but a believer in prayer and in the potency of Nature, and he suffered a man's wound to do as it pleased and to throw off the dead tissue in a flux of matter. We had our wounded laid in the corridor, and the stench of their wounds drifted in at the windows, and sometimes gave me a queasy stomach, but Morgan welcomed it. He said that such festering smells were the product of Nature's healing juices, and that a wound that was odourless might be a dealer of death.

It pleased me to be alone at times, and to wander out and gaze upon our cornfields. The wheat was standing tall and straight with their myriad ears gleaming, and stalks beginning to go blue in the sunlight. Oh, peaceful fields, pride of the husbandman! I longed to see the sickles at work, and armfuls of ripe corn laid ready to be stooked. Should we garner all our corn? It would be a race with time and with our enemies.

And in the orchard apples were swelling on the trees and claiming colour. There was one particular tree which bore fruit of an especial sweetness, and I could remember Igerna the child sitting on the grass below the tree while I climbed it and dropped golden apples into her lap. We had called the tree Hesperides. It pleased me to sit when Igerna had throned herself, and to look up into the branches where the young green apples would turn to gold. Would Igerna ever eat of this sweet fruit? My dream was that some day she would.

But we were not idle. More lost men joined us, and Lob was busy at the forge. We drilled and hardened our bodies, and kept our patrols working. Lob and Morgan and I rode again to Londinium to find the gates shut and barricaded as before. Morgan stood holding his cross, and claimed entry that he might speak to the City Fathers, but they would not let us in. And for once I saw a Morgan who was angry. He held his cross high, and I thought he would curse the city, but he turned away with a smoulder in his eyes.

'Too much wealth corrupts. When a man's belly becomes a money-bag, there may be no courage in him.'

Lob was more candid. He pointed to his lost ear.

'See that, you fellows. I have one ear left—but it is not the ear of an ass. Asses seem to grow in your city.'

No news had come from Artorius, and I sent Caradoc into the west to tell Artorius how we fared, and to bring news of him, but Caradoc rode no further than Calleva, for there he fell in with a body of horsemen whom Artorius had sent to strengthen us. They were a hundred strong, and when Caradoc returned with them I was proud to be their Dux.

Looking back upon those strenuous summer days, and upon the sentimental moods of cornfield and orchards, I have to admit that life can be an ugly business and man a blind creature groping in a dark forest. Our prophets are few, and sometimes false, and if Morgan could not see three days into the future, I was far more blind than Morgan. Artorius's men were sure that he would be with us before we joined battle again with the Saxons, and I allowed myself to believe that all was well with my world. Twice we had beaten our enemies, and maybe I was growing over-confident; a young man whose fine feathers had not been clotted with blood and mire.

Yes, I did not foresee or forefeel what I was to suffer in body and soul, and I went blindly towards my fate.

Once again the weather had changed its temper, thunderstorms, squalls, clouds bursting on us, and I rose one morning to see our corn flattened, and the orchard littered with fallen apples. Mabon, who had been in charge of the watch, told me that it had hailed in the night, and that the hailstones had been as big as hazel-nuts. I was sad about the corn, but the sickles could deal with it if the weather bettered, and the corn did not sprout in the ear. In the orchard I saw a circle of green apples on the grass below Igerna's tree.

Lob led the eastern patrol on that fatal day. The storm of the night might have forecast to us other storms, and the morning was heavy and hot, and turgid with thunder clouds. Morgan and I had gone forth to look at the laid corn, and to console the men whose bivvies had become sodden in the night. Many of them were in a state of nature, and trying to dry their clothes and clean their harness.

Assuredly Fate caught us in a state of nakedness.

Lob had been gone less than an hour when I heard a horn blowing on the hills, a note of warning. Morgan and I looked at each other. And then we saw Lob and his riders hastening down the hillside, and we knew in our hearts that evil was upon us.

Lob looked grim.

'They come, Master, and in strength, yes, by the Green Way. We had to ride for our lives.'

'Are they many?'

'Some hundreds, Master. Their shields were like poppies in the corn.'

I found Tobias beside me.

'Blow, blow, Tobias. We must arm.'

Arm we did, and with furious haste, and while we did so Morgan, Lob, Artorius's captain and I held council. Should we fight or abandon Sweet Water and retreat. I was all for fighting, and Morgan was with me, but I saw that Lob was less sure, though he had too much stuff in him to confess to his doubts. I wanted to save my house and home, and maybe I was over-confident after the fight we had won at the White Bridge.

In times to come this fight was to be known as the Battle of the White Down, and it was fought in a thunderstorm, with the rain beating in our faces. In truth we and our enemies blundered into each other through a curtain of drenching rain, and in a sense the surprise was mutual. We had just climbed the hill to the great ridge, and both horses and men were somewhat winded, and we had no time for tactics. Nor did we catch our enemies unready as we had done at the White Bridge, and in numbers they were stronger than we were. Moreover, it was fortunate for us that we met only the vanguard of their host; the main body being still at the river crossing.

We both won and lost this fight. I remember the flash of lightning and the crack of thunder overhead as I went in with Artorius's men. It was a scrambling cavalry charge, for I hoped to break their ranks for our foot to follow, but these sea-wolves were ready for us. They had armed themselves with long spears, ash saplings cut from some thicket and pointed with iron, and when we rode at them they planted these pikes and stood firm. It was too late to change our plan, and I had a mass of horsemen thundering behind me. We crashed in on them, and broke the first ranks, but the fellows behind held us.

And here I struck disaster, for I was a horse length ahead of my fellows, and all that happened to me was a blur of blood and confusion. I met a bristle of spears. One took my horse in the chest, and he went down like a spitted boar, and the battle boiled over me.

I had taken spear thrusts in the leg and the arm, and in my face, and in the turmoil and trampling I lay there dazed and in great pain. The fight went over me and past me, and I was saved by our foot-men coming in and helping the cavalry to push the Saxons back. I could not see, for there was blood in my eyes, and I do not think I realised that the point of a spear had stabbed my left eye. Men were leaping over me, shouting and pushing forward. I had tried to rise and was knocked flat, and after that I think I must have fainted.

Then I remember Morgan kneeling by me, but my vision was so blurred that I knew him by his voice. Again I tried to rise, but fell back.

'Lie still, my son, lie still.'

The fight had gone somewhat in our favour, and I was lying among other men who were dead or wounded. I was conscious of Morgan leaving me. I heard the sound of rending linen. I had put my hand to my face, and then it was that my groping fingers found something round and warm and soft lying on my cheek. The spear-point had forced the eyeball out of its socket.

Morgan was back with me, and binding my arm and leg with the linen he had torn from the dead. The noise of the fight and its carnage seemed to grow faint. Our enemies were in retreat, and we had won the battle, but at what a cost. We lost more than a hundred of our people in dead and wounded.

Morgan was kneeling by me, and I knew that he was looking at my face. His silence had a dreadful meaning for me, dazed though I was.

'There is something you must bear, my son.'

'Yes, Father.'

I was dimly conscious of his dilemma, but the grim choice he had to make was inevitable.

'It has to be, Geron.'

I think I nodded at him. He had a knife at his girdle and he drew it, and I felt the cold metal touch me. It was done with one swift and gentle stroke, and my useless eye lay in Morgan's hand.

Of what do wounded men think? Of a cause, a crisis, other men or themselves? They had laid me upon a litter of branches, and were carrying me down the hill to my home. All that familiar and lovely landscape was blurred to me, though I could distinguish the shapes of the men who walked at my feet. Was I going blind? I put a hand to my face, and rubbed at my other eye, for the lids felt stiff and glued together.

Then it was that I felt a hand upon my shoulder.

'Blood, my son, clotted blood, not blindness.'

Oh, blessed words! For there is horror in physical mutilation, and that blob of white tissue lying on my cheek had made my soul and stomach squirm. I, who had thought myself a comely fellow, had a bloody hole in my face where the light of an eye should have been.

A deep cry came from my inward self.

'Igerna, oh—Igerna!'

How would she see me were we to meet again? Should I appear repulsive to her, a blemished creature, only to be pitied? Maybe, I was weak from pain and loss of blood, but I had no spunk in me, no man's pride.

Nature herself was playing at tragedy. The storm broke again as they carried me down the hill, flashes of brilliant lightning, and thunder. The rain came down, and someone covered me with a cloak, and since it covered my head as well as my body I felt like a corpse on a bier. I dragged the thing from my face, and when the lightning flashed the world seemed red. Then I remembered that I had lost my horse, the good Cæsar, who had carried me so often and so far, and the shield Dame Julia had given me, but my sword lay with me on the litter.

I was aware of voices, vague and far away, though they were near me, and they seemed to speak like the voices of tragic actors on a stage. They were the voices of Lob and Morgan. Artorius's captain had been slain, and so had the poor lad—Tobias. I was to hear of our horses later.

I listened to the voices, and to me they were indeed the voices of tragedy.

'We cannot hold them down yonder. Let us load what we can and go while we may.'

This was Lob's voice, and Morgan's answered it.

'True, my friend; we have lost too many. Our hope is to join with Artorius.'

So, my house was to be abandoned, and left to be plundered or set on fire by our enemies. Yet what else could be done? Yet the truth was like another wound to me, and I could have wept, so broken was I in spirit. Disaster was in the air like that rending firmament, and the rain that came down upon us all.

I was indeed like a dead man who yet could see and hear and feel all that went on about him. I was carried into the courtyard and laid in the portico. I gather that the urgency had been too grim for the salving of those others who had been desperately stricken. Haste and noise and turmoil were all about me. Men were loading waggons with food, and harnessing horses. I heard other men groaning and cursing. The rain rattled on the pantiles of the portico, and, as I say, I felt like a dead man in the midst of all this flare and haste and fury.

Then Morgan came to me, and put a cup of wine and of milk to my lips.

'Drink, my son. I will dress your wounds again before we lay you in a waggon.'

131

I drank, like a sick and consenting child.

'I am useless, Father. Why not leave me here?'

He patted my shoulder.

'Foolish words, my son. You shall live to fight again.'

So he dressed my wounds with oil and clean linen, and washed my face, and bandaged that bloody cavity. His hands were gentle, and I felt that his spirit was undismayed. It was the succour and the sustenance that I needed, and I felt my manhood stirring.

'Forgive me, Father, for puling like a child.'

He smoothed the bandage on my head.

'Sick men are but sick children. All that will pass.'

Presently they came to carry me to one of the waggons, and to lay me on a bed of hay. The rain had ceased, and I saw with my one eye a great shaft of golden light striking the house and valley. This was Fate's *Vale* to my home, for never did I think to see it again save as a mound of blackened stone and ashes. Two other wounded men were laid with me in the waggon, and one of them kept up a constant groaning, but the other lay still as death.

I felt the tug of the traces and the play of the wheels on the courtyard stones, when a sudden whim seized me. I called to Morgan, and another voice answered me, the voice of Coel. He had climbed up into the waggon.

'Yes, Master.'

'Bid them leave the gates open.'

'Open?'

'Yes.'

I somehow felt that the open gates would be a challenge to fate.

So, we set forth along the valley road towards Astolat, Artorius's horsemen guarding our rear, and the footmen and servants marching with the waggons. I listened to the rumble of the wheels and the plodding of the horses, and the shuffling of men's feet, but in all else there was silence, and I felt it to be the silence of bitter and beaten men. That fight on the downs with its dreadful losses had taken the heart out of our people.

132

Coel sat on the waggon's rail, and I heard him humming a song, an old country love song. I felt stricken by it and angered. How dared this red-headed fop croon such words in my hearing when such bitter happenings were like sour wine in our bellies.

'Coel.'

'Yes, Master.'

'Get down and march with the rest. You have no wounds to vex you.'

For the moment he was pert.

'Does not my master lust to hear of love?'

'Get down and out,' said I, 'or I will have you thrown out. If fighting-men can march, so can fops.'

He obeyed me, but at his leisure, and still humming his song, and there was a sauciness in his singing.

Morgan and Lob came and sat in the waggon with me, and now that I felt more than a poor and bloody rag, my urge was to speak with them of what should be done. I was for sending Caradoc westwards to carry the news of our peril to Artorius, and to urge him to hasten to our help. Then, should we try to hold Astolat and the river-crossing there? And had we the strength and the heart to do it? Now that the clotted blood had been washed away my right eye could do its duty, and I saw by Lob's grim face that he was doubtful of our holding Astolat.

'We might lose all, Master. Better to save what we have.'

And Morgan was of his way of thinking, for even a saint can be shocked into caution by the blood and death and anguish he had witnessed.

I bade Lob call Caradoc, and when Caradoc came to us I gave him his orders. He was to take the best horse we had left to us and ride hard by way of Pontes into the west. Artorius would come by the great road, and at all hazards Caradoc was to find him, even if he had to ride as far as Corinium. He was to tell Artorius of our condition, and say that we planned retreating upon Colleva. The city had stout walls, and we could rest there, and gather strength and be ready to join up with Artorius.

'Much rests upon you, Caradoc.'

'And may God be with you,' said Morgan.

When Caradoc had gone a great weariness seemed to overwhelm me. My wounds began to twinge and stab and the movement of the waggon jarred me, even though I lay on hay. I wanted to be at peace somewhere, and I doubted whether I could bear the journey westwards. In fact, my weariness was such that I would have welcomed a bed in the deep fern, with trees overhead, and no company but that of the wild things and the birds.

We rumbled into Astolat to find the place deserted save by a few strong dogs. Its people had fled, and not a soul remained in the little town. I must have had a fever mounting in me, for when we came together again to hold council, I felt too weary and confused to help in the choice of action. This melancholy little town was like a grey symbol of despair.

In fact we did not unload our waggons, and Morgan, Lob and Mabon were still speaking together, with our weary men lying where they could, when two of Artorius's horsemen who had been left behind to scout, rode in with grim news. The Saxons had crossed the White Bridge in full strength, and were marching in pursuit of us, and no doubt they wanted vengeance for the slaughter we had made of their vanguard.

This was grave news. It would be madness to remain at Astolat, and when the choice fell upon me an utter weariness clouded my spirit, but out of that cloud shone a sudden ray of light. My body rebelled at the thought of miles of jolting in a waggon. I wanted to lie still somewhere and meet death—if death it was to be—in silence and in peace.

I called Morgan to me.

'Father—I shall be nothing but a useless body. Go, all of you, and meet Artorius.'

'And leave you alone, my son? That is not——'

'I am very weary, Father, but I know of a place where no enemy is likely to find me.'

'Where is that, my son?'

I told him of a little island that I knew of in the marshes south of Astolat. It was surrounded by water and marsh-land, and a narrow causeway linked it with solid ground. On it stood a fisherman's hut, a thing of wattle and daub and reeds, screened by willows. I had fished there as a boy. I had a strange and almost prophetic yearning in me to lie at rest in some such secret place.

'Coel can come with me, and look to my needs.'

'But—at Colleva, my son——'

I put out a hand to him.

'Father, I wish it. Maybe—a wounded body is wise as to its own needs.'

'So be it, my son. Would you have me bide with you?'

'No, Father. You are a man to whom Artorius will listen. And if you see Igerna——'

'We should meet with Artorius—nearer than Corinium.'

'Maybe—you will, but some day—and if I die—tell her I died loving her.'

'I will, my son, but may death be far from you.'

There was no time to lose, and food and gear were put into my waggon, and Morgan, Owain and Coel climbed in, and we set off for my refuge. It was no great distance, and Coel sat by me, a suddenly kind and considerate Coel, who seemed to have lost his sauciness in my dire need of him. So, we came to the marshes, and the grassy causeway, and they laid me on a litter and bore me to the island. It was green and peaceful in the midst of the still water, with no sound save the voices of the water-fowl. Owain carried a truss of hay, Coel bread and meat and jars of wine and milk in a great pannier. Morgan had brought linen and oil, and the wagon-ner carried my sword and two horsemen cloaks. We found the little hut clean and weatherproof, and they spread the hay and laid me down.

Morgan spoke to Coel.

'Let well alone. If there should be much fever, uncover and cleanse the wounds, and bind them with clean linen.'

Coel was obsequious.

'It shall be done, O—Father.'

Then I bade them go, for their need was urgent, and I wished them God's speed, and Morgan bent and kissed me.

'You must live, my son. We shall return.'

So weary was I that when they had gone I fell asleep.

XIV

I—CARADOC—a farmer turned soldier, and a simple fellow, have written at my poor lord's request the story of my journey in search of Artorius. I hold myself fortunate to have escaped unwounded from that bloody fight in which we won what the ancients described as a Pyrrhic Victory. Yes, I had received some schooling at Corinium, and could quote my Homer and my Virgil.

Well, to the story. I was wet to the skin when I began that ride, and my backside was sore before I had finished it, and my horse was pretty well foundered. I lodged and slept the first night at Colleva, and between you and me I have no great love for cities, and the men of Colleva had no spunk in them. Nor had I that night, though a pretty sewing-wench made eyes at me, and at other times I would have obliged her. I was off soon after dawn on a clear, calm morning, with the sun on my back and the great road before me, and hoping to meet my lord Artorius and his host. But no armed men did I see, only a few merchants and pedlars and country folk going about their business. Strange business it seemed to me after the bloody scrimmage from which I had escaped.

Well, to cut the story short, not an armed man did I meet on the road to Corinium, an odd hundred miles, sir! The island might have been at peace, and merchant ships unloading their cargoes at Londinium, and the country folk getting ready for the harvest-home, and oysters being peddled from Vectis. I spoke to some of the wayfarers whom I met, and when I told them of the havoc and slaughter I had seen, some of them would not believe me.

I could not understand why my lord Artorius dallied, for he was not a man of procrastination, but when I took the White Way and came in sight of Collis Alba, I rubbed my eyes, as I would have rubbed oil into my sore backside. I had hands of leather, and I could jump a five-foot gate, but my buttocks were not those of a cobbler. And what did I see? The meadows stippled with tents and booths, rows and rows of horses, and a multitude of men cleaning harness and arms, or drilling, or sunning themselves on the grass. It was—indeed —a sight for sore eyes, and it made me think of our poor Dux's lost eye, and that bloody hole in his fine young face.

Well, I rode through the crowd to the great gate, and from one big booth came a savoury smell of cooking. It ran from my nostrils down to my stomach, for I had a hell of a hunger on me, having eaten nothing but a crust of bread that day. Yet no one paid any attention to me, though I could have told them things fit to raise the hair on a mangy dog.

The porter on duty was known to me, and he was spooning up a good meat broth with bread in it.

'Hail, brother,' said he, 'what do you here?'

He had a cheerful countenance, and I could have stolen his soup.

'You look pretty comfortable,' said I.

'Passably, passably.'

'That's more than we have been. We have been fighting, my friend, while you were sitting on your bums.'

'What else should we sit on, brother?'

'Hot coals, if you ask me. But I want your master. I have news that would raise the dead.'

'My lord is at supper.'

'That's where I would be. Take me to him, or I'll kick your bowl of broth to Hades.'

So, seeing that I was hot and urgent, he put his bowl aside and led me up the steps into the great white house, and bade me wait in the atrium, and I looked at the pictures on the walls, and the pictures on the pavement, and wondered whether I stank and was too travel-stained for such fine company. I had not long to wait, for the porter came and beckoned to me, and I followed him up the great corridor to my lord's state chamber.

It was a noble room, with white pillars and curtains at the further end, and Artorius sat alone at the table. The platters and dishes were of silver, and I noticed that two empty chairs stood opposite to his, with platters and drinking cups laid on the table, and I supposed that Artorius had rid himself of guests before he spoke with me. Three servants stood by the gilded serving table, and when I stood before him he dismissed them.

'Well, Caradoc, my friend—you have ridden far?'

'I have, sir, more than a hundred miles, and my news is as sore as my posterior.'

'Bad news?'

'Indeed it is, sir. We have fought twice with the heathen, and the last battle was bloody. We beat them back, but lost too many men. And my lord Gerontius is wounded near death, for he was more forward than any of us.'

I saw Artorius glance at the curtains, and half rise from his chair, but I was full of my news and I continued:

'My lord—Gerontius has lost an eye, and has two other great wounds, and the captain of your horsemen was slain.'

He raised a sudden hand, as though bidding me be silent, but the warning came too late. I saw a trembling of the purple curtains, and then one of them was plucked aside and a dark girl stepped through them. She had a lovely and tragic face, hair black as charcoal, and eyes that were as dark as her hair. It was the Lady Igerna whom Gerontius had brought to the House of the Holy Women at Corinium.

She stood there, staring at me as in a kind of stupor, and I realised that my news had brought this horror into her dark eyes. Artorius had risen from his chair, and from behind the curtains came Dame Placida, that most noble and saintly lady, to lay an arm over the girl's shoulders.

'Come with me, Igerna, my child.'

Child indeed! Never have I seen a more sudden transformation. The dumb and frightened child became woman. I saw her great eyes flash, and her lovely mouth came alive.

She took two steps nearer to me, and looked steadfastly into my face.

'Tell me the whole truth.'

'I have told it, lady.'

The thing that astonished me was that both Artorius and Dame Placida stood helplessly by as though this young girl was mistress of the moment.

'Gerontius is dying?'

I felt confused by her fierce questions.

'Not dying, please God, but sorely stricken.'

'Where is he?'

'I left him with our people near Astolat. Saint Morgan was with him.'

Again Dame Placida would have put an arm about Igerna, but the girl, with deliberate gentleness, put the arm aside. She looked at me, and she looked at Artorius.

'I must go to Gerontius.'

Artorius made as though to speak, but before he could utter a word she turned to pass back through the curtains. Dame Placida followed her, and Artorius and I were left alone together.

He shook his great head at me.

'That was ill timed, but it was no fault of yours, Caradoc. I should have been wiser. Yet how could I have guessed——'

'Well, sir,' said I, 'she should be suffered to go where she pleases.'

He looked grave and clouded.

'Impossible. A battlefield is no place for a woman.'

'But, maybe, sir, she would find Gerontius at Colleva. They were heading thither, if Astolat could not be held.'

Again he shook his great head at me.

'We march in three days. Women must be left behind.'

I was silent, but my goodwill was with these lovers.

I went to the bath and I needed it, though my chafed skin smarted, and Artorius sent for me to sup in his state chamber, for he had questions to ask me. I was served royally with wine and meat, and Artorius sat by a window and listened while I told him all I had to tell. The purple curtains were drawn

SC—K

back and the ladies had gone, and we men could speak without caution. I told Artorius of Londinium and its barricaded gates, and how its gentry appeared to have no spunk for fighting, but there were many other things he wished to know: in what order the sea-wolves fought, how they were armed, and how our men had fared in combat. The lamps had been lit before I went to my bed in the guest-house, where a kind servant found me unguent for my chafed backside.

Weary I was, and I had drunk much wine, and I slept till cock-crow, when someone shook me by the shoulder.

'Are you one called Caradoc?'

The roughness of the morning's salutation peeved me.

'I was christened such! And who the hell are you?'

'My lord has urgent need of you.'

I sat up, and felt as stiff as an old horse.

'Why so early, fellow?'

'That is my lord's affair.'

I cast a cloak over myself and followed the man to Artorius's sleeping chamber, to find him striding up and down and looking black.

'So—you were safe in bed, Caradoc.'

'Most certainly I was, sir.'

'Do you know aught of what happened in the night?'

'I know nothing, sir, save I slept till your fellow clawed me by the shoulder.'

He looked hard at me.

'I believe you. Someone stole a horse in the night, one of my best saddle-horses.'

'Who was the thief, sir?'

'Igerna. She is not to be found. Do you know aught of this?'

'I know nothing, sir, but to be honest—my good wishes are with the lady.'

XV

WHEN I woke from my sleep a little dreary wind was blowing, and the sky fled grey with drizzling gloom. From the doorway of the hut I could see the water like tarnished silver, and the ruffled woods on the hills about us. Yet I was glad to see even this grey dawn and to know that I was not blind, but had the use of one eye left to me. My wounds felt stiff, and the lids where my lost eye had lived were glued together.

This island with its mere and marshes was like a pattern rimmed on all sides by the hills. The causeway was no more than a narrow green bank, hardly visible at a distance, and the hut might have been a pile of faggots. I could have chosen no safer or more secret place, and I could lie here at peace, waiting upon death or life, as God should choose for me. My head felt clear, and I had no fever, and a healthy stomach asked for food.

I saw Coel come to the doorway carrying a brown pitcher of water, and I was glad of Coel.

'Coel, I would drink and eat.'

'Yes, Master.'

He spoke to me gently, and I thought that my wounds had moved the man in him. I managed to sit up, and he scuffled up some hay for my support. Then he brought me meat and bread—and a cup of milk, and I felt grateful to him.

'You are a good man, Coel. It shall be remembered.'

'I am here to serve you, Master.'

'Have you seen aught of our enemies?'

'Not a sign, Master.'

When I had eased my thirst and my hunger I laid me down and besought him to cleanse my eyelids, and kneeling he washed the blood and matter from them and anointed them with oil. His hands were gentle and skilful, and I blessed God for such a servant. This was a different Coel. He had shed his vain vapours and his sauciness.

Presently he sat himself down in the doorway, and busied

himself with cleaning my sword, and helmet and harness. There were bloodstains upon all of them, and when he had washed the blood away, he polished the metal with oil. It pleased me to see my harness being cared for, for it was part of a memory, my ride to the west with Igerna.

I spoke to Coel.

'I wonder if I shall wear that harness again.'

His red head was bowed over my sword.

'Why, yes, Master. Such gear is for the young and lusty. It is handsome armour.'

'Which I am not.'

'Why, yes, Master—you will be.'

I lay thinking of Igerna. Would she and I ever meet again in this world? And then I saw Coel put my helmet on his head.

'That makes a man of you, Coel.'

He gave me a sidelong smile.

'I wanted my lord to see that my hands have made it shine.'

'They have, Coel.'

I fingered my chin and its bristles.

'I should be shaved. Have you a razor with you, Coel?'

'No, Master, I fear not. We fled in such haste.'

'Well, I must go hairy.'

I sent him across the causeway to scout around, and feeling drowsy I fell asleep. My wounds were aching, and my sleep was shallow and uneasy, like a thin plaster laid over the wounded flesh, and when I woke again I was alone. Heavy rain was falling and the wooded hills were dim, and the rain came through the thatched roof and began to drip upon me. I moved to one side on my bed of hay, and when I moved my wounds were stabbing spurts of pain.

So I lay and let my thoughts drift, and wondered whether Igerna would hear of my desperate state. If she was shut up in that Holy House Dame Placida might keep the news from her, and I might die and Igerna not know of it. And would my death wound her? I remembered that last moment between us in Corinium when she had run to me for a last farewell, and then had gone to lay her hands upon the cross. Oh, moment of sweet bitterness and lost love!

Then the rain ceased and the sun came out and I saw the world glistening as though its eyes were full of tender tears. I, too, wanted to weep with the one eye that was left to me, for my wounds and my heart were hurting. In no way could I find ease upon my bed of hay; it seemed to have grown hard and lumpy, and needed shaking up like the down in a mattress.

And what had become of Coel? Had he gone scouting or searching for food? I called to him and got no answer.

Time seemed to crawl, and there was vague fear in me. What if Coel had been caught by our enemies, and I—stricken to death—left helpless and alone? I looked at my sword and harness lying near, and it seemed to mock me. I lay and listened for footsteps, and when they did not come I became a creature of weak despair.

The water-jar lay near, and some food on a platter. I reached for them, and let out a groan as the movement made my wounds give me grievous pain. I managed to reach the jar, and struggle up, and hold it to my lips, to find that it was empty. Oh, God! I was thirsty and had no water.

I called aloud.

'Coel, Coel, I am thirsty and there is no water.'

No one answered me, though I heard some water-fowl call to its mate.

I lay and listened, until a feverish fancy must have fooled me into imagining things. I heard the water lapping at the reeds and sedges, and the birds calling, and these sounds became voices. Coel was coming, bringing friends with him, but no Coel came, and more clouds covered the sun, and rain came down once more. I lay and listened to the drip from the thatch until it became like the sound of a hammer beating upon my brain.

From great weariness I must have fallen asleep. I woke hungry and thirsty, and I remembered that there was no water in the jar. I called again upon Coel, and no voice answered me.

My mouth and tongue were dry and the one thing I craved for was water, and water was so near. Well, I could try crawling to the mere's edge, and crawl I did, for my thirst was fiercer than my pain. I sprawled over a little, placid inlet of the mere, and suddenly I saw my face reflected in the water, and for a moment I forgot my thirst in looking at my disfigured self. Was this—I—Gerontius, swollen and one-eyed and unshaven? I had a kind of horror of myself, and then my thirst came back, and I spooned up water in my right hand and drank and drank.

Then I crawled back to my bed of hay and cursed myself for a fool for not having taken the water-jar with me, but I was too exhausted to do more. Nor had I any stomach now for food. I felt confused and helpless, sunk in a sort of lethargy. Sleep seemed my only solace, if my wounds would suffer me to sleep.

I must have slept, for when I woke again, my world seemed dim, and for the moment I thought that blindness was upon me. Then I realised that night was falling, and like a child feared the darkness. My body had gone numb. I could do nothing but lie huddled up in the hay like some wounded beast deserted by the herd. I had given up all hope of Coel, for I believed that Coel had fallen into the hands of our enemies. Yes, Coel might be dead, and I was lost and alone in this solitary place.

I lay and watched the oblong doorway of the hut grow dark, though it was less dark than the walls. The water-fowl were silent, but I heard an owl hooting, and rustlings in the reeds and rushes. A strange sense of unreality possessed me. Was this . . death . . . which was coming to me like some shadow-shape stealing across the marshes? And was I afraid of dying? The open doorway had become like a picture which someone had covered with a black cloth.

Then came a change, and I lay and watched and wondered. Little burrs of light burst out like sparks upon this background. What were they? Was I gazing upon actual things, or was this phantasy, illusion flickering in a fevered self?

These yellow burrs grew bigger, and took on a reddish tinge, and suddenly I knew them as distant fires burning where Astolat should be. Was Astolat going up in flames, or were these the watch-fires of a Saxon host?

I lay and watched them, for they fascinated me. They were like live things, dancing in the darkness, and like dancers they separated themselves into two groups ever against each other. The smaller fires seemed to be on the hills, the larger fires below in the valley, and these valley fires grew into Medusa heads of spurting flame. Astolat was burning, and those other fires were camp-fires on the hills. For one moment I had wondered whether the camp-fires might be those of Artorius, but burning Astolat dispelled that hope. The sea-wolves had set fire to it instead of lodging in its houses, for these savages had a strange way of avoiding our towns and villages as though such places were cursed and haunted, and like the wolves they were they chose the wild woods and the hills.

I wondered if Coel had ventured into Astolat, and been caught there and had his throat cut, and been thrown into one of those funeral fires. Poor, red-headed, saucy, posturing Coel! I should never see his face again.

And there I lay in the darkness with my enemies so near, and in the stillness of the night I fancied that I could hear a distant burble of voices like the faint thunder of a mill-stream.

Dawn.

It came gradually with a greyness that was suffused with a gradual golden glow. I woke and lay gazing. I could see the reeds and rushes and the still water like a silver shield, and glittering woods, and smoke rising from what had been Astolat. There was smoke on the hills, and I fancied that I could see movement there as of a multitude of coloured beetles busy in the dawn. My wounds felt stiff, but they had ceased to pain me, but my mouth felt dry and parched with thirst. Water—water! Again I cursed myself for not having filled the pitcher, for, if I crawled out to drink I might be seen, yet my thirst was so urgent and inevitable that I was driven to take my chance, and I crawled out of the hay and across and through the rough grass to the water's edge. I was hidden here by the high reeds.

Before I drank I looked at the reflection of my face in the still water, and it shocked me. My chin was all black stubble, my hair clotted, and my left cheek blue and swollen, and the eye socket oozing matter. I drank and filled the pitcher, and then dashed water over my head and face as though I was washing in Jordan. We Roman Britons were a clean people, and the yellow scum on my eyelids and my filthy hair revolted me.

I crawled back to the hut with the pitcher, and crouched in the doorway. Astolat was smoking, with the sun lighting up the smoke, and I could see movement on the hills above. Were my enemies preparing to march, and if so—which way would they go? To Pontes, or along the great west down? And if Artorius was coming eastwards, where would the two hosts meet?

But I had other problems to challenge me. Should I try to dress my own wounds or leave them to Nature? And what of food? I opened the food wallet, and saw that I had enough meat and bread for a day or two if I hoarded it, though the meat might go bad and the bread grow dry or mouldy. I cut myself a small portion and sat in the hay and ate. I could watch the hills and the causeway across the marshes from where I sat.

But I soon found that movement had stirred up my wounds, and that I was quickly wearied. I lay down, and in my solitude and helplessness I began once more to despair. What would happen to me if Artorius dallied, or if he were vanquished in battle? I might crawl about here like a wounded water-rat, but unlike a rat I could get me no food.

Then I saw my sword lying there, and the challenge of destiny seemed to be mine. Would it be better to rot and starve, or fall on my own sword like a Roman?

I sat staring at the mere, considering the fatal choice, and my judgement for the moment was in favour of the sword.

XVI

ALL my food had gone and my wounds had begun to stink. Once a day I crawled to the water and washed my face, and a desperate and haggard countenance it was. All the youth had gone from it, the smoothness and the colour, and I looked like some wild, starved, mutilated outcast whose inevitable end was death. There was nothing about me but wild nature, the water and the grasses and the trees, and the wild things, and I began to realise how apart was man and how little the green earth was concerned with his joys or his sorrows. I tried to pray, and my prayer was like the Lord Christ's—'My God, why hast Thou deserted me?'—but I had no ultimate courage left to me on my cross.

I was a foul creature with my stinking wounds; disgusting even to my sapless self. Matter oozed from my empty eye-socket down upon my cheek. The linen on my other wounds was frayed and dirty and sodden with discharges, yet the wounds themselves had ceased to be acutely tender. My hunger was becoming a pain. So savage was it to begin with that like Nebuchadnezzar I tried eating grass, which seemed to turn sour in me, and the strange thing was that after a time my hunger passed and my stomach seemed to go to sleep. But I was growing weaker and my crawl to the mere for water became more and more an effort.

The weather was fine and the sun shone, and the water glittered and the air was warm, and I lay hour by hour on my hay in a state of half-aliveness. I remember a moorhen coming to the doorway of the hut and looking at me with a beady eye, and then walking off with tranquil unconcern. Did the bird know that the creature man was dying and no more dangerous than a log of wood?

But the simple incident tantalised me. If that bird had been some man or woman I might have become once more man, and not a stinking and incipient corpse. I remember bursting into silly tears, and burying my face in the hay.

'Oh, God, let me die.'

And yet there was a part of me that yearned passionately to live.

I seemed to lose all sense of time. My clock was the sun, dawn, full noon, twilight, darkness. To begin with I counted the days, but as they passed I lost count of them or ceased from counting. The life of nature went on about me, but I was nothing to nature, and God's earth was as heedless as some dead planet floating in space.

It may have been an illusion, the fancy of a clouded consciousness, but a curious feeling came to me that I was being watched. Once, when I crawled out to the water I seemed to hear a sudden rustling of the reeds, but I set it down to an otter or some water-fowl, and yet the feeling remained with me. I might have been a dying beast with some other hungry beast watching and waiting for me to die.

Another day passed, a serene and sunny day, and towards evening I fell into a kind of stupor. I did not feel my body or my wounds, and my self seemed to float out into the sunlight.

Sun and moon and stars, midnight, still water, a shadow of death floating across it, the thing I called my soul. And then it was that I heard voices, and I thought them to be part of my dream state or voices from another world. I lay and listened, but the voices drew nearer to me, live, real voices, a man's and a woman's.

A strange spasm went through me.

Igerna's voice!

Well, veritably I was dreaming, and hearing sounds that human ears were not made to hear.

'Stay there, Owain. It is for me to look.'

'But—lady——'

'Stay there, the fate is mine.'

Then a figure darkened the doorway, and I saw Igerna with her clouding hair, clad in a cloak of saffron, with a purple girdle about her slender loins. For the moment I thought it was a vision, and that I must be very near to death.

Then I heard her utter a low cry. She was down on her

knees beside me in the hay, and I gazed at her in wonder. How could this be true?

'Oh, Geron, my dear love.'

'Igerna.'

I heard her call to Owain.

'Owain, Owain, come quickly. He is here and lives.'

Then it was that I remembered my filthy face and all my squalor, and a horror of myself possessed me. I writhed over in the hay and buried my face in it.

'Leave me to Owain. I am no fit sight for such as you.'

But leave me she would not. She put her hands upon my shoulders and turned me over, and took my head into her lap, and so weak was I that I was at her mercy. And what mercy it was! I felt something wet upon my face; her tears, for Igerna was weeping. Owain was standing there, looking at us, and then he turned away as though he knew that this great moment was ours—not his.

'Why weep, Igerna?'

'Because you live and shall live, my beloved.'

'I? But I am a foul thing——'

She bent and kissed me, and to me that kiss was God's own revelation.

'Geron, never speak such words. Were you blind—I would love you.'

'Igerna.'

'I love your wounds, all that you suffer is mine.'

'Darling. But how did you know and come to me?'

'It was Caradoc. But you shall hear of that later.'

Then she called again to Owain.

'Owain, Owain! Wine, food, water, linen.'

Trust a woman for foresight. They had brought a pack-horse with them, and the panniers were laden with food and gear. Igerna kissed me a second time, and got to her feet, and I lay marvelling at life and at love. I—with my filthy face and stinking wounds was no foul thing to her, and the blessedness of loving was revealed to me.

I heard their voices, and no longer did I feel a dying man left to rot in solitude. My heart seemed to gather strength, and my blood to grow warm. I sat up and stretched myself, and spread my hands and gave thanks to God, not in mere words, but with an exultation that welled up from within me.

Owain came into the hut with a great basket of food.

'Greetings, Master.'

'God be with you, Owain.'

He laid his basket down.

'Where is Coel, Master?'

'I know not. He went forth and did not return. Maybe our enemies caught him.'

Owain was silent, and went forth for more gear, and I felt my stomach stirring, and a live hunger yearning in it.

Igerna was back with me.

'When did you last eat, Geron?'

'For days I have had nothing but water.'

'Then we must go softly. Milk, Geron, and a little bread soaked in it, and a sip of wine.'

For the first time for many days I laughed, but it was a strange, dry cackle.

'I could eat a haystack, Igerna.'

'Leave that to me, Geron. Then I will dress your poor wounds.'

She fed me as a mother might feed a sick child, or a bird its young, slipping little pieces of bread soaked in milk into my mouth, and her slim white fingers touched my lips. Then she gave me wine, a little from a flask, and I felt my stomach grow warm and I understood her wisdom, yet she was young to be so wise.

'Presently you shall eat meat, Geron.'

I smiled at her.

'I have other food than meat, Igerna. But, tell me, how did you come?'

Having fed me, she too, ate, sitting on the grass beside me.

'It must have been God's own wish, my dear. I was at Collis Alba with Dame Placida when Caradoc came. We were in the alcove behind curtains, and I heard Caradoc's news.'

'But—how——?'

'They would have held me at Collis Alba, but that was not to be.' And then she laughed and looked at me slantwise: 'I was not a tame dove in a cage.'

'Then—you——?'

'I stole a horse in the night and ran away.'

'Igerna! Alone?'

'Yes. It was easy to follow the great road, and they did not catch me. I had money for the hostels, and this morning—early—I fell in with Morgan and your people, camped, and waiting near the Great Down for Artorius.'

I was dumbfounded. This girl whom I had given to God, had spread wings like a young falcon and flown in the face of fate.

'My darling, you were in great danger.'

'Was I, Geron?'

'Had I known I should have been sweating blood. But, surely, Morgan did not suffer you to——?'

'I did not ask Morgan. I spoke secretly to Owain, who is your good servant.'

I stretched out a hand to her.

'Igerna, I love you, I love you more than life, and now there is new life in me. Owain shall take you back to Morgan, and then return to me.'

She shook her head and smiled.

'No, my love. I stay here with you.'

I tried to reason with her, but she would have none of my reasoning, and perhaps my pleading was half-hearted. Her peril in staying with me might be far less grave than I pretended, for no one had been near the place, and if Morgan and my people were camped near the Great Down the Saxons must have turned north, perhaps to cast a leaguer about Londinium. No city in the island could promise them greater plunder. And then there was other and sudden exultation in me. If Igerna had fled from holiness and the House of the Good Woman, and had become falcon in place of dove, then she might be for ever my Igerna.

But she was both dove and falcon.

'Now—your wounds, Geron.'

'Owain shall deal with them.'

She shook her head at me, and I—conscious of those filthy bandages—would have rebelled, but she would have none of my squeamishness. Almost she was the severe nurse dealing with a fractious child.

'Now, Geron, don't argue. I know what to do.'

'Who taught you that?' I asked.

'My mother—when I was but a girl.'

'And what are you now?'

'Women should know these things. Owain, Owain!'

Owain came to the door.

'Owain! Water, oil, clean linen, wool.'

Owain smiled upon us, and was meeker than I was.

Igerna had a little knife at her girdle, and she bade me lie flat while she cut the knots of the bandages. The linen was crusted and glued up with blood and matter, and when Owain came with what she needed, she took wool and soaked it in water and wetted the stiff linen. Very gradually and with gentle fingers she peeled the stuff away, while I shut my eye and wondered how it was that my foul self did not disgust her.

'Am I hurting you, Geron?'

'No,' said I, and I was somewhat puzzled by this lack of pain.

I opened my eye and saw her set and intent face. She was frowning as she softened and peeled off the last swathings, and suddenly she drew her breath in sharply, and I guessed that the filth beneath was revealed to her. I closed my eye again. I heard her call Owain.

'Owain. Look. Have you any knowledge of wounds?'

'Yes, lady. We woodcutters sometimes suffer hurt.'

'Look.'

Owain was silent for a moment, and I, wondering and fearing the worst, opened my eye.

'Blessing of God, they look good, lady.'

It was so. Those gashes had clean pink lips that seemed to be glazing over, and I remembered Morgan's saying that Nature could be wiser than man. Igerna's frown had gone, and her eyes were gently smiling.

'They are clean, Geron.'

'Thank God,' said I.

'It is your health and strength.'

'And Morgan's wisdom.'

She tossed the clotted dressings to Owain, and taking clean linen wrapped it softly round my wounds, and I lay and watched her, and felt an infinite peace descend upon my soul. Already my man's strength seemed to be returning. I might be a man of one eye, but I should bear arms again against our enemies.

'Owain.'

'Yes, lady.'

'This bed has seen its service. We passed a little haystack in the meadows.'

'Yes, lady.'

'Bring fresh hay, and let us burn this bed.'

But here I had to warn her.

'Better not light a fire, Igerna. It might be seen by our enemies.'

She nodded at me, and Owain nodded with her.

'I will fetch fresh hay, lady. That stuff can be thrown into the mere.'

Owain went to and fro across the causeway so loaded that he looked like a walking haycock, and they made me a new bed, and the smell of the mellow old hay was sweet. Igerna stuffed a small sack with it to serve me as a pillow. Owain had tethered the pack-horse to a willow, and I could hear the beast cropping the grass. It made me feel hungry.

'My sweet,' said I, 'I could eat again. I want my strength back.'

She sat there on a pile of hay with another saddle-bag beside her, and a platter on her knees.

'It is coming, Geron. This is for you.'

'But you have not eaten yet, Igerna.'

'We will share it,' said she, with a loving look at me.

And for a while I forgot my hunger in looking at her and in marvelling at her loveliness. Igerna was woman, glowing, lustrous, with more colour in her skin and sparkle in her eyes. No longer was she the meek, milk-white maid, but a woman with all the bloom of her youth and love fragrant in her. She could be fierce, and she could be gentle, and even her sweet neck was rose as well as lily, and her clouding hair like a cloud about the moon.

'Igerna.'

'Yes, Geron.'

'How lovely you are.'

She gave me a quick, deep look.

'I would be—to you, Geron.'

'It makes me marvel. Do you remember the night at Corinium, when I left you——?'

She was silent for a moment.

'I shall never forget it.'

She turned on her knees, and put the platter of food on mine.

'Eat, Geron.'

'If you will share it.'

'I will.'

'Your fingers first. Do you know what is in my mind, Igerna?'

Her smile was downward under deep lashes.

'Tell me.'

'This—is like a holy sacrament, Igerna. All that I can pledge I pledge to you.'

'Yes, Geron.'

'And—whatever fate may have for us, if you will it—I will ride with you again to Corinium.'

She did not answer me for a moment.

'Do you wish that, Geron?'

'No. I would rather die in battle.'

She bent and touched my forehead with her lips.

'You shall not die in battle, my beloved. I—I—am woman, not a frightened girl. What you have to bear—I will bear with you, ever and always.'

I spoke just one word—'Igerna'—but into that one word went all my soul and body.

The very weather was kind to us. The sun shone and a little breeze whispered in the willows. Owain had his hatchet with him, and he cut willow boughs and built three little booths, one for Igerna, one for himself, and another for the horse. They matched the green of the island and were inconspicuous, and were unlikely to catch hostile eyes. I had my hay-bed moved nearer to the doorway of the hut, and I had long sight and an eye left to me, and I watched the downs and the hills for any sign of our enemies. Owain went foraging for us, and ventured as far as Astolat, to come back with the news that Astolat was a mound of ashes.

I could not understand why Artorius lingered, and I spoke of it to Igerna.

'Is he not strong enough to march?'

Her calmness comforted me.

'Artorius would be so strong, Geron, that our enemies will not stand against him. I know—because Mother Placida is his sister.'

'Do all sisters know the hearts of all brothers?'

She gave me a glancing smile.

'Placida and Artorius are twins.'

My wounds were healing well, and the eye-socket had ceased to weep, and my strength was returning. Early in the morning and at dusk I would go out and hobble about the island, for at these hours I should be less likely to be seen. My leg was stiff and twinged when I put my weight upon it, but I could bend my arm without discomfort. Igerna would stand and watch me like a mother watching a toddling child.

One morning I missed Owain, and asked what had become of him. Igerna told me that she had sent him with a message to our people to say that all was well with us. This troubled me, but I said nothing of it to Igerna. Our fortunate star seemed to be in the heavens, and yet—with all that I had seen and suffered—my world had its dark valley of doomed and deathly things.

Lying there on the sweet hay, with my hands under my head, and my one eye closed I seemed to see against the darkness the incredible and swift happenings of the last few weeks.

SC—L

This Greek tragedy had broken upon us like a storm in the night, yet now I could see its inevitability, and wonder at the blindness of our peaceful past. We, a fat, rich, easy country, had bargained with the barbarians, and bribed them into our service, as though gold and soft words could buy loyalty and faith. Even I, a strong man, had ridden from Venta after buying wine, to have my fool's innocence shocked by death and horror. I thought of Igerna sitting so near me, and how— by the frailest of chances—she had escaped that pile of corpses. A frightened, soot-smothered child hiding in a furnace-room, with all those dead above her! Londinium cowering behind closed gates. Our one hope—Artorius—and those more valiant and hardier men from the west.

I opened my eyes and saw Igerna sitting with my helmet in her lap; she was polishing it, with a little smile playing about her lips. I remembered Coel burnishing that same headpiece. Poor Coel! Where did his bones lie?

Igerna's head lifted suddenly. She was looking towards the causeway, and the smile had gone from her eyes and lips. From where I was lying at the moment I could not see the causeway. She put my helmet aside and stood just inside the doorway.

'Someone coming?'

She nodded and held up a hand for silence.

'Owain?'

She shook her head, and spoke in a whisper.

'A man. Keep still, Geron. I do not know yet whether he is one of ours. He does not—come—as though he knows this place.'

I whispered back.

'Something strange about his way of coming?'

'Yes, like someone's spy.'

I rose from the hay and stood behind her in the shadow, and I could see the man upon the causeway moving slowly towards us. He appeared to be a cautious creature, for now and again he paused, and stood to look and listen, and I wondered why he should be shy of so wild and peaceful a place. He was still some distance from us, and as far as one could judge he carried no arms, but might be some lost countryman seeking sanctuary. And yet there was something familiar about his figure, and suddenly his head caught the sunlight and glinted red.

'By Gemini, it is Coel!'

Coel it was, and he appeared to be gaining confidence, and he came loping towards us, and I, holding Igerna by the hand, stepped with her out into the sunlight.

'Coel, hallo. All is well, my lad.'

Then an astonishing thing happened. Coel stood stock still, staring at us; we might have been two ghosts. Not a word did he utter.

'Come on, man,' said I, 'we are not spectres. What happened to you? Where have you been all these days?'

He did not answer me, and he was near enough for me to see a curious smirk spread over his face. I took three limping steps over the grass, and suddenly he turned and ran, looking back once or twice, but not as though he feared me.

'Stop, you fool,' I shouted, 'we are not dead, but living,' for I could think of no other reason for his fleeing from us, but he did not stop, and I watched him until he had crossed the marshland, and was lost to sight behind some willows.

I turned back to Igerna, and was struck by her set and frowning face.

'The fellow must be mad. Maybe some terror has put him out of his senses.'

She stood looking past me into the distance.

'I wonder. Is Coel to be trusted?'

'Trusted? Why, the man has been my body-servant for years. How could he hurt us?'

I met her eyes, and there was a stark gleam in them.

'I do not trust red-headed men.'

'But, Igerna—how could the fellow harm us?'

'I wonder,' said she. 'I wonder.'

We went back into our hut, and sat on the hay, with the causeway under our eyes. There was a restlessness about Igerna that puzzled me. To me Coel was no more than a smirking jay, and I still believed that he would return.

'I like this place no longer, Geron.'

'Because——?'

'It would be better for us to leave it.'

'Just because a frightened fool——?'

'He might be more than that.'

I reached for her hand and held it. She had shown such courage in coming to me that I did not believe that she was afraid.

'What makes you think evil of Coel?'

She looked at me and smiled.

'Women have feelings about some things, Geron.'

'Some women, yes. We men may feel the same. But Coel is just a peacock of a fellow, and——'

I felt her fingers tighten suddenly on mine. My eyes were on her face and she was gazing at the track across the marshes.

'Look, Geron.'

I looked and saw and dropped her hand. Two figures showed on the causeway, armed men with helmets and red shields, and I knew them at once for enemies. Saxons! Had Coel betrayed us to our enemies? I felt a vast rage rising in me.

'God in Heaven, you were right, Igerna.'

I took her by the shoulder, and drew her into the shadow of the hut.

'Quick!—buckle my harness on me.'

I saw that she had her hand on the handle of her knife.

'You cannot fight, Geron. You are too weak.'

'I can fight as I never fought before. Quick, my harness.'

She cast it on me and fastened the buckles with swift fingers that did not tremble. She placed my helmet on my head, and then she kissed me.

'I shall not live if you die, Geron.'

I understood, and I kissed her on the mouth.

'You—shall—live.'

She slipped my shield upon my arm, and I took my sword, and went forth to meet my foes.

It has been well said that the spirit can be stronger than the flesh, and a sudden wild strength raged in me. I thought of

Coel's treachery, and wished that he had been one of those two. I might be fighting mad, but there was a cunning in me, and I remembered the knife in my love's hand. She should not die nor be at the mercy of these swine. Almost, my nostrils were blazing fire.

I went quickly to a narrow part of the causeway where there was deepish water on either side, and there I waited with my sword upon my shoulder. I had the sun behind me, and it shone in my enemies' eyes.

I looked straight at them as they came towards me, and I seemed to see in their hairy, red-smudged faces all that was evil and cruel and vile. They were not young men, and one of them had grey hair in his beard, but they were stout and lusty, and they grinned as they came, and their eyes were the eyes of beasts ready for the kill. One fellow had yellow fangs with gaps in them, like a broken palisade. Each carried a hand axe, and a dagger at his girdle. I knew how deadly those axes could be.

Now in this narrow place there was not elbow-room for two men without their being half-bogged in mud and water, for at some time the causeway had given way here, and I had my plan and it was like an arrow on a taut bow. I would meet these fellows where the two of them could not well rush at me together. They came towards me leaping and laughing and mocking me in their coarse lingo, for, no doubt, they thought me an easy victim. I had one eye, and a bandage on my leg, and as Igerna told me afterwards, a dead white face, but its pallor was the pallor of fury. It was my nature to go bleached of face in battle.

I did not wait for the beasts to attack, but leaped upon the first of them, my shield up and my sword pointed, for the point of a sword can be deadly. Maybe the suddenness of my charge, and the white fury of my face gave me the moment of surprise that was so precious. The fellow swung his axe, but was slow with his shield, and the point of my sword shot over it and caught him in the throat. It was a lucky thrust, and he staggered forward and fell, and in falling blundered against my legs. That was not so fortunate, for the second man was on me before I had got my balance. His axe shore through my shield and gashed my arm, and my second thrust went astray.

This new wound sent me mad. I threw myself against him like a bull, body to body, and he went down, but he clutched my legs and I fell on top of him. He had dropped his axe, and his hand had gone to his dagger, and I had shed my shield and sword, and grappled him. I had to have that dagger. We slithered down into the water reeds, and I got a grip of his wrist, and we struggled together like wild beasts. He was the older of the two and not so supple in strength as I was, nor so fighting mad. He tried to get his teeth into my throat, but I rammed my helmet under his chin, and twisted at his wrist, and bullocked a knee into his belly. Then he lost the dagger, but it slithered into the water, and we fought with naked hands. I got a grip of his throat, and shut my one eye, and held on though he clawed at my face. I was on top and forcing his head down into the water. With one knee in his belly I slowly got him under, and held him there in spite of all his writhings and struggles. He began to weaken. My hands at his throat and the water smothered the life breath in him.

I kept a knee upon him and my hands on his throat, and saw bubbles break the surface, and I held him there until I was sure that he was finished. Then I tried to scramble up, and suddenly all my strength left me, and I pitched forward into the water on top of the dead man. That furious effort had exhausted me, and I was trying to hold my chin above water when Igerna ran to me. She, too, seemed to have come by superhuman strength, for she got me on to the causeway close to where the other man lay with his throat slit and his blood staining the grass.

'Oh, my love, your arm!'

It was a mere gash, and with her help I managed to reach the island, though my head was swimming, and my legs dragged heavily. My stomach was heaving, and my heart going at a gallop, but with Igerna supporting me I reached the hut. And then I fell flat on the hay, and the world went black.

'Oh, Geron, my brave love.'

Her voice seemed far away, and for a moment I thought that death had me.

This was Igerna's hour. She put the wine-flask to my lips, and made me drink, and then she brought water and bathed my face, and presently the faintness and nausea passed, but I had no strength left in me. I lay there with my head low, so weak that I could not lift a finger. Igerna was kneeling. She loosened the straps of my harness—my helmet and shield were in the water—and then she washed the wound in my arm, poured in oil, and dressed it with clean linen, using her knife to cut the strips. I had my eyes closed, and suddenly I felt her lips on mine.

'Oh, Geron—my brave Geron, live, my beloved, live.'

I looked at her and smiled.

'Could I die—with you beside me?'

She held the wine-flask to my lips and as I was drinking I remembered Coel. Had Coel the traitor betrayed us to our enemies? Was that why he had come, to spy upon us, and so that he could bring those brutes to butcher me and carry off Igerna? And what now? Coel might be over yonder like some lurking wolf, and there was a sudden great fear in me. Exhausted as I was I should be at the mercy of that treacherous gadfly. The island had ceased to be a refuge, and had become a trap.

And Owain had taken the horse with him.

I drank greedily of the wine, hoping it would warm me and give me back some strength.

'Igerna, you were right.'

'How, Geron?'

'This place has become a trap. I had forgotten Coel.'

I saw her young face go hard and fierce.

'Coel! Was it he who betrayed us?'

I nodded.

'Give me food, and more wine, Igerna. Yet I may not have the strength. There is still—Coel. Go, Igerna, while you can.'

Her eyes blazed at me.

'And leave you?'

'Yes, go, my beloved.'

'I go, and leave you to that dog? Never.'

Nor had my pleadings any effect upon her.

'If Coel should come, leave him to me.'

'But—Igerna——'

'I am no soft child, Geron. Eve is not always fooled by the serpent.'

Yet I was profoundly troubled and fearful for her sake, for, if Coel came and saw me as I was he might see himself as master—and I—a poor slave. Or he might bring more of the Saxons upon us. I tried to sit up and my head swam, and with a little cry Igerna laid me back upon the hay.

'Give me more wine and food. My strength—must—come back to me.'

She gave me more wine, cooked meat and bread, and I made myself drink and eat, though my stomach felt queasy. My thoughts were on Coel, a Coel who must have gone fawning upon our enemies and betrayed me. Why had they not cut his treacherous throat? But maybe he had said to them: 'I will show you where Gerontius lies wounded, the man who helped to slay so many of your comrades. If you lust for revenge and blood—I can give it to you.' Yes, and more than that. Coel had seen Igerna, a lovely prize that might dazzle his lustful, faithless soul.

Again I tried to sit up, and my head went round, and in my desperate fear I pleaded again with Igerna.

'Go, Igerna, while there is yet time.'

She sat beside me and her eyes were both fierce and tender.

'Save your dear breath, Geron. I stay with the man I love.'

She was watching the causeway, and presently I saw her shoulders stiffen, and her head lift, and I guessed that her eyes had seen that which I dreaded.

'Coel comes.'

Her voice had a strange softness, and her face was almost serene. She rose to her feet and stood at gaze.

'Geron.'

'Yes, Igerna.'

'Lie still. Do not move. You are wounded to death, and helpless.'

I had a strange feeling that our fate was in her hands, and that she had some desperate plan that yet might prove our salvation. I saw her toss her hair and walk out into the sunlight, while I lay there in the shadows.

I moved myself on the hay so that I could watch the causeway and I saw Coel quite near to us, a jaunting, swaggering Coel. He stopped where the dead men lay, and seeing my shield and helmet lying half in the water, he bent and recovered them, put the shield upon his arm and the helmet on his head, and in my helpless wrath I cursed him. Then he picked up one of the Saxon battle-axes, and came striding on, arrogant and smirking.

Igerna went to meet him, and I gritted my teeth. Oh, ye gods, how I yearned for the strength to take that false beast by the throat! And how he had fooled me!

I saw Coel pause, with the axe upon his shoulder, and his blue eyes smiling. I heard Igerna speak, and her words wounded me.

'Why, Coel, you look a fine figure of a man.'

He gave her an ironic yet half servile salute.

'Hail, lovely lady.'

Impudent beast! My hands clenched themselves. I heard Igerna give a little laugh.

'Am I lovely, Coel?'

He smiled at her.

'How is our dear master?'

I saw her shrug her shoulders.

'Stricken unto death. And he is no longer a man upon whom a woman can look with pleasure.'

Coel grinned.

'Am I such?'

I saw her nod.

'You might be. I need a strong young man in these evil times.'

Coel walked close to her, and I saw them gazing at each

163

other, and from Coel's face I knew that she was looking at him as at a man who pleased her.

'I am dark, you red, Coel. That is as it should be.'

'My blood is hot and red, my lovely.'

Again she gave a little laugh, and beckoned to him.

'Come and look upon the poor thing yonder.'

I saw Coel hesitate.

'Did he slay those two?'

'Yes, and got his death wound. My eyes can no longer look on him as a woman would.'

Coel came two steps towards her, and his face was a lustful smear.

'You women are fickle.'

'Women ask for a man.'

'You are a wanton wench, my lovely.'

'I am—woman, and young. Besides—he is ugly now, and an offence to my eyes.'

They seemed to swing together, and her left arm went round him, and his right arm round her. He was leering in her face.

'I am a good man at the love game. Let us look upon my lord and master.'

So, linked together, they came to the doorway of the hut and gazed upon me, and I saw Coel's false eyes gloating.

'Hail, Gerontius. Who now is master?'

I lay quite still, trying to will my strength back.

'I am still your master, Coel.'

'Ha-ha,' said he, 'no more of that. I took the kick and the commands. Now, you are down in the mud, and I am the man for a lady.'

I clenched my hands.

'You are a foul coward,' I said, 'and a traitor, and had I the strength——'

He spat at my feet.

'Ho, ho, Master Gerontius. Lie there and rot. A woman knows a man when she sees him. Why—were you to live no old beldame would look at your face——'

Then I saw what Coel had not seen: Igerna's hand going

to the knife at her girdle. Stealthily she drew it, and I saw it swirl and flash, and drive upwards into Coel's throat. He staggered and clutched at his throat, whence blood was spurting. Igerna had torn loose, but Coel was not done for. He swung his axe, and in that moment my strength seemed to come back to me. I clutched my sword and heaved myself up and struck at Coel's legs. The swinging blow brought him to earth, and crawling to him I put the point of my sword on his chest, and with both hands on the pommel, drove it home.

I can still see that evil, anguished face, with the cold blue eyes bulging at me, and the red lips curling back from the teeth. I was straddling Coel's legs and I felt the death spasm under me. Then I must have fainted.

When consciousness came back to me I was lying on the hay, and Igerna with me, and her arms were about my body. And she was weeping, and I felt the tumult of her bosom. I laid my hand upon her head.

'Igerna.'

She raised her head and looked into my face, and then hid her face against me.

'Oh, Geron, do not die.'

'Who speaks of dying?'

Her voice was broken.

'Oh, beloved, forgive me for the words I had to speak. I shall hate myself—even though I lied that you might live.'

I caressed her head.

'Igerna, you have the blood of heroes in you. My God, you gave me my chance to crush the head of that treacherous snake. And now—give me time and my strength will be sufficient. A great peace comes to me.'

She raised her head and kissed me on the mouth.

'Oh, live, Geron, live. I feel that I could carry you in my arms like a child.'

'No need for that, Igerna. Give me more wine and meat. We must be out of this place before nightfall.'

XVII

IF man is but the creature of his senses, and his senses are the slaves of material things, then indeed is he but chaff blown by the wind, or a belly waiting upon the trough. Here was I—once more wounded, unshaven, foul with fighting, and my face scarred by human claws; and yet a woman's love carried a mysterious lamp whose light seemed to transfigure all my blemishes. I lay there watching Igerna and wondering at her and what our fate would be, for Igerna was busy upon a strange business; she had stripped Coel of my helmet and shield and was sitting in the doorway of the hut cleaning them and my harness.

Now, things may be symbols, and some simple act a kind of sacrament, and as I lay there resting and watching Igerna, I came by a new feeling for the ultimate mystery of translunary things. Here was a young girl who—in the nearby past—had been but a pampered daughter, proud of her young beauty, and seeing life as a pageant revolving about Igerna, and I had been but a galliard, cocksure boy full of my own youth and the vanities thereof. There came to me words of Saint Morgan's which had puzzled me—'Tomorrow not Yesterday should pull a man towards God.'

Three dead men lay out yonder, and I—who had been so near to death—felt a sudden pity for them, even for that false wretch Coel. His vanity and his jealousy had been his undoing, and his malicious soul had thought to be revenged upon the man whom—with secret hatred—he had called master. But then my mood changed as I remembered what might have befallen Igerna, and again I felt the savage exultation of driving my sword's point into Coel's chest. Assuredly man's moods fly hither and thither like a dragonfly over summer water.

The sun was well in the west, and I saw more mystery in the glowing hills and woods. Igerna sat there against this golden background, with my sword across her knees. It was she who had plucked it from Coel's body.

I sat up and stretched my arms.

'Igerna—I am stronger now. We must carry what food we can in a wallet.'

She sat at gaze, her dark hair clouding. It was the fashion for women to pin it in coils at the back of the head, but Igerna loved her hair to be free.

'And your arms, Geron.'

'I doubt if I can bear them.'

'I shall bear them for you.'

In truth that is what she did. She slipped my corselet over her slim body, and girded on my sword, and set my helmet on her head.

'I go armed, Geron.'

'A veritable Minerva!'

She gave me a loving look.

'I am no Minerva. I have filled a wallet.'

'Then let us go,' said I, 'there is much woodland near where we can lie in safety.'

I struggled up and slung the wallet over my shoulder, and she bade me lean upon her, but that I would not do. My first steps past those dead men were weak and limping, but more strength seemed to come to me as we crossed the causeway. Igerna kept step with me, and I felt that our spirits were in step, and the beauty of the evening sank into my soul. I had but one eye, yet it saw the green earth with a new vividness.

So I hobbled along across the meadows with my gaze on a great clouding wood that rose before us, oaks, beeches, yews, birches, all fringed with fern. No human figure showed to threaten us, and the sky was without a cloud.

'Thither is our sleeping place, Igerna. The trees will be our friends.'

She smiled at me.

'And the green fern shall be our bed.'

My legs began to labour under me when the ground grew steeper, and Igerna would have taken the wallet, but that I would not suffer. I felt as I had often felt at the end of a foot-race when the world begins to go black and one's lungs are near bursting. Coming to the shade of an old gnarled thorn I sat down suddenly like a small child not sure of its legs. Somehow it made me laugh as one can laugh in desperate moments, and my sudden laughter set Igerna off, and our laughter was like gushing water that has been pent up in a cistern.

'Oh, Geron!'

I lay flat and laughed.

'Ye gods, what is there funny in a pair of wobbling legs! And yet——'

She flung herself down beside me, her face close to mine.

'Laugh, my love, laugh. Maybe man's laughter is like woman's tears.'

'Would you weep while I laugh, Igerna?'

She kissed me on the forehead.

Presently I sat up, with my breath coming easily, and I saw the valley cupped below us with the marshes, and the island and the pool. The green causeway was a slender thread, and upon it something glinted, perhaps the helmet of the first dead sea-wolf. And yonder stood the little haystack whence Owain had pulled hay for us. So peaceful did that valley look that blood and death might have been illusions.

Igerna's hand held mine.

'Oh, Geron,' and her face had gone dark and strange, 'to think that I helped to slay a man!'

'Does it lie heavy on your soul, Igerna?'

'No, because——'

I raised her hand and put my lips to it.

'That would not have happened but for you.'

She nodded.

'Love can be fierce, Geron, and yet so gentle.'

So we went on, and up into the great wood, and with the covering of evening a wood may become more and more a place of mystery, with its green glooms shot through with shafts of light, and its canopy of leaves eyeletted with gouts of gold. Even the colours grow more deep in contrast, the browns and greens and greys, the blue blackness of midnight colorades. There may be a great silence everywhere, and then a little wind may come, and the trees become like trees in some sacred grove where God walks in the cool of the evening while the trees are moved by the breath of the great spirit. So it happened when we came to a grove of beech trees, ancient trees with great grey trunks and their roots like monstrous talons gripping the ground. There had been a great stillness, and suddenly a little trembling took the leaves, and a sibilant rustling spread above us.

Igerna stood still with a hand on my arm.

'Listen, Geron. We are welcome here.'

'The trees are our friends, Igerna.'

'What do they say? Peace be with you, children. God is here.'

A beech wood may be a stately and mysterious place, but it is no temple for those who would spread a woodland bed. There is a coolness in the air, and it is draughty under these splendid trees, and no grass or flowers flourish, and even the fern fades out of sight. We passed on up a woodland track, and presently we came to an open space, a great glade into which sunlight slanted, and here we saw six old yew trees like sombre tents with their red-black trunks for tent-poles. But we saw more than that, a little booth built of faggots and roofed with boughs which had served some woodmen for shelter.

I held Igerna back and, taking my sword from her, went to make sure that the place was empty, and empty it was save for some dry fern which the woodmen had left behind them.

'Our luck is good, Igerna; even a bed of dry fern is spread for us.'

The booth had a centre pole set with the ends of lopped-off boughs to serve as pegs, and I hung the wallet on one of these. The old yew trees stood on guard about us. Igerna hung up my harness, and I planted my sword in the ground, and its crossed pommel was a symbol.

'Lie down and rest, Geron.'

Obedience was more than virtue, for I was at the end of my

169

strength, and never was my bed more welcome than that pile of dry fern.

'God bless the fellows who left it here.'

Igerna was emptying the wallet, and when it was empty she stuffed it with dry fern, and put it under my head.

'I must find water, Geron.'

She took the water-jar, but I was not happy about her going alone.

'Wait awhile, Igerna, and we will go together.'

She held up a slim white finger.

'Listen!'

I sat up sharply, thinking she had heard sounds of someone moving in the wood, but she smiled and shook her head at me.

'Listen! What do you hear?'

I heard it, too, a little, moist, gurgling sound as of water gushing from a bank. I knew that these hills were full of woodland springs.

'Water, Igerna, and near.'

She went forth with the jar, and in a moment or two I heard her voice.

'I have found it, Geron.'

'God is giving us everything,' said I.

She came back with a full pitcher, and a light like the play of sunlight on water in her eyes. Then she knelt and set out our simple food, and we ate together in that little darkling booth. There was a great silence everywhere, and the light was fading, and our sentinel yews standing black and still. Igerna's hair was as black as the trees, and her face like some white wood-flower shining in the dusk.

Then a moon rose and made more mystery, and I have never known a more still and noiseless night. Our woodland world might have been encased in crystal, blackly brilliant and like moonlit ice. We sat together holding hands. I was weary but with a peaceful weariness, and my love sat at my side. It had begun to be chilly, and the damp was rising round us and we had brought no bed-gear with us, for we had none to bring.

'Oh, Geron——'

Her fingers pressed mine, and I wondered if she was afraid.

'Yes, Igerna.'

'Ants.'

'Ants?'

'Yes, our food. We have so little.'

A wood can be full of great ant-heaps, and emmets might raid our food in the night.

'Put it in the wallet, Igerna, and hang it on the pole.'

'Yes, but ants can climb.'

They could—the brutes, and metaphorically I scratched my head, but the inspiration was Igerna's.

'Your shield, Geron. Will it hold water?'

'It should do so.'

'If I fill your shield with water, and set your helmet in it, and put the food in your helmet——'

What a practical maid was this!

'It should be a safe defence. Put them to peaceful uses.'

She glided off into the moonlight with my shield, and came back with it brimming with water from the spring, and placed it with care in a corner of the booth. I saw her wipe the inside of my helmet with a wad of grass. Then the food went into it, a couple of stones kept the helmet steady in the centre of this improvised moat.

'The wisdom of Minerva, Igerna.'

She gave a little laugh, and stretched herself beside me on the fern. I heard her yawn.

'Sleep well, Igerna. You must be weary.'

'I am.'

'Peace be with you, beloved.'

We snuggled down into the fern, and I felt that she had no fear of me, which made my love glad and strangely exulted.

'Hold my hand, Geron.'

We fell asleep, holding hands.

XVIII

DAME FORTUNE had been kind to us, but our woodland idyll was not destined to be all moonlight and music. I woke with my wounds feeling stiff, and with an ache in my head, and a sharp thirst upon me, yet I must have slept late for the sun was up and the booth empty. I missed the water-jar, and guessed that Igerna had gone to fill it.

I lay still, listening. I could hear the spring making a moist murmur, and as I listened other sounds came to me: distant voices, and they were the voices of men. I sat up, with a hand to my head, feeling giddy.

Where was Igerna?

I called to her, and no answer came to me.

I staggered up and out, and hobbled in the direction of the spring and found it gushing from a rocky cleft in the hillside. The water-jar stood beside it, but there was no Igerna. I picked up the jar and drank, and going back to our shelter set the jar down and looked at Igerna's larder. The food was safe, but a big blackish beetle was swimming in the water, and I flicked the beast out into the sunlight, where it lay on its back with its legs busy.

I sat down in the fern and drank from the water-jar and listened to those distant voices. They were angry, clamorous voices, making me think of a pack of hounds giving tongue. I did not like that sound. It seemed to come from the marshes in the valley below.

Then I heard the sound of someone running over the dead leaves in the beech wood, and there was a promise of fear in this brittle rustling. I put the water-jar aside, and stood up, to see a fleck of colour moving like a shuttle between the great grey trunks. It was Igerna. She dropped to a walk when she reached the grass and saw me standing there. Her eyes were big and black in a dead white face.

'Geron—the Saxons.'

She was out of breath, and I saw fear in her eyes.

'Down yonder?'

'Yes, a score of them. I had gone to the edge of the wood to look if it was safe to——'

'Have they seen you?'

'No, but they have seen their dead.'

That explained the animal noises down yonder, and that these sea-wolves were howling for blood. Igerna was leaning against me and I felt her trembling, for there are some sounds that freeze the blood.

'Are you sure they did not see you, Igerna?'

'I was behind a tree, and they were busy about their dead.'

I held her close to me and thought hard, and she let her head rest on my shoulder.

'It would be better to go deeper into the wood, Igerna.'

Even as I spoke the voices of our enemies came nearer, or so it seemed to me, and I wondered whether we had left a betraying trail behind us.

'Quick, into the fern. We must take our gear with us.'

We gathered up our possessions and waded into the tall fern until we were deep in a green fortress, and suddenly a jay began screaming at us, and I cursed the bird. Moreover, I remembered our bed of litter, and that it might betray the marks of sleeping bodies, and I hobbled back to the shelter and tossed the dry fern into a heap. I could hear the voices of our enemies, and they seemed nearer to us as I dived back into cover. Our passing had parted some of the bracken fronds, and with swift stealth I set them straight and covered our tracks so that the canopy of green plumes looked unbroken. That accursed jay had winged its way off, and a little breeze came bustling through the wood.

We crouched there, listening to the wind in the oak trees about us, and watching the waving fern. I had my sword by me and knew that if I had to use that sword it would spell death for both of us. I could still hear the voice of our enemies, but they had come no nearer to us. I looked at Igerna, and she at me, and there was question and answer in that look.

'If they should find us, Geron, kill me.'

I drew her to me and kissed her on the mouth.

'May that fate be far from us.'

We had our little store of food and water with us. I would have made Igerna eat, for when a great fear is with you it is good to give the body exercise, but she would not touch the food.

'We have so little, Geron, and it must be for you.'

'I will not eat unless you eat.'

And seeing that I was stubborn about it, she shared out a part of our store, and halved it, but I saw that she had given me the best of the meat, so I snatched that which would have been hers and gave her mine, and with a gentle and loving look she humoured me.

Then that accursed bird returned with a family of jays and squawked and scolded at us, and I dared not clap my hands and drive them off. The feathered brutes must have thought that the wood was theirs—not ours, so we sat still, and listened for any sound in the valley.

Silence! We looked at each other and wondered, and presently the suspense was too much for me. I wanted to see what was happening down yonder, and I crawled through the fern, but not by the way we had come. The jays still scolded at me and I had to suffer their impudence, but before breaking cover into the open space by the yews I parted the fern and peered. The little glade was empty, and I crossed it and took to the beech wood, moving from trunk to trunk. My feet made a slight rustling amid the dead leaves of yesterday, but with the breeze overhead the live leaves smothered the little sound below. The jays did not follow me into the beech wood. Maybe they believed that they had routed man.

So I came to the edge of the wood where the branches drooped to the ground in a green fluttering curtain. I parted the leaves and looked down into the valley, and what a shock was mine. In the meadow nearest the marshes were waggons, horses and men, scores of them, and they were not friends. Men were pulling hay from the little haystack that had saved us, and on the island I saw others digging a grave to bury the Saxons I had slain.

That was enough for me. I could not say whence these enemies had come, whether they were part of a new horde or belonged to the great company that had gone north and found Londinium too strong for them, but what was only too plain to me was that our countryside was in their hands, and that they might be swarming all about us. I wondered what had happened to our people, and to Owain in particular. I hoped to God that the good fellow had not come back and fallen into the clutches of those brutes.

I was about to leave the edge of the wood when I saw happenings down yonder which made me tarry. A group of our enemies were moving towards a waggon where two fellows had removed the waggon pole and appeared to be nailing a cross-piece to it. Then I saw that a prisoner was in the centre of the knot of figures, and suddenly he was seized and thrown down upon those pieces of timber, his arms forced out, and his legs lashed together. It was Owain, and of that I felt sickly sure. A man with a hammer was nailing Owain's hands to the cross-beam; two other fellows were digging a post hole in the ground. I watched all this with cold horror, saw the cross raised and planted in the ground, and poor Owain hanging there.

The savages stood round and mocked him. Their shouts came to me and seemed to be—if interpreted:

'Hail Christus, God of the Britons.'

And what could I do? Nothing.

But my fear was for Igerna, for I knew what her fate would be were she to fall alive into the hands of those beasts. The very thought of it moved me to a cold madness. I knew that I could not tell her about poor Owain, and as I made my way back towards her hiding-place I tried to decide what was best to be done. Should we stay where we were? But what of food? We had but little left to us. I cursed my wounds and my lack of strength. It seemed to me that it would be better for us to remain in hiding, and then, when the moon was up, to make our way across country, and to take cover again when dawn came. And were Morgan and Lob and my people still in leaguer west of the Great Down? And what of Artorius? I was moved to curse Artorius for not marching more swiftly to our rescue.

Once more the jays had gone, and I slithered through the fern to find Igerna on her knees, eyes closed, hands together. She looked so lovely and devout that I, too, got on my knees and prayed, and my prayers were for her and for poor Owain. How long would he hang there before merciful death came to him?

Igerna opened her eyes at me, and I tried to smile at her. We were beginning to look like two wild creatures, and much less sleek than those handsome jays.

'There are many of them,' I said; 'there is nothing for us to do but stay here till night comes.'

I must have been looking dark and grim, for there was no smile in her eyes.

'But food, Geron?'

'I know,' said I, 'but it is not safe to move in daylight. We shall have to go fasting.'

'And your poor wounds?'

'Oh, curse my wounds—I can lie here and rest. When the moon rises I think I can find the way towards the Great Down. And we may come upon some deserted farmstead, and discover food of sorts.'

'No nuts, no blackberries.'

'Too early in the year. Nothing but grass, Igerna,' and I made myself laugh, but there was no live laughter in me as I thought of Owain.

So we lay down side by side in the fern, holding hands, and looking at the green boughs above and the blue sky showing in patches through the waving foliage. It was still and peaceful until the flies discovered us, for though green fern is supposed to keep flies at a distance it did not deter our particular pests. I had been sweating, for in my weak state I sweated easily, and I and my wounds were the bait, and the brutes settled on my bandages and the lids of my eye-socket. Igerna was more virgin to them, and sweeter of body than I was, and she sat beside me and with a bunch of fern fanned the flies off me. She had covered our little store of food with my shield.

These pests added to my restlessness. We might have slept the daylight hours away had the fly-world been less voracious. The voices of our enemies kept up a distant burble in the valley below, and I thought of Owain hanging on that cross, and wondered if he had a cloud of flies about his poor, anguished face. And why should Igerna have to sit there fanning the black pests from me?

I sat up, feeling angry and desperate.

'Let us go, Igerna. Your arm must ache.'

'And whither, Geron?'

'Anywhere but this accursed wood, and away from those voices.'

She must have been as tired of the flies as I was, poor darling, and maybe her mood was mine.

'Yes, away from those voices.'

So we gathered our things together, and wading through the fern took a trackway that led over the hill and away from the sun. I had wanted to leave my harness behind, for it was heavy and could be recovered later if we lived to more fortunate days, but Igerna bade me carry it, and carry it I did for a while until we came out into wild, heathy country, and the sun grew hot. The plated mail was too cumbersome, and, coming to a stunted, solitary fir, I had my way, and hung the harness on the peg of a broken bough, like a scarecrow in a field.

I took a look at the country, while we lay in the heather, with the wind blowing over us in a world that seemed free of flies. I had hunted in these parts, and I knew the lie of the land. It was one of those blue days, beautiful and limpid, with a clarity that was exquisite, and it seemed so strange to me that terror should be abroad, and man more dangerous than any wild beast. Moreover, I could not get poor Owain out of my thoughts, and the anguish and thirst he was suffering. The Great Down swelled against the northern sky, and far in the west I could see smoke rising. A crumple of hills and valleys waved westwards, and more to our left I could see the height of the Five Hills, blue and distant and mysterious. It was wild country, but I knew that in some of the valleys there were little homesteads and one or two manors where we might find food and shelter, even if they were deserted, for food was our great need. Nor could I see any live thing moving, and it was not country that would tempt our enemies with plunder.

Igerna was looking at me with tender, anxious eyes, for I must have seemed a ragged, haggard creature, dirty and unshaven, and she, too, was looking like a wild country wench, yet lovely as ever.

'Let us go,' said I, 'I like the wind in my face.'

We found a sandy track which led us down into a valley. There was little cover on the hillside, but we had to dare the risk, and Igerna's eyes looked this way and that like the eyes of a wild fawn. My one eye was apt to ache, having all the work to do, and was easier if I looked into vague distances. It was slow travelling, for I had to limp on my wounded leg, and this crawling irked me, for I had always been swift on my feet.

Yet once again good fortune was with us. In a little secret valley about two miles to the west we came upon cornfields and meadows, and saw the white walls of a small homestead sheltered by elms and poplars. A brook threaded the valley under the shade of thorns and elders, alders and willows, and we took to the bed of the brook. It would bring us in secret close to the homestead, for it was a green and secret tunnel, and the shallow water was fresh and cool to our feet. I heard a cock crowing, and the quacking of ducks, and these country sounds were reassuring. No marauders could have plundered the place.

The green canopy overhead opened out suddenly where the brook widened into grassy ledges, and leaving Igerna hidden by the bushes I got my chin over the high bank and scouted. The little homestead with its outbuildings and wattle fence was not fifty yards away; it was a timber and plaster house with a great thatched roof sloping nearly to the ground.

Ducks were waddling across a paddock. I saw an orchard and tranquil trees, but no sign of human life, and I judged the homestead to be empty.

'Igerna.'

'Yes, Geron.'

'Duck, my dear, and an orchard. Stay there while I explore.'

I took my sword with me, and went limping across the little paddock, and the ducks halted in line and eyed me with beady eyes. 'Something for the pot,' thought I. The gate in the wattle fence hung open, and there were flowers in bloom, and two hens scratching among them. I found the oak door locked, but I broke a window with my sword-hilt, got a hand in and lowered the latch, and stood listening. There was not a sound, and I wriggled into a neat, clean room paved with red tiles. I saw a meal still laid on the table and stools set about it, but the place was silent as death, and its very silence was welcoming.

I unfastened the door and went back for Igerna.

'Food and drink, my dear,' said I. 'Can you roast a chicken?'

I helped her up the steep bank, and when she saw the ducks she blew a kiss to them.

'Aren't they sweet, Geron?'

'I hope so,' said I. 'Roast duck, oh—beloved!'

'Oh, a shame, Geron!'

'My stomach is without shame.'

Now the house was ours for the using, and use it we did in measure, but I knew that it might prove a trap for us should marauders happen upon it. Its people had fled, and that was a sufficient warning for us. They had taken their cattle and their pigs with them, and their horses and their waggons, but the ducks and the fowls remained. There was a well with windlass and rope and bucket, and bed-gear, and some food in the larder, and I will confess that the first thing we did was to fall upon that food and eat like a pair of greedy children. We had found butter and cheese as well as bread, and I laughed when I saw Igerna with butter on her chin. She was even more hungry than I was, poor darling, and she might have buttered herself to the eyes, and I should have loved her.

I felt much more of a man after that hearty meal, but a dirty fellow, and leaving Igerna to clean up the platters I went down to the brook, and stripped myself and washed. Moreover, I discovered a little grassy bank which was dry and shaded by bushes, and I saw it at once as a secret and safe refuge where we could spread hay, and borrow bed-gear and sleep in peace.

XIX

MAYBE I had over-tired myself or over-eaten, but my latest wound grew very stiff and sore in the night, and its throbbing kept waking me, and when I did sleep I had evil dreams. Poor Owain seemed to haunt me in these dreams, and once I started from sleep with his voice calling: 'Master, Master, save me.' The moonlight filtered through the leaves, and the brook ran softly below our little plateau, and Igerna lay beside me, and I could see her dim and tranquil face white amid her clouding hair. Wake her I could not, poor darling, for she was sleeping so peacefully.

But I was worried by the pain in my last wound, and by a feverish feeling, and the haunting horror of Owain. The wise tell one that the life spirit is at its weakest before cock-crow, and that melancholy and cowardly thoughts rise to the surface like the drowned dead when their bodies begin to swell. Was my wound poisoned and giving me fever, and how could I lie sick when my whole duty was to watch over Igerna? So, towards dawn, I became a creature of restless, shivering gloom, and I left my bed and climbed up into the meadow and walked to and fro watching the eastern sky go grey. There had been a heavy dew and the grass was cool to my feet, and a peerless day was in promise, but my head began to ache and cold spasms passed down my spine.

Was Owain still living? Had he called to me, and had I heard his voice? Even this secret dawn, and the golden glow in the east seemed fantastic and unreal. I had a fever on me, and the world was distorted and unhappy. I began to fancy that I heard voices and footsteps, and when hens started cackling somewhere I went stiff and frightened. Were our enemies about? Was there death in the dawn?

Then I heard an actual voice, Igerna's.

'Geron, Geron.'

There was fear in her voice, and fear in me lest it should betray us. I turned and hobbled to the brook, and saw her white face appear above the edge of the brook's bank.

'Hist!' I whispered. 'Make no sound.'

I slithered down the bank, and my fresh wound gave me such pain that I let out a half-stifled yelp.

'Someone is lurking about the house. Back to cover, Igerna.'

Her face went tender and troubled, and she put an arm about me.

'Your poor wound, Geron. And you are shivering.'

'Curse my wound,' said I, 'the thing would not let me sleep.'

She helped me to lie down, and kneeling, put a hand to my forehead. Her hand was cool and my forehead hot.

'You have a fever, Geron.'

'Maybe I am imagining things. Keep still. Let us listen.'

I was conscious of her watching me as we listened, but there was nothing to be heard save the sound of softly running water. Maybe I looked what I was, a man in a fever both of mind and of body, with his chin and upper lip black with bristles, and his face crumpled with worry and pain. She laid a sudden hand again on her forehead, and I could feel that she was sorely troubled about me, not as a tired and oldish woman might be, but with the strength and tenderness of youth. She did not say 'Oh—wretched man—what ails you now?' but went and soaked a kerchief in the brook, and laid it on my forehead.

She said: 'I wish Morgan were here.'

181

My God, so did I, for I had a forefeeling in me that I was
to be a sick man, and helpless, and such thoughts added to
my fever.

'Morgan, if he lives, cannot be far from us.'

She did not answer me, but busied herself with preparing
food. We had found bread and cheese and butter in the
house, and eggs in the fowl-house, and some milk that had
gone sour, and this morning Igerna gathered dry wood
together to make a fire. We had feared to light a fire, even
in the brook bottom, lest the smoke should betray us, and I
questioned her daring so, but she had a strange, silent look
about her, and she smiled at me. Her face might have been
the face of a sybil.

'God shall bless our fire, Geron.'

She had more in her mind that I knew of, for she had found
flint and steel and tinder in the farmhouse, and I watched her
kneel and blow upon the first flames until the wood was well
alight. She had brought a skillet with her, and first she boiled
me eggs, and then warmed up the sour milk. I was still
troubled about the smoke from the fire, and when it had
served she scattered the ashes.

I had not much stomach for my food, and flashes of heat
and spasms of cold played over me. Igerna still continued
strangely silent. She shared the meal with me, but there was
food left over, and she placed it beside me, and then went to
wash her hands in the brook and to comb her clouding hair.

'Can you sleep, Geron?'

'I will try, Igerna.'

She brought back a cool wet cloth, and laid it on my
forehead.

'Sleep, beloved, for you are very weary.'

Sleep I did in a fitful kind of way, though it was more like
a dream doze than deep slumber. Both spirit and body had
surrendered. My consciousness was blurred. Igerna was there,
and then she was not there. Her absence did not trouble me
to begin with, and I kept dozing off and dreaming. The sun
swelled high in the heavens, and I saw its light scattering
through the bushes. My refuge was like a little cool green

cove, with the water running softly, and the hay smelling sweet below me.

It came to me suddenly that Igerna was not with me. I sat up, holding my head. I waited, listened, and felt fearful.

'Igerna—Igerna.'

No Igerna answered me, and suddenly I felt desolate and alone. I lay down and covered my face, and broke into foolish, frightened tears. So little manliness was left in me. I became a creature of wild conjectures. Igerna was lost; Igerna had fallen into the hands of our enemies; Igerna had deserted me. But the devil of doubt was a mere phantasm of my fever, and all the man that was left in me cast out that scurrilous thought. Then, fool that I was, I turned my eyes on the food and the drink she had placed for me, and I came near to guessing the truth. Igerna had gone in search of help.

I lay down again and closed my eyes—I found that I always thought of my two eyes. The day drowsed on; I was hot and I sweated, and my conscious self drowsed like the day. A kind of apathy descended upon me, and I accepted my fate—whatever it might be. I could do no more; I was a sick man and useless.

The sun went west. The ducks had come down to the grassy space where the brook broadened, and I heard their exultant quackings. A cock crowed now and again, and into my dulled consciousness these nature sounds seeped like soothing music. Peace and security were here while these feathered creatures splashed and paddled near me. I watched the sunlight blinking through the leaves, and listened to the brook, and for some strange reason—I know not why—a feeling of peace descended upon me. It might have been the happy stupor of a man who was dying and who welcomed death and its last assuagement, but I did not feel death near me. A voice kept saying to me—'Igerna comes, Igerna is near. She has dared all that you feared for her.'

It must have been towards sunset—I had been dozing—when I heard voices.

'This way, Father.'

It was Igerna's voice, and I seemed to wake and hear another voice saying in me:

'Igerna, Igerna.'

She came gliding through the green gloom, and after her came Morgan, and I lay and gazed at them as in a dream.

'Hail, Father.'

They knelt down beside me, and Igerna kissed my forehead.

'I had to go, Geron.'

Morgan was smiling.

'Your love is brave, my lad. Now, let us look at you.'

'My love is very brave,' said I.

'And so have you been, my son. Now you can rest in peace.'

He nodded at Igerna, and she rose and left us, but I was anxious about her going.

'Is it safe, Father?'

'Very safe, my son. Twenty of Artorius's horsemen are with us, and there is not a Saxon this side of the Great Down.'

He had his old brown leather satchel with him, and I could remember it as a boy when he had dosed me when I had one of the spotted fevers.

'Now let us look at you.'

He felt my pulse and my forehead, and uncovering the last of my wounds, frowned over it and looked solemn.

'Ha, here is the trouble, my son. We must see to this.'

'Is it poisoned, Father?'

'Some foul humour. It must be suffered to discharge and obey nature. Now, let us look at the others.'

He found them clean, and so was my eye-socket, and he nodded reassuringly.

'You have had your share, my lad. Now you can leave it to others. And in a day or two you shall see a sight that will make you glad.'

'Artorius comes?'

'He does and in great splendour.'

'It is high time.'

'Ha, Artorius has the wisdom of the great. Deliberation,

slow, sure ruthlessness. Only little men fuss and are in a hurry.'

'Then I must be a little man.'

'Not so. All men praise you.'

Then it was that I remembered poor Owain, and pleaded eagerly and fiercely with Morgan.

'Let men go and see if he is alive, Father. No, Igerna does not know of that horror. I could not tell her. Maybe he still breathes on his cross.'

Morgan's eyes flashed.

'I will go myself, my son, and take men with me. But I fear——. Think of our Lord Jesus.'

'But a spear was thrust into His side, Father.'

He nodded.

'I will take Artorius's men. You will be safe here till we return.'

I put out a hand to him.

'Wait. The Saxons are strong there.'

'I think not,' said he, 'our enemies are in retreat.'

Morgan left me, and in a short space I heard Artorius's cavalry ride forth and wished that I could see them, but Morgan had bade me lie still. Then Igerna came to me and sat by my side and asked whither Morgan had gone and for what purpose, and I could not tell her. She had seen enough horror, and I lied to her and said that Morgan had gone scouting. The light of a windless evening lay upon the earth, and dew was falling, and I could smell the sweet herbage, and watch the glittering gold upon the leaves. A great peace possessed me.

'I am happy, my love,' said I, 'for you are safe, and I can lie and look at you.'

Her dark eyes were tender.

'And you, too, Geron. I have a hero for my love.'

'A very unhandsome hero.'

At that she bent and kissed me on the mouth, though I was all raw hair.

'Is love so light?' said she.

I took her hand and kissed it.

'Tonight you will sleep under a good roof.'

'And you.'

'No. I have a liking for this place, and the brook and the green world.'

'Then *I* bide here, Geron.'

'But why, Igerna?'

She smiled at me.

'I am your nurse, to watch over you. Morgan has bade me poultice that wound, and there is water heating in the house.'

'But you need sleep, Igerna.'

'Do I? Do I look sleepy-eyed?'

'You are the moon and the stars, and all that is lovely. My dear, I have one desire.'

'And that, Geron?'

I laughed.

'To be barbered and feel clean.'

So the gentle hour passed, and the dusk came, and I lay holding Igerna's hand, and listening for the return of Morgan and his men. They had not had far to ride, and in the twilight I heard the sound of horses. Igerna would have risen, but I held her hand.

'Stay with me here, Igerna.'

I wondered what the news would be, and whether poor Owain had been rescued alive, but there was doubt in my heart. I kept hold of Igerna's hand, for she had seen enough of death, and waited until the horsemen had passed round the homestead. The twilight was deepening and it was growing dark under the bushes.

Igerna tried to loosen my fingers.

'I must go and get your poultice, or it will be too dark.'

'We can have lights tonight, Igerna.'

I let her hand go, for I heard footsteps on the bank above, and knew that Morgan was coming. Igerna left me, and Morgan took her place. His face was dark, and I knew that Owain was dead.

'Too late, my son. We found him hanging there.'

'Poor Owain. Our enemies had gone?'

'Yes. They are gathering all their scattered groups together

186

somewhere on the Green Way. We found Coel, too, lying dead on the island.'

Coel the traitor!

'Did you bring Owain back, Father?'

'We brought both of them.'

That shocked me, for I had realised that Morgan did not know of Coel's treachery, and of Igerna's courage. Maybe she had not wished to speak of it to Morgan.

'Our men are digging a grave in the orchard.'

'For Owain, Father. Let them not be buried near each other. Owain was a good man, Coel a foul traitor.'

Then I told him the truth, and I saw the smoulder in his eyes.

'I will see Owain buried, my son, and say a prayer over him. As for the traitor, he, too, shall be buried, but with no prayer.'

XX

I CANNOT say whether there was magic in my brookland sanctuary, or whether it was Morgan's wisdom and Igerna's care of me, but I sweated the sickness out of me in the night. The fever left me, and there was no pain, which goes to show that the spirit may be master of the flesh, and a happy heart the best timepiece. Man can never be so foolish as when he thinks himself clever, and half our dogmas are blind assertion or the mere products of prejudice. Having read the philosophers, I have fled like a bewildered child to God and a faith in some mysterious purpose, for words can be like a juggler's balls, pretty things to play with, but mere baubles cheating the senses. What is it that man sees and hears and touches?— just the surfaces of things which may not be what they seem. How much is there that his senses cannot know? This may be trite stuff to the seers and the thinkers, but to me it came as a sudden revelation as I lay there in the cool shade, and felt my head clear, and my body at peace.

Yes, mystery everywhere. Why was Igerna Igerna? Why should a compound of flesh and bone and blood appear a creature more incredible than any other woman in the world? Why did ducks quack and fowls cackle, and blackbirds sing like strange spirits out of Heaven? I felt myself in a haze of mystery, and floating with the brook under the green boughs and the summer sky.

In fact I was the first up, and kneeling by the water and washing myself while Igerna lay asleep in the shade. I had found a placid piece of water for my mirror, and as I looked at my reflection in it I marvelled, which—in nan—is a sign of grace, that any woman could love such a bruised, hairy and one-eyed scoundrel as I appeared. And suddenly I laughed, and when a man can laugh at his sacred self the beginnings of a wise maturity are at work in him.

But my laughter woke Igerna.

'Geron, what are you doing?'

Was I to be scolded and tenderly so? That, too, moved me to lovely laughter.

'I am healed, Igerna. You and Morgan——'

She shook her hair into a cloud, and as she stood I saw her torn clothes and her scratched ankles, dear signs of her wild dash to find help and Morgan.

'You will lie down again—at once—my dear.'

'Let us compromise,' said I. 'I will sit. And I wish to God someone could find me a man with a razor.'

She gave me a loving look.

'You worry too much, Geron, about appearances.'

'I may be an ugly devil, but why should I be a dirty one?'

'You are neither,' said she, almost with severity, 'and if you love me you will rest.'

'There is no other answer to that, my queen.'

And I returned with proper humility to my bed.

Igerna smiled and left me, and went a little way along the brook. She thought I could not see her, but I will confess that I could. I saw her slip her clothes down to her waist and wash, and her white, virginal beauty gleamed in the green gloom. And suddenly she turned her head, and I went flat, a little ashamed perhaps of gazing at so pretty a picture.

Artorius's men were up, grooming their horses and cleaning harness, and I heard them laughing and talking. These men had not been in battle, and did not know what wounds were, but a cheerful innocence may be helpful to a fighting man in his first scrimmage. I lay rubbing my hairy chin, and feeling provoked by those loud and hearty voices, for, in spite of my wounds I lusted to ride with Artorius against the heathen. I had poor Owain's end to remember.

Then Morgan came, and stood looking at me with the eyes of a physician, and I grinned at him.

'Find me a barber, Father, and I shall be fit for battle.'

'Not you, my son. If I can borrow a razor I will barber you myself.'

He felt my pulse and my forehead, and examined my wounds, and seemed astonished.

'Some Saint might have laid healing hands upon you.'

'Are you not that Saint?'

He gave me a shrewd look.

'Flattery goes to the head.'

'And kissing by favour, and I am not fit to be kissed.'

He tweaked my nose.

'That is an infirmity I can help to cure.'

He left me, to return with a razor borrowed from one of Artorius's men, also soap and a clean napkin, and he was busy on his knees while I lay flat when Igerna came back to us. She sat down on the grass and watched the shaving, and Morgan's tongue was teasing.

'Here is a fellow who quarrels with a beard. Now why should that be, sweet maiden?'

Igerna's eyes were dark and deceiving.

'How should I know, sir?'

'There speaks innocence.'

Morgan was holding my nose while he dealt with the fur on my upper lip, and I, perforce, was mute.

'Vanity, vanity,' said Morgan, 'and yet—young blood should be proud.'

189

'I am very proud,' said Igerna.

'Of your comely self, my dear?'

'Yes, and of other things.'

Morgan's mood of mischief was not ended. He had brought a box-mirror with him which he had found in the house, and he produced it from a pocket in his robe, and offered it to Igerna. The barbering was over, and Morgan had wiped my face with the clean cloth.

'Youth looks at life,' said he. 'How does my work please you, sir?'

Igerna had opened the box. She did not look at herself in the mirror, but moving on her knees, held it out to me.

Said Morgan: 'I see two mirrors here.'

Igerna gave him a flashing look.

'Yes,' said he, 'the eyes of a woman. Which do you prefer, my son?'

I laughed and looked at Igerna.

Morgan sent two of Artorius's men back to the leaguer near the Great Down with a message to Lob and Caradoc. They were to come with a horse-litter or light waggon to carry me from the farmstead, for though our enemies were going east, there might be peril from straggling parties of them. Morgan told me that we had spies or traitors in our country who had warned the sea-wolves of Artorius's strength. Yes, there were other Coels, and always there will be Coels in a world in which vain and ambitious men are jealous of the great.

Morgan himself set off with a dozen of Artorius's horsemen to scout around, and gain what news they could of the Saxons. The heathens were cunning brutes, and all this talk of a retreat might be meant to fool us. Instead of going back they might come forward.

Meanwhile I sat in the shade by the brook with a good and growing hunger in me. Igerna was busy in the farmstead, and someone had whispered of roast meat and honey-ale. I heard a pother among the hens, and supposed that Artorius's men were culling a dinner. The ducks were down at the pool, so they—good creatures—had escaped the slaughter. And I—carnal man—was thinking of roast chicken and other slaughters. Already I was planning to ride with Artorius.

It was high noon before I heard the sound of waggon wheels and of horses. Igerna was with me, and looking over the brook's bank she told me that Lob and Caradoc had come. I would have gone to greet them, but she would have none of it, and I—having schemes of my own—played the good disciple. It heartened me to see these good men, Lob with his black grin and great limbs, and Caradoc the gay and buxom. They came down to me, and kneeling, pressed my hands, and were a little humble about the whole business of the marshes.

'We should have been with you, Master. As for that foul traitor Coel—I would have broken his back.'

I held a hand of both of them.

'My good comrades, a word in your ears. When the great day comes I would be with you.'

They looked at me with affection.

'But, Master, you have done enough. We would have you sound and safe.'

'Thanks, Lob,' said I, 'am I to stay behind with the women?'

'That's as it may be, sir. You won't be in petticoat land and without glory.'

So we left the farmstead and my green refuge which had served us so well. Lob carried me in his arms to the waggon, though I was capable of walking, and Caradoc bore my arms. They had piled hay in the waggon so that a soft sweet bed should save me from jolting. I saw that Caradoc had his eyes on the ducks, but I spoke for them.

'Let the birds be. They have quacked courage into me.'

Caradoc grinned.

'Such medicine was not your need, Master.'

Igerna joined us, and sat with me on the hay, and we rolled forth in the summer sunshine past cornfields which were waiting for the sickle. I was more happy now about these fields and our precious harvest. I wondered if my own fields were growing golden-eared, and if my house still stood, or was but a pile of ashes.

So we came to Lob's leaguer. There were many rich villas and homesteads west of the Great Down, and Lob had lodged our people in one of these, a comely place with many buildings and a view about it. My people gathered round the waggon and raised their hands to me and gave me greetings.

'Hail, Master. We who serve are glad of your safe return.'

Somehow I knew that I was indeed the master and the leader of my people, and that my wounds were badges of honour and of lordliness.

Now, nothing seemed too good for me so far as my fellows were concerned. They had made me a bed in the villa's state room with its painted walls and purple curtains. Silenus grimaced at me from the floor, and there were wine and silver cups upon the table, though why the master of the house had not taken his silver with him or buried it was beyond my comprehension. Maybe, he had been in such a devil of a fright that he and his had bolted like rabbits. Such spunkless creatures were of no value to us in these tempestuous days.

Then the sleek Gildas came in to me, and bowed and rubbed his hands. He was an Agag of a man.

'I trust my lord is comfortable? We are very glad of my lord's safety.'

I am afraid that I was curt with my steward.

'I am very comfortable, Gildas, thank you. I shall be glad of a dish of oysters.'

He gaped at me.

'Oysters, lord?'

I laughed and dismissed him. For, if fortune proved kind, I planned to make Lob my steward, and send Gildas to grind corn with the women.

Dinner was served, and Igerna came to me. I got up to sit at the table, and she bade me stay on my bed. Well, how could a man not humour so lovely a mistress, for Igerna was no longer the wild wench of the woods. She had been to the bath, and her hair was dressed, and so was her dear body in rich and borrowed garments. Her gown was of saffron, her shoes of green leather, and her black hair was perfumed.

I lay and gazed at her, and suddenly she looked coy.

'Why do you stare so, Geron?'

'Stare!' said I. 'Please God I am guilty of no such rudeness. I look where I cannot help looking.'

And she blushed, which reminded me of a saying of my father's: 'Never marry a woman, my son, who cannot blush.'

Then Morgan returned and sat at table with Igerna, while I dined on my bed. Morgan's tidings were good. They had seen no sign of our enemies, and Artorius was at Pontes.

'Tomorrow you may see a great sight, my son.'

I remembered to be grateful for my one good eye.

XXI

ACCORDING to Saint Morgan, Artorius could have marched on Londinium and made that great city secure and himself the master of it, but his urge was of more mighty a temper. Always in the history of our island the courage and genius of one man has saved her when she has been in dire straits, especially so when a committee of little men have haggled and gabbled and divided their forces. A mob is of less significance than a muck-heap when great perils press. The man of destiny is he who can think bold thoughts and take bold action. So Artorius had taken time in gathering the western clans together, men who had not been sapped of sense and valour by the sour savours of the city. Master Urbanus is a fine fellow at chattering about his rights and privileges, but a shabby creature when good red blood is needed. Artorius had waited until he had felt himself strong, and now he was for no pretty manœuvres, but for meeting our enemies in the field and driving them into the sea. In days to come the mob of Londinium was to cheer Artorius when he had conjured the fearfulness out of their bones, only to belittle and sneer at him when their bellies were full and their tongues like bell-clappers. The little man, when scared, will acclaim his hero, but discover the great man an offence when swords have given place to yardsticks.

That unforgettable day began with a rain shower, and the face of summer was refreshed when the sky cleared and the sun came out. There was a secrecy in Morgan's actions, and I suspected that Igerna was in the plot. I gathered that Artorius was marching south and that we were to meet upon the Great Down, and as we broke fast I saw through an open window a waggon pull into the courtyard like a state galley on wheels. It was dressed with green boughs and swags of wild flowers, and even the heads of the horses had their favours. I caught Morgan winking at Igerna, for even a saint may flick an eyelid when God is in a good humour.

'My lady's chariot?' I asked.

'No, my lord, your triumphal car. We meet Artorius in state.'

I am not a very modest fellow, but the idea of being stuck up in that bower on wheels bothered me.

'Forgive me, Father, but I am not a May-day doll.'

'Shame,' said he, 'think of the lady.'

I looked at Igerna, and her lashes were lowered.

'Well, someone must blush for me.'

'That's as it may be,' said Morgan.

So men may jest before going into battle, hoping to hide the more solemn thoughts that lurk like ghosts in the dark places of the mind. I had my own ghost and my own temptation, for as I looked at Igerna and knew that she mattered to me more than life itself, I became for the moment a coward. Why should I risk all my dear desires, I who had fought and suffered wounds, when men would think it no shame for me to stand aside and leave the last great fight to others? And yet I could not bring myself to stay behind with men like Gildas, the scullions and the women.

The house had a little chapel of its own, and before we sallied, Igerna and I knelt together before the Holy Cross, and held hands, and once more I was tempted, for I divined in

194

Igerna a belief that I was not pledged to battle. Her face was serene and happy, and her hand held mine as though she was sure that no other peril would part us. And there was sudden anguish in me and a yearning to stay with her and tempt fate no further. Her fingers held mine firmly, and suddenly she leaned her body against mine, and I was a coward in fearing to hurt her.

'No more wounds for you, dear love.'

I put an arm about her.

'No more wounds for you, Igerna.'

'For your wounds are my wounds.'

I could not bring myself to tell her that I must go with Artorius or suffer secret shame.

So, before I climbed into the waggon, I called Lob to me and told him of my choice, and he looked black and unconsenting. Lob could be a blunt, gruff fellow who called an axe an axe, and he argued with me. Had I not done enough? Of what use should I be in a bloody fight with my wounds still unhealed?

'Moreover, Master,' said he, 'you have a duty to think of the lady, and the children she should bear you, children that this island will need.'

'Lob,' said I, 'you are a little previous. Maybe——'

'Maybe, and rubbish to you, sir. Why get yourself killed and break a fair maid's heart? And if any man doubts your courage, I'll tear the throat out of him.'

Then I had my inspiration.

'Lob, my friend, there are some things a man must do or spit in secret on his own soul. Listen. Why should not this waggon be a war chariot? Give me a long spear and a dozen men, and we'll play the Carthaginian elephant.'

He looked hard at me and grinned.

'Sir, you were always wild-headed as a boy. But, damnation, the notion tickles me.'

'You and I and Caradoc, and a few stout fellows. Let Artorius's horsemen break in and we can rumble after them.'

Lob knew that I would have my way, and that he yet would

have some say in it, for he nodded his head at me and fondled his beard. I warned him to keep the matter secret, and again he grinned at me. Maybe he thought me a headstrong simpleton, and that he and Caradoc and Morgan would see to it that I did not lose my other eye. In truth, before we moved off I saw those three good friends of mine with their heads together, and Morgan's hand was resting on Lob's shoulder.

But what a day was this! We marched, horse and foot, up the southern slope of the Great Down, and there were four horses in my waggon team. Igerna sat beside me, and Morgan led us with his cross. When we came to the crest of the ridge we halted there, and a great silence fell upon all our people. The sight we saw was fit for silence. Down below us where the country was wild yet flat we saw a glitter and a moving mass of colour, Artorius and his host about to climb the Great Down. A glorious sight it was to men who had borne the heat and the peril, and were but few compared with the multitude of fighting men whose harness and spears shone in the summer sunlight.

Artorius's host was but part of a great picture, and its coloured shields flowers of the forest. Green woods, green fields, dark heaths, and distant cornfields turning gold, a blue hazed distance. We sat and gazed in silence at those rippling ranks, the dragons of war trailing their shining harness up the long slope to the great chalk ridge. Helmets and spears flashed, and horses' heads went up and down, and behind the host a mass of waggons rumbled, guarded by files of foot-soldiers. Artorius himself rode in the van, with chiefs and notables, and with a great white cross carried before him, and the sound of their coming rolled up to us like thunder.

Then trumpets brayed. It was a salutation to our little band of fighting men, many of whom carried their wounds like badges of honour. I saw Morgan go forward with his cross to meet that other cross, while Igerna and I sat like two spellbound children.

Artorius was mounted on a great white horse, which caused me a pang in remembering poor Cæsar. He wore gilded harness and a sky-blue cloak, and a white plume in his helmet.

He and Saint Morgan saluted each other, and then Artorius rode straight to our waggon, and Igerna and I stood to greet him. He raised his right arm and I raised mine.

'Hail, Gerontius—hail, Igerna.'

He was smiling, for Artorius was no tragic figure, but a man with jocund eyes and a mordant mouth. You felt that he saw the whole of you, both within and without, and that in his human wisdom he was profoundly man.

'We are here at last, my friend. You have had much to suffer, and all fighting men salute you.'

I bent my head to him, and he turned his eyes upon Igerna.

'Well, young woman, what have you to say for yourself?'

Igerna was head in air to him.

'Just—that I am a woman, sir.'

And Artorius laughed.

'How profound is your justification. A child runs away in the night, and to become a lioness and hunt beside the lion. Such madness shall be our salvation. And are you satisfied, young lion?'

'Very well satisfied, sir.'

'Good. But let us put words in the baggage train, and go on to battle. We hold that you have done enough, Gerontius. Sit, my lad.'

I smiled at him.

'Is that a command, sir.'

'It is.'

'Then, I may have to play the part—of Igerna.'

He looked at me shrewdly.

'That choice, I think, lies between the two of you.'

So we sat there in our triumphal waggon, with Artorius and the notables beside us and watched the British host pass by and spread along the great green trackway. These men from the West made my heart feel good and my stomach tighten as they tossed their spears to us and shouted:

'Hail, Gerontius—hero.'

Was I a hero? I looked at Igerna and her eyes were flashing,

197

and never had I felt life to be so good. All carefulness had gone from me, and my blood was whimpering, and I knew that it was to be my lot to go with these fighting men.

I saw a squadron of horsemen ride out along the Great Down, a scouting party, while Lob came and was questioned by Artorius. The Notables had gathered round our waggon and they spoke with me and were full of courteous flattery. Some of them were oldish men, yet all of them looked with commendation at Igerna, and Igerna smiled upon them and knew that she was pleasing to their eyes, and such knowledge may be good for a woman.

The rest of the host had halted to rest their horses and their legs, and to drink and eat. The wains trailed along the green way like a great serpent. Men were building and lighting fires and setting great cauldrons over them. The horsemen had planted their spears in the turf, and they looked like a forest of young trees, or the masts of ships in a harbour.

Igerna and I were alone for a moment, and her face was bright with colour and her eyes flashing.

'Beloved,' said I, 'maybe you feel as I do.'

'How, Geron?'

'That I must be part of this great day. Wounds or no wounds—I must share in it.'

Her face and eyes went dark of a sudden and her fingers closed on mine.

'You have done enough, my love.'

Her clouded eyes hurt me.

'Igerna, how can I hold back?'

I felt her slim white fingers gripping mine.

'I will not let you go, my love. That is too great a thing to ask of me.'

There lay my choice, like white-hot metal from the furnace for man's hand to dare the ordeal. So ravaged was I that when I found that I could not move her, I left the waggon and limped about in search of Morgan, for Morgan should be my counsellor and father confessor. I found that our people had built a little chapel of green branches for the Saint, and that he had set up a rude altar there, and upon it was a silver chalice

and platters of bread, for Morgan would administer the Holy
Sacrament to those who followed the Cross into battle. He
happened to be alone and kneeling by his altar and when he
saw me he bade me enter.

'What would you, my son?'

'Counsel, Father.'

'Kneel down, my son, and open your heart to me.'

So I told him of the choice I had to make, and his eyes
watched my face, and when I had finished he put forth a hand
and signed me with the cross.

'Follow your urge, my son, whatever it may be.'

'I would go with Artorius, Father.'

'Then go.'

'But Igerna? She has borne so much for me.'

He smiled at me, and his face had a serene radiance.

'Maybe Igerna will more than forgive you.'

'How, Father?'

'Pride, my son, pride in the valour of those we love. A
woman may say nay and yet, in secret, applaud the yea. And
I shall be with you.'

'You, Father?'

He smiled once more.

'I have spoken with Lob and Caradoc. Our waggon shall
bear the Holy Cross into battle as a sign and a symbol. We
go together.'

I bent my head over the altar.

'That comforts me, Father. Will you suffer me to take the
bread and wine?'

'I will, my son, and let Igerna taste of them with you. Bring
her to me, and there shall be peace between you.'

I found Igerna in the waggon watching the great host
camped about us, for I reckoned that Artorius had gathered
together the strength of two Roman legions. She had a
listening-look, as though she had heard what Morgan had said
to me, and held some secret of her own.

'Igerna.'

'Yes, Geron.'

'Saint Morgan is serving the holy bread and wine. Will you take it with me?'

She rose and stood above me, looking over and beyond me to the blue distances, and with a strange, still dignity. Her eyes were dark and mysterious but unclouded.

'I will come with you, Geron.'

I did not suspect what was in her mind, or that her words had another and poignant meaning. I put up my arms to lift her down, and she accepted them, but with a strange, dark reticence.

'You must forgive me for being man, Igerna.'

'And I shall be forgiven for being woman.'

So we went together to Morgan's green chapel, and kneeled down, holding hands, and Morgan served the Holy Sacrament to us, and blessed us, and I waited for Igerna to rise. But she remained kneeling, and I saw her slip the gold ring she wore from her finger, and hold it out to me.

'I would be your wife, Geron.'

I was dumb. I looked at her, and I looked at Morgan, and he smiled upon us.

'What say you, my son? Do words fail you?'

I took the ring from Igerna, and raised her hand and kissed it.

'Marry us, Father. My love is such that I am dumb.'

So Morgan made us man and wife, having called in two soldiers to bear witness, and when it was over I looked at Igerna, and she turned her face to me, and we kissed. But she did not rise from her knees.

'Father, we have pledged ourselves to stay together in love until death do us part?'

He bent his head to her.

'That is so, my daughter.'

She was smiling now, and there was a tender triumph in her smile.

'Thank you, Father. So my husband and I cannot be parted, and where he goes—I go.'

I think Morgan caught her meaning before I did, for his face went strangely solemn.

'Do you claim that right, my daughter?'

'I do,' said she, 'so I go with my man into battle.'

I was dumbfounded. I had been playing the solemn hero, and now found myself a sweet simpleton who had been out-witted by a woman. But what a woman! My impulse was not to take her seriously, and I looked at Morgan, thinking he might solve the riddle for me. Igerna had linked her arm in mine, and was looking at the ring I had replaced upon her finger.

'Father,' said I, 'I may be a devoted simpleton, but a man does not take his wife into battle.'

'It is not a normal procedure, my son. I fear that in many instances the battle is between man and wife.'

Igerna let out a little laugh and I went hot about the ears.

'This is a most grave issue, my sweet.'

'Are we to quarrel, Geron, we who are bride and bride-groom?'

'There will be no quarrel, Igerna.'

She pressed my arm with hers.

'That is generous of you, dear husband. I will take it as a wedding gift.'

'You will do nothing of the sort.'

'Oh. Geron, how can you refuse me this, when my heart is set on it?'

'Because I love you, Igerna.'

'Do you love me as I wish to be loved?'

I was dumb for a moment, and I caught a smile deep in Morgan's eyes.

'If I love you, Geron, I would share all things with you, peril and pain, and the great adventure. You cannot say me nay, my love, because I will take no nay.'

I looked helplessly at Morgan.

'Reason with her, Father.'

He held his hands over our heads.

'Reason, my son, may be no sign in the heavens when great happenings are willed by God. Seeing madness may be rightness. Honour your wife, and defend her.'

I looked at Morgan and I looked at Igerna, and suddenly the great issue which lay before us seemed to blaze up in me.

'By my God—I will.'

XXII

OUR scouts brought back the news that our enemies were encamped in strength on our side of the White Bridge and that it appeared that they were waiting to give us battle, but Artorius was in no haste. His plan was to give his men a day's rest after the long march from the west, and let them be fresh for the fight. He called a council of war in the pavilion that had been pitched for him and to it he called such men as knew the lie of the land about the White Bridge. Lob and I could tell him all he needed to know, and taking a pen he drew a rough map upon a scroll and pondered over it. The White Bridge lay in a valley, with Stone Street crossing it, and it could be approached from the downland bluff to the west, and along the valley from north and south. Artorius, having heard all we could tell him, studied his map, and put before the Chiefs and Notables a plan of battle. It would appear that we outnumbered the heathen and had men to spare for strategy. I told Artorius of our fight there, and it pleased him. We would attack with our main force down the long slope to the bridge, but two other bodies could swing round into the valley above and below the White Bridge, and storm in on the flanks.

So our plan of battle was agreed upon. We had scouts out watching our enemies to report upon any movement they might make, but all we heard from them was that the Saxons had lit fires, and built bivvies and had their waggons in leaguer. In fact, our enemies appeared to be over-confident, remembering the slaughter they had made of the Kentish men about Durovesum and Durobrevis.

Our plan was to march at dawn along the crest of the downs whose wooded heights were screened by trees along the Green Way. We should have our scouts out to warn us of any surprise the heathen might have in store for us. Our hope was to catch them out of battle array, or—if they were ready and stood to meet us, to make such a slaughter of them that our island might have peace for many a day.

The night was calm and clear and the sky brilliant with stars, and Igerna and I lay on our bed of sweet-smelling hay in the waggon, and were man and wife together. All about us the host slept, and the sound of their breathing came to us like the sound of the sea. I held Igerna close, with my lips to hers, and the sweet shudder that had swept her white body had filled me with strange sadness. There are moments when a man does not gloat over the tender struggles of his love-mate, and though the vulgar have jests to make upon man's passion and its exploit, I somehow felt that I had sinned against the child in her.

'Forgive me, beloved.'

With her warm, soft bosom heaving she held me fast.

'Forgive—and what, Geron?'

'You—who were to be a saint—to be soiled by man.'

She kissed me, and fondled my head.

'You are a strange man, Geron.'

'I?'

'So boisterous in battle, and so modest in loving.'

'My love is more than that.'

She held my head against her shoulder.

'That is how I would have it, Geron.'

A sweet lassitude possessed me, and I fell asleep, to wake in the night to feel her body pressed to mine.

It was a halcyon dawn. No trumpets blew to salute the sun or rouse our warriors from their sleep. There are days when men wake of themselves because of some inward fire that flares into flame—as fear—or ardour or hate or a savage lust to fight and to avenge some horror. But we had a better cause and a nobler symbol, the Cross, and the peace and happiness of our homes in this green island. The Great Down seemed tremulous with men's voices, vibrant and vigorous. No boastful voices these, but the quiet talk of men who were steadfast in purpose and had good, if bloody, work to do. Igerna lay asleep with a little smile upon her face, and I did not wake her but knelt in prayer for a moment beside my wife.

Then, suddenly, there was a strange stillness, and I saw Morgan standing on a little knoll, holding his cross high, and all those stalwart men moved into a great circle about the figure of the Saint. Some were in harness, others not yet armed, but there they stood in a great, silent congregation, faces upturned, eyes gazing upon Morgan. He was in white garments, and the slanting light of the rising sun fell upon him, and the cross. I heard his voice.

'Kneel, my children, kneel.'

I was kneeling beside the sleeping Igerna.

Artorius and the Chiefs and Notables joined the great circle, kneeling together in a little band, and Morgan prayed to God to bless and preserve all men who went into battle. He stood with his eyes closed and his hands outstretched, as though waiting for the Holy Spirit to descend upon all of us. And then—indeed—a most strange thing happened. A white pigeon came winging out of the blue, and with fluttering wings perched on the cross which Morgan had set before him. There may be many who would scoff at this story, but happen it did, for my own eye and those of thousands saw it.

Artorius was on his feet, his right arm holding his sword high, and I heard his deep voice.

'Men of Britain, we have seen a sign from Heaven. Today shall bring us victory. To arms, all of you.'

Then the white bird rose in the air, and after circling over us flew towards the east as though winging us towards victory.

I had been so spellbound that I had not realised that Igerna was awake and on her knees. She, too, had seen the white bird float down and perch upon the cross. Her face was upturned and her eyes deep and dark as though some great mystery had been revealed to her.

'God is with us, Geron. To such saints as Morgan miraculous things can happen.'

I was silent, thinking that to the greatly wise and to men of supreme sanctity life may be other than it is to mere carnal man.

XXIII

I HAD armed myself with Igerna's help when Lob and Caradoc came to the waggon, and with them were a score or so of picked men, all mounted. Lob had chosen six of our own fellows who were stout-hearted to ride the horses and help man our ship-on-wheels. The British host already had sent out its vanguard, with their faces to the rising sun.

'Hail, Master,' said Lob, 'I bear a letter from Artorius.'

He passed the tablet to me, and I opened the box and read it. I was to command the reserve guard of the army, and Artorius gave me orders. We were to stand fast upon the bluff above the White Bridge, and watch how the battle sped, and not commit ourselves unless our enemies held the ground where they stood. Then we were to come down and deliver a blow that should turn the fight in our favour.

I rubbed my chin over this sheet of wax. Was Artorius tying me to Igerna?

I passed the tablet to her, and told Lob of our orders.

'Well, Master, we shall see all the fun.'

'Fun!' said I. 'I see nothing funny in being left behind like a baggage-train. Moreover, Artorius has said nothing of what we should do if the heathen breaks and runs.'

Lob grinned at me.

'Sir, I should say that Artorius has left that choice to you.'

So we set out to follow Artorius and the main host, leaving charred Astolat behind us. We had some miles to cover, but our men were fresh and in great heart, and it was part of Artorius's plan that we should not lie too near our enemies during the night, but make a forced march and surprise them. For, as I had discovered, the Saxons could be stupid brutes, all hair and belly, with no subtlety in their tactics, and it was more than probable that Artorius would surprise them, and revenge the treacherous slaughter they had made of our King and his nobles.

We were now in my own country, country that I loved and knew so well, the great sweep of the chalk hills with the Green Way winding along the crest between thickets of thorn and of yew and woods of beech. On the southern slope the grass was rank and deep, with bushes of Wayfaring Tree and little junipers, and clumps of broom and bramble. It was a blue day and the distances were superb. We could see the south downs across the forest of Anderida, and the wooded and healthy heights between us and other valleys. And suddenly my stomach yearned in me, for down yonder lay my house and lands, cornfields and orchard, barns and cottages. We were very near it now, and I feared to look down into that deep valley lest I should see ruin, ravaged crops, and the blackened shells of burnt-out buildings.

I think Igerna divined what was in my mind, for when we came near to a break in the woods and thickets through which a trackway led down into the valley, she beckoned to Lob and spoke in his ear. Lob halted our waggon and helped Igerna down and together they went to the lip of the hill and stood at gaze. I watched them and waited, and I must confess that I expected them to return to me with set and silent faces, having no good news to tell me.

Then I saw Igerna turn and wave to me, and I leaped down and went striding down the turfed track between the banks of fern. She came to meet me, and her face and eyes were glowing.

'Come, look, Geron.'

Lob sneaked off and left us, and we stood on the lip of the hillside, holding hands, and I saw all that I had not dared to hope for. There, in the deep green valley, stood my house, white-walled and red-roofed, and the barn and buildings, and the orchard and the mill. Even the cornfields were untouched, and yellowing for the harvest. I could see the great pool and the island and its willows and the island house, and the black barge half hidden among the reeds and water-flags. There was no wind blowing, and the scene was clear and still as crystal, and steeped in a mysterious peace.

Igerna put her head upon my shoulder.

'Oh, Geron, I had prayed for this. How lovely and good it looks.'

I kissed her on the forehead.

'Our home. I would call it an omen of the things that are to come. Do you remember——?'

'The island and the little house. It seems so long ago.'

'And yet—like yesterday. I have much to make good to you, Igerna. Please God, I shall.'

We stood for a little while gazing upon this small world that was ours, lovers and mates, two sentimental creatures, yet somehow wise as to the elemental things that make life good. Then we turned slowly and walked back to the waggon, suddenly conscious of the eyes of the men who were watching us. I smiled at Lob and raised my hand to him.

'Now, brothers, we go on to win a battle.'

We were lumbering along towards the great bluff above the White Bridge, with silence about us, a silence that seemed strange when we thought of those thousands of men ready for battle. Almost I began to wonder whether our enemies had not beaten a retreat in the night, deeming it safer to withdraw to the island about Rutupiæ, and I was about to send a horseman forward when a messenger came to us from Artorius. Our enemies were camped by the river, busy breaking their fast, with their waggons drawn up beyond the bridge. Maybe they were wiser than we knew, and more cunning, and pretending to be unaware of our nearness, for each man had his arms beside him, and they were ready to leap into battle order.

We had halted to hear the news, and I remember a green woodpecker gliding into a tree and looking at us as it clung to the tree trunk. I could see the bird's black eye, and the red tuft on the green body. Then it flew off with its laughing cry, and I wondered whether it was laughing at us.

This was to be no day of laughter, but of blood and sweat, tears, tumult and anguish.

The woodpecker's laughing cry seemed to wake the whole welkin, for no sooner were we on the move again than we heard a tumult of voices and the thunder of horses in the valley ahead of us. The battle was joined, with wild and shouting men rushing upon each other. I bade our drivers whip up the horses, and I felt my belly harden and my heart beating fast. Such stern sounds roused the wild man in me. I was standing, leaning on a spear, and waiting for the woodland to thin so that we could see into the valley below us. Igerna was beside me, and I felt her arm clasp mine.

'Be patient, Geron.'

I gave her a quick, fierce smile, for I knew what was in her heart, and that she herself was a pledge for my patience. With such treasure beside me I could take no wild-cat chances. I was aware of movement beyond the trees, as of columns of men passing down into the ends of the valley, and I guessed that these were Artorius's squadrons who were moving to take our enemies in the flank.

When—at last—the woodland opened before us, and we looked down the green hillside to the valley and the river, I saw a sight that made my hair bristle. There were those two moiling masses of men locked together in a great swirl of colour and of flashing metal, a screaming, cursing whirlpool, with horses rearing and plunging and rolling to earth. For the moment these knots of wild men were in a vast tangle, but as I watched I saw a thing that chilled me. The hurlyburly had been static, and then I realised that it was moving slowly towards us. Our enemies had been ready, and had met our charge with a counter-charge, and our people were being driven back. I felt Igerna clutch my arm, and I heard Lob cursing.

'Oh, Geron, look.'

I felt my bowels squirming.

'Wait. There are the others.'

I saw our two flanking forces swinging round and in, and as they did so more of our enemies rose from the river bank where they had been concealed. Tough brutes these heathens, and cunning. They had been ready for some such strategy, and had kept a rear-guard to counter it.

A second battle boiled up behind the other, but our people had numbers in their favour, and as I watched I saw the second blurr of steel and colour, of horses and of men merge into the main battle. Our people had driven the Saxons back and in, and had got between them and the river, but that did not mean that the bloody business was over.

Far from it. Artorius had our enemies encircled, but they were like a blob of boiling metal or a knot of flame eating into the circle of fighting men. I could see the ranks nearest to us thinning, and a sinister bulge showing in the great, boiling mass spreading up the hillside. The sea-wolves were threatening to break through and throw our host into disorder, and the crisis was bitter and calamitous. Nor was that all. I saw a horseman pressed like a drop of colour from the battle. He was lying forward on his horse's neck, and two soldiers were with him, trying to hold him upon his charger's back. Artorius? His gilded harness, and the blue plume in his helmet were those of our Dux.

That was enough for me. I tossed my spear and shouted. There were some five hundred of us, enough to restore the fight.

'Forward. Our time has come.'

Lob and Caradoc climbed into the waggon, and as they did so I took Igerna by the waist and would have lifted her over the tail-board, but she struggled with me with sudden fierceness.

'No, no, where you go I go, Geron.'

'Ye Gods,' said I, 'a man does not take his wife into battle.'

'Give me a spear and I can fight.'

So lithe and strong was she and so utterly set upon being with me that I bade her lie down in the waggon, for it was moving and the need was urgent. I shouted to the men upon the horses to get them into a gallop, for we were rolling down-

209

hill. Our footmen followed behind, and our horsemen led the charge in a closely set squadron. We shouted and cheered, and passed Artorius on his horse. He heard us; he was wounded and not dead, and he raised himself for a moment in the saddle and lifted his arm. I saw his blanched and bloody face before he sank down again upon his horse's neck. The thinned and desperate ranks of our people must have heard the thunder of our onset, for they swung back and cheered, leaving us a passage for our charge. I saw the wild faces of our foes, and in we went like a stone from a catapult, and drove in with the weight of our rush downhill. I expected our horses to go down and the waggon by itself on top of them, but it was not so. We ploughed in, for our coming seemed to take the heart out of our enemies. Our footmen followed, and so did all those who had swung back to give us free passage.

I caught Igerna round the waist, and flung her down into the hay, but she was up again with a spear in her hand, yet we in the waggon were like an island in stormy water. Our fellows were round us, and our enemies were being crushed back in desperate disorder. Our people were pressing in on every side, and the business was becoming a fight to the death and fierce slaughter.

For that charge of ours down the hillside gave us the victory, and when I saw what was happening, the horror and the splendour of it, the despair and the butchery, I remembered the woman in my wife. This was no ghastly sight for the eyes of Igerna. I sat down in the hay, and pulled her down to me, and held her in my arms with her face against my body. I could not close her ears to the shrieks and curses of the men who were being slain, but I could keep all this horror from her eyes.

We were alone in the waggon, for Lob and Caradoc and the rest had leaped out to share in the killing.

'Lie still, Igerna. Peace be with us now.'

Her fierceness had passed, and she lay in my arms almost like a frightened child. The uproar and the screams of the dying and the wounded, and the shouts and curses, horrified her. She put her fingers in her ears.

I could see over the rails of the waggon, and I was less sensitive than Igerna, and that which I saw filled me with grim exultation. The battle had become a slaughter, and the heathen were like faggots with the flames of our wrath pressing in on every side.

'Kill, kill,' was the cry.

It was a veritable blood-pool and slaughter house, piled with bodies, limp or twisted in the agony of death. And I thought of the wounded Artorius, and wished that his eyes could see the victory that was his.

Then a strange silence seemed to fall. It was the end. I doubt whether more than a score of our enemies got away across the river. I saw men tossing spears and swords and shouting, others standing breathless, some bent with exhaustion with their hands upon their knees. Others were holding wounded arms, or bloody heads, and in the midst of it all lay that mown crop of dishevelled dead, hundreds upon hundreds of them, and for a moment I felt sick in my stomach.

But Igerna must not see all this. I gathered her up, and bade her keep her eyes shut, and sprang down with her out of the waggon. My strength seemed to have come back to me and I did not feel my wounds. So I carried Igerna up the hillside to the peaceful shade of the woods, and there I found Artorius sitting with his back against a tree. His face was bloody, but his head unbowed.

XXIV

ASSUREDLY I should have said that Igerna had seen enough of blood and wounds, but when she looked upon this memorable man, the brother of the beloved Placida, and Britain's man of destiny, she was woman. The two fellows who had helped Artorius out of the battle were standing by like two obfuscated loons, for Artorius was bleeding still, and that gashed cheek was not his only wound. A spear had thrust through his harness and smitten him in the belly.

In fact he was biting at his beard with pain, and his face was blanched and twisted behind its mask of blood. He had heaved himself up against the tree to watch the great finish of his book of battle, but now both body and soul were exhausted.

'Lie down, great sir,' said I.

But Igerna was the mistress. She turned on the men.

'You—find Morgan, if he lives, and bring him here.' For Morgan had left us and carried his cross into battle.

To the other she said: 'You have a sword. Cut ferns and make a bed for your master.'

They were like sheep at her service, and this time it was I who was commanded.

'Geron, there is wine in the waggon, and some clean linen in my wallet. First help me to lay him down.'

I did as she desired, and left her sitting with Artorius's head upon her knees, and went running down the hill to that pool of death. Our people were collecting their wounded and putting an end to such enemies as still lived, for a dead Saxon was—in our estimate—the only good one. And here I came upon Morgan, very much alive, but minus his cross; his vestments were bloodstained, as were his hands.

'Father, Artorius needs you. I fear he is stricken unto death.'

After I had gone to the waggon for wine and linen we set off together up the hill and I asked the Saint if he was wounded, and he looked guilty.

'No, my son, I fear I fell from grace, lost my saintliness and became carnal man.'

I could not help grinning at him.

'You joined in the battle, Father?'

'Yes, my son, I did. May the Lord Christ forgive me, but our need was desperate.'

'But, Father, Cross and sword may be one—in a good cause.'

He was silent, but later I was to hear that the good Saint

had cast his cross into the scrimmage, possessed himself of a battle-axe and fought like Satan.

So we came to the soft green shade where Igerna sat, like the soul of compassion, with Artorius's head upon her knees. She had unstrapped his helmet and his harness, and the grey showed in his hair. Blanched he might be and bloody, but the spirit of this memorable man shone in his compelling eyes, and he smiled a twisted smile at Morgan.

'Hail, Father, it is good to see you.'

Igerna's eyes were large and anxious.

'Thank God, Father, you are alive. But you, too, are wounded.'

Can one chuckle on such grim occasions? Had the business been less tragic I could have prodded the good Saint in the ribs.

'A mere nothing, my child,' said he. 'I have been with the wounded.'

Incomparable man! He was down on his knees beside Artorius, but his own hands were bloody, and he was loth to touch Artorius until he had washed.

'Here is water, sir,' said a voice.

The fellow whom Igerna had sent to cut ferns had found a spring and filled his helmet with water, and Morgan blessed him, and washed.

'Now, sir, let us look at you.'

I had passed the wine and the wallet to Igerna, and suddenly I saw her close her eyes and go pale.

'Come,' said I, 'I will serve.'

She gave me a grateful glance, and I slipped into her place, and bade her go and find the spring, and wash and rest in the shade. Morgan was turning back Artorius's harness and tunic, and uncovered a gaping wound. For a moment he hesitated, and then thrust a finger gently into the wound and probed it. I watched his face, and a shadow seemed to pass from it.

'God be thanked. Mere flesh. Your good harness saved you, sir.'

Artorius's grim face relaxed into a smile.

Our waggon was to serve in a good cause, as were the waggons and horses we captured or rather recaptured from our enemies east of the White Bridge. Some of our wounded, and there were many, were too grievously stricken to be moved, and these we housed in the hostel by the White Bridge and in the booths the Saxons had built. Six men lifted Artorius gently into my waggon where he lay on the soft hay, with his face swathed in linen, yet his eyes were alive and capable of flashing with sudden humour.

'It seems, my children, that I travel in a triumphal car.'

For so it was, with its green garlands and swags of flowers.

Igerna sat beside him and moistened his lips with wine and water, and I perched myself on a rail. Morgan we left behind us, for he had gone back to succour the wounded and pray over the poor dead.

Artorius looked at Igerna, and then at me.

'Gerontius, I have not yet scolded this young woman for flying by night.'

'I have no quarrel with her courage, sir.'

'Neither have I. I would say that your wife will bring pride to a proud house.'

'More than that,' said I.

'Much more, my son. I hold that——'

Then Igerna laid two slim white fingers on his lips.

'You must not talk too much and tire yourself.'

Artorius kissed those fingers.

'Do I make you blush? Were I a young man I should crave more than fingers?'

Igerna shook her head at him.

So we rolled westwards along the Green Way, and when we were near the trackway leading down to my home, a green woodpecker, maybe the same bird, flew past us, winging up and down and laughing.

Sunlight, dust and silence. I had taken the key of the house from Gildas and given it to Igerna to carry in her wallet, and it was she who unlocked the door of our house and was the first to cross the threshold. There was a strangeness and a

214

rightness in all this, and Igerna stood with a finger on her lips, looking at me with eyes that made mystery.

For if a house can speak, the house of my fathers spoke to us. It said: 'Welcome, man and wife, welcome, Mistress and Master. You feared me dead, but I am alive and happy, if a little dusty. Enter, Gerontius; enter, Igerna. May you be blessed with peace and plenty.'

We had left Artorius in the waggon, and he, wise even when wounded, had spoken to me like a father.

'Go, my son, and take your wife to her new world.'

I put my arm about Igerna, and together we wandered through all the familiar rooms, and saw the dust dancing in the sunlight. Igerna's face had a strange tenderness. What could be more lovely than a homecoming such as this, for even the silence and the solitude were ours.

'Geron, isn't it strange?'

'What is strange, beloved?'

'That familiar things should be so mysterious?'

I held her close to me.

'Like you, Igerna.'

Her eyes had a tender sheen.

'Am I like that?'

'Yes, and always will be.'

And then she laughed, soft, secret laughter.

'Maybe I shall be the mother of children. And shall I seem strange then, or like a familiar bed?'

I kissed her.

'What now is—matters.'

We carried Artorius into the summer-room and laid him upon a couch there until a bed could be made for him. There were linen sheets and blankets of wool in the linen room, but we found the door locked and I had to force it open.

'Forgive me, O Queen,' said I, 'but locks can be mended.'

The house had not been plundered and there was grain in the granary, and eggs in the hen-roost, and cheese in the larder. Moreover, we had a tree in the orchard that bore early and sweet fruit, and Igerna gathered apples while I set a man grinding grain at the hand-mill. In the wine-cellar I found the wine-jars untouched, and I filled a flagon and carried it and a goblet to Artorius.

He was lying with his eyes closed, and the sunlight shining in upon his bandaged face.

'Wine, sir, if you wish it?'

'Wine is good for old men, my son.'

'Where is the old man, sir? I do not see him. Is the sun too strong for you?'

His eyes laughed at me.

'Can one have too much sun in this green and cloudy island?'

I poured out wine for him and supported him while he sipped it.

'I am both a masked and a marked man, Gerontius. Your wine is good.'

'If you are marked, sir, they are badges of honour.'

I laid him down again, and drank from the goblet he had used.

'Where is the lady of the house, Gerontius?'

'Busy in the kitchen, sir, and the linen store. We shall have a bed for you and speedily.'

He drew a deep and contented breath.

'Your lady is quick to play her part. Peace after stormy days. May God bless this house.'

So, too, Morgan blessed it when he came with a waggon full of our wounded, for Igerna made it a house of mercy. We had hay spread in the portico, and some thirty stricken men laid there, and Igerna and I went round at night with lamps and saw to their good comfort. As for Morgan, he was once more the man of peace. I caught him early one dawn, stripped to the waist, and washing the bloodstains from his outer garments in the kitchen conduit.

'That could have been done for you, Father.'

He shook his head at me and smiled.

'*Peccavi*. I wash out my sins, my son.'

'Were they sins, Father?'

He scrubbed away at the cloth.

'Friends who can forget are wise.'

I laughed.

'Friends who can remember the good things are also wise.'

I think I shall remember to the end of my days how Igerna and I walked through our cornfields in the cool of the evening. She had a white flower in her dark hair, and a red flower at her bosom. The wheat was golden-speared, million-headed in the sunlight, and not a stalk moved, for the evening was calm and still. Igerna put out a hand and touched the wheat ears as we passed along the path. All about us a royal peace reigned, and the wooded hills were as still as the corn.

'How lovely it is, Geron.'

'Very lovely,' said I, looking at my wife.

'Corn in Egypt. Honey and wine in——'

'This—our island. The fruits of the earth, my beloved, should be man's inspiration and his joy.'

She smiled up at me.

'And the labour?'

'When man loses his joy in labour, he is better dead, for there is something dead in him. I, too, can use a sickle.'

'As well as you use a sword?'

'May God give us sickles, and no more need of swords.'

I plucked an ear of wheat and rubbed it between my hands, but the seed did not come out into my palm.

'Not yet ripe for reaping, Igerna.'

'It looks ripe.'

'Very soon it will be. My sweet, I have a sudden desire in me.'

'Yes, Geron?'

'To cross that mere of ours to the island, and stand by the willows—and remember.'

She put her hand in mine.

'Let us go, Geron, and remember all that is good

THE END